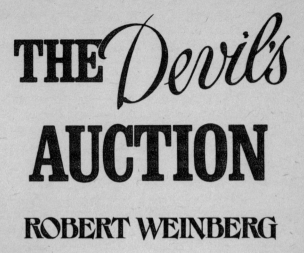

THE *Devil's* AUCTION

ROBERT WEINBERG

LEISURE BOOKS NEW YORK CITY

To Phyllis

A LEISURE BOOK ®

August 1990

Published by

Dorchester Publishing Co., Inc.
276 Fifth Avenue
New York, NY 10001

Printed in the United States of America.

THE *Devil's* AUCTION

CHAPTER ONE

The pain hit Jake Lancaster in a wave that swept across his chest. It burned deep within him, a sharp, intense shock unlike anything he had ever experienced.

Terribly scared, he stood motionless in the center of the kitchen. He had felt fine all day. Supper had been at Levine's Deli on the corner. None of his usual cronies were about, so he had come home early. As always, his first stop had been the kitchen. Mrs. Davidson, his housekeeper, had turned on the lights and left the mail on the kitchen table before going home for the day. Jake was a creature of habit. Checking the mail was the first thing he did when he got home, even before he removed his coat. He had just lifted the letters from the table when the attack started.

Now he staggered to a kitchen chair. The burning within him grew worse. It couldn't be a heart attack, he thought; his heart was in fine condition. He had just gone through a complete physical last month and been pronounced in exceptional health for a man his age. There was nothing wrong with him, yet the pain was increasing. His neck and shoulders were on fire and the heat was spreading up his neck to his head. Suddenly, he knew what was coming. "No, not again," he begged, but already it was too late. With one hand clutching desperately at the letters, the other at the top of the kitchen table, he was swept up by the dark force of a premonition.

The fury of the vision roared in his mind. It lasted only a bare instant, but that was long enough. Jake bit his lip hard, tasted salt. He tried to sort out the incredible mélange of images that assaulted his senses.

Time and space condensed, as the present and the future swirled together and combined into something that held a trace of both. Jake felt nothing and yet felt everything. Then the future engulfed him in a powerful embrace.

Incredible, devastating pain swept across his body again. Jake screamed, his bones cracking and breaking in a dozen places, blood spurting from a dozen wounds, agony searing through his mind as flesh and muscle ripped and tore. He felt huge teeth clamped onto his neck. Even as he screamed, loud and terrible cries rang in his ears. Jake recognized his own voice, echoing back to him from the future.

Whimpering, he fell from the chair to the floor. He knew without thinking that death claimed him with that final scream—a violent, terrible death.

The vision departed as swiftly at it arrived. Jake's eyes cleared. The kitchen looked no different; his body felt unharmed. The premonition had lasted only a few seconds.

For the third time in his life he knew what the future promised. As with his previous visions, this one warned of approaching death. In the other two instances, though, he had experienced the death of others.

At sixty-seven, death no longer had any fear for Jake Lancaster. A short, slightly overweight man with a thick thatch of white hair and bright blue eyes, he had accepted the inevitability of his passing long ago. Even a master of the black arts did not control mortality. Magic might prolong life a few years, but it could never defeat old age. Age brought a certain wisdom. His wife had died six years before, and many of his close friends had passed to the great beyond. He worked in a dangerous field; only a few magicians ever survived to their sixties, since no one retired from the black arts.

At times, when he felt very lonely and his work overwhelmed him, Jake wondered if perhaps death might not be a welcome rest. But not tonight. Not after that vision of his end. Tonight, Jake Lancaster wanted very much to live.

He stared at the letters he still held. Death's messenger was in this sheaf of mail. The touch of one had been the trigger which fired the psychic gun.

He forced himself to his feet. For the first he realized his lip was bleeding. Depositing the mail on the kitchen table, he went over to the sink and got a drink of cold water. He rinsed his mouth out several times to get rid of the lingering taste, then washed his hands and splashed a little water on his face. Feeling somewhat better, he returned to his chair. Now he was ready for the worst.

Quickly he sorted through the letters. Two bills, a flyer from a record club, an advertisement sent to 'Occupant,' an aerogram from Conrad Stein in England, and an ornate, hand addressed letter with no return address.

Jake dropped everything but the letter. He just stared at it for a moment, then ripped open the fancy envelope. A card fell out. Except for the dates, the card was exactly the same as the one he had seen in his friend Vassily Romanov's study thirty years ago. He had been smart that time and had not gotten involved. Romanov should have given the invitation away, but hadn't been able to resist the temptation it represented. Unfortunately, he had not been powerful enough to hold it.

Jake remembered his friend's funeral quite well. There had been several that month, all the result of the mad scramble for possession of that invitation. Now the cycle was starting again. Jake's murder would be only one of many. Death was an integral part of the Devil's Auction.

Closing his eyes, Jake let the feel of his house filter into his mind. Was his adversary already about? From room to room his sixth sense explored, carefully searching for anything unusual. His mental probings encountered nothing out of the ordinary. Whatever stalked him was not here yet. He had a little time. He was not sure exactly how long, so he had to act as if every moment were his last.

Rising from the table, he returned to the front hallway and locked and bolted his door—not that such precautions would stop his attackers. It was habit, and habit settled his nerves. He had lived in this house for over forty years and followed the same routines nearly every day. His wife and daughter, and now his housekeeper, humored him in this one quirk. Magic was ritual and ceremony, and doing things by habit strengthened his magical abilities. The more he could do by habit, the better. It left his mind free for the more difficult tasks.

Needless to say, this was not something he could ever tell Mrs. Davidson. Like most people, she thought black magic and sorcery were the stuff of horror novels and movies. She had no idea the nice old man whose home she kept clean was actually a powerful warlock. Mrs. Davidson was a pleasant if somewhat simple-minded woman, and Jake was glad she wouldn't be back till Monday morning, four days from now. At least she wouldn't be involved in whatever happened. Let her live in peace in her ignorance of the darkness all around us, Jake prayed as he stood by the front door.

He kept the deadly invitation with him as he hung up his coat and hat. More habit. He risked a brief look outside through the front door's peephole. Nothing. It was dark already, though it was only a little after seven. Night came fast in Chicago in October. Night, when the powers of darkness were at their greatest. At best, he had an hour. Probably less.

There were no false hopes to which Jake Lancaster might cling. He was too old and too much of a realist to fool himself. His life was forfeit. Twice before premonitions had touched him. In both instances, he had known death would strike someone he loved. He had tried to change the future, but in both cases his efforts came to naught. A true vision was not a glimpse of what *might happen*; it revealed what had actually *occurred* in the future. A premonition never lied due to the nature of its creation: violent death always releases a burst of psychic power. Unable to travel beyond its origin point, the scream of mental agony escapes across energy links into the past. It occurred often enough, Jake knew, but few individuals ever sensed the terrible cries.

Jake possessed that power. When his father lay dying, more than fifty years ago, he had felt such a calling. He remembered vividly the gut-wrenching pain in his chest while he sat in class. He had rushed home from school to find his father in the midst of the heart attack that had taken his life. That was the first time he felt the helpless frustration of knowing what the future brought. As he held the dying man in his arms, unable to do anything but pray, he'd cursed his own fate.

Six years ago, he had suffered the same frustration a second time. While sitting at the desk in his study, he experienced a sudden flare of intense heat as terrified screams echoed through his mind. The warning was again a grim joke of the gods. Jake had immediately called the airport, but it was too late. His wife's flight had taken off over an hour ago. Jake's frantic urgings prompted the terminal to radio the pilot, but the message went unanswered. They later learned that a bomb had been in the luggage compartment, planted there by a disgruntled ex-employee. It exploded only a few moments after Jake's call.

That phone call had brought Jake under close scrutiny by the police investigating the bombing. Fortunately, all of the evidence pointed in other directions. With no motive or opportunity, Jake was an unlikely suspect. Still, it had been a trying period until the true culprit had confessed.

Friends in high places made sure that all traces of the investigation into Jake's business were quietly lost or misfiled; the story of his premonition never made it to the papers and he sank back into the obscurity he desired. There was no way to stop the vivid nightmares that lasted for many months afterwards, though. While other practitioners of the Black Arts actively strived to master such psychic flashes, Jake felt his two experiences seeing the future were more than enough.

Now he had just experienced his third premonition. He knew, without any doubt, that it presaged his own end. Just because he'd received an invitation to a sinister auction that only a select few could attend, someone was going to kill him. He had no doubts that the invitation was the cause of the coming attack: it was necessary for admission to the auction, and only a few were ever sent out. After that, the law of survival took over: it was the same thing that had happened to Romanov so many years before. The auctioneer didn't care if the holder of the invitation was the person to whom it was originally mailed. Possession of the card was all important, since only the most powerful practitioners of the black arts were welcome and the strong kept theirs. Those who did not receive one, if they were ruthless and deadly enough, killed to obtain it. Romanov had deluded himself into thinking he was one of the strong ones. That mistake had cost him his life.

There was no time to curse uncaring fate. Too much remained to be done. He swiftly climbed the stairs to the second floor, footsteps echoing through the huge old house. Finally he arrived at the study where he relaxed in the evening.

From his desk he took a large manila envelope. He thrust the invitation into that. He was determined that his killers would not have it. His eyes made a quick circuit of the room. Not very many good hiding places if someone was dedicated in his search.

Finally, in desperation, Jake scribbled a few lines on the outside of the envelope and pasted on a few stamps. He quickly brought it downstairs to the front closet. The mailbox opened into a box by the coats. He stuck the envelope up into the container so that it rested just below the mail slot. His postman would find it there tomorrow when he delivered the mail. It was the one place his attacker would never think to look.

Breathing heavily, Jake made his way back to the study. A cold, numbing sensation was creeping through his body. Jake had practiced the black arts for too many years not to recognize the signs: the cold came from a psychic attack. He could combat the malignant energies being directed against him, but not from this room. Before he went upstairs, though, he had one last thing to do.

Palms sweating, he picked up the phone and dialed, keeping a careful watch on the corners of the study. Strange entities could sometimes materialize in the darkness. It was unlikely that his enemy would resort to such manifestations, but an attack could take many forms. He listened intently, but there were no sounds in the house. All was still, as though waiting for something to happen.

The phone rang and rang. Finally, on the sixth ring, a machine answered.

"Hello." It was his daughter Valerie's voice, deep and husky, but with that odd self-conscious sound of someone talking into a microphone with no one else around. "Valerie Lancaster is not able to answer the phone at present. If you have a message to leave, please hold on until you hear the beep. The recorder is voice activated and you can leave as long a message as needed. Please leave your number if you want me to return your call. If you are phoning about business, please contact my office during business hours. In any case, thanks for calling."

"Valerie, this is your father." Jake paused for an instant, hoping that she would come on the line. He knew she used the answering machine to monitor her calls. Tonight, however, there was no click indicating that she was home; he was only talking to the machine. She was probably out of town on a modeling assignment, he figured. Sucking in a few deep breaths, he forced himself to think things out. He had hoped to have a few last words with his daughter. Now, he felt very much alone. The tape machine made things more difficult, since any message he left might be heard by others. Anyone with power could easily trace his call. His message had to be clear and concise, but reveal nothing to any unwanted listeners.

He knew his daughter better than she ever realized. Valerie was very much like him. All his life he watched her and saw his own youthful mistakes. He knew Valerie would demand justice after his death—justice that law could never administer. Blood for blood still held true in magical circles, and Valerie had all the necessary talent in the dark arts, if not the training, to catch the murderer. Now he'd make sure she knew why he'd been killed. He had told her the story of Vassily Romanov and the Devil's Auction years ago. He hoped she still remembered it.

"I've just received a very interesting invitation to an auction. From Vassily Romanov. Remember, I told you about the rare curio auction he participated in thirty years ago? Another is going to take place later this month, on Halloween, at his estate north of Chicago. I have a feeling that I won't be able to make it. I suspect a gatecrasher might take my place. Wish I knew his identity, but I don't have a clue. If you decide you want to attend, remember you need an invitation to be admitted. Do me a favor and ask Professor Warner from the University to accompany you. He's been a good friend the past few years. You should meet him. You might need a hand. Good-bye, my dear. Remember that despite our differences, I love you very much. . . ."

The phone went dead. Jake punched the dial-tone button, but there was no sound. Either the cable had been cut or dark powers had been used. Overhead, the lights flickered. Annoyed, Jake waved a hand and muttered a few words under his breath. The electricity stabilized. The phone remained dead, though; the line must be down. Calling the police, for what little help they could provide, was out. He debated leaving some other communication for his daughter and then decided against it. Any other message would be seen by his enemy, not by Valerie. He had done all he could.

Rising from his chair, he sighed and looked around the study one last time. It had been a good place to work.

As the coldness within him grew stronger, he knew there was no winning this fight. Still, he had never been one to give up. Tonight would be no different. He would not surrender, *could* not surrender. If he was to die, let him die fighting. Muttering to himself, he climbed the rear stairway to the third floor.

A heavy-duty combination-lock guarded the only door. Jake had never bothered memorizing its code. A very selective, personalized spell twirled the tumblers and popped the lock open. Gripping the doorknob, Jake strained to pull the heavy door open: the seemingly frail wood concealed a solid steel core. The entire third story of his house had, in fact, been reinforced with steel plating years ago, floors and ceiling included. There were no windows. The one huge room was effectively a sealed fortress which only Jake could enter. As he stepped into the chamber and pulled the door closed behind him, the tumblers clicked as the door locked automatically.

A quick glance assured him that nothing was amiss in his sanctum. Floodlights illuminated every inch of the room, and there were no patches of darkness lurking in the corners. The dust coating the long shelves filled with esoteric volumes of occult lore lay undisturbed. Most important, though, his wand and other tools of the trade still sat safe in their glass case. He breathed a bit easier, seeing them undisturbed.

The coldness within him had begun to sap his strength. If he let it continue much longer, he would be easy prey for whatever horror was approaching.

He crossed to the full-length closet at the far end of the room and removed a long black robe, which was inscribed with arcane symbols and words of power, from the single hook. When he slipped it on over his street clothing, the warm material clung to his pot belly like a second skin. At once he felt more confident, more self-assured; performing the basic rituals of magic always restored his mental balance.

Flexing his fingers, he went to the case holding his staff of power. He picked up the hazel shaft, capped with steel at both ends, as though it were made of solid gold. A great deal of effort had gone into making that wand, and it was his most powerful magical instrument.

Clutching it in his left hand, he took a piece of thick white chalk from one of the bookshelves with his right. He felt slightly more confident as he knelt on the floor.

With a steady hand, he drew a huge circle, ten feet in diameter, going clockwise from east to south to west to north. It was not a perfect figure, but pretty good for one drawn freehand.

Finished, he put the chalk in a back pocket and raised his wand.

He touched his forehead and began to recite the invocation of power. "I dedicate this circle of power to the Lord High God, Tetragrammaton, Creator of the Universe and all that exists." He touched his solar plexus with the wand, his symbolic sword. "He is the Ruler of the Kingdom." Next, a tap of the wand against his right shoulder. "He is the Master of all the Powers." Now, a touch to his left shoulder, completing the occult cross which represented the four elements. "May his Truth and Glory endure Forever and Aye."

Jake could feel the strength start to flow back into his body. Through the occult chant, he proclaimed his mastery of the four elements, the cardinal points of the universe. He clasped his right and left hands together, pointing his magic hazelwood wand upward. "Let Him rule forever and ever for all the ages of the ages. Amen."

As the last words of the formula were completed, Jake felt the familiar rush of psychic energy. Confidence and some of his old arrogance returned as power coursed through his veins once more. He might only have a few minutes left, but he would go down fighting. His magical powers were strong now. The circle was nearly complete.

In his mind's eye he envisioned his marker

not as a simple hazel wand but as a great cross-handled sword like those used by the Crusaders. His voice rang with authority as he proclaimed, "In the Name of the High God, Tetragrammaton, Creator of the Universe, I take in these hands the Sword of Power for defense against all evil." No longer did he think of himself as an old man whose most athletic endeavor was climbing the multitude of stairways in his huge house. Instead, he imagined himself a young knight of Christendom, eager for battle: a strong, lean face, burned dark by the desert sun; a massive, muscular body, supported by legs like oak trees. He was sheathed in steel armor, the chain mail of the righteous. A fiery red cross was emblazoned on his chest. He was a Crusader of blood and iron.

Now he faced the east. He raised his wand high over his head. "May the mighty archangel, Raphael, protect me from all evil approaching from the east." He turned to the south. "May the mighty archangel, Michael, protect me from all evil approaching from the south." Then to the west, this time naming Gabriel, and finally to the north calling upon Uriel.

The first line of his defenses complete, Jake tucked his magic wand into his belt. He knelt on the floor again with his chalk. The spells of protection were overly dramatic, he felt, but they served their purpose. They were powerful counter-charms against psychic attack. And, in going through the recital of the invocations, he always felt a renewal of purpose. Like all of ritual magic, the performance of the actual ceremony was a part of the final result.

Jake began to inscribe a large triangle inside the circle. Just as he finished, he stopped for a second and looked around. The room looked the same; nothing had changed. Yet, something had impinged on his consciousness.

A cold chill tightened the muscles across his back as he realized what was wrong. *It* was in the house. His killer was downstairs.

This sanctum was soundproof, so he couldn't hear anything, yet he could sense some dread creature violating his living quarters. His mouth went dry and the muscles in his chest grew tight. Whatever it was, the thing wasn't human. He could sense its essence. It was evil, and filled with a dark, ugly hunger.

His body flashed hot and cold. Sweat seemed to ooze out of every pore.

Hurriedly, he drew a second triangle, crossing but reversed from the first, forming the six-sided star known as the Seal of Solomon. His fingers trembled as he inscribed his secret name in the top of the six triangles formed by the crossed lines. In each of the other five he wrote one syllable of the great name of power, Tetragrammaton. His heart pounded fiercely.

The veins above his eyes throbbed. Memory of the terrible pain he would soon suffer haunted his every thought.

Stiffly, he rose to his feet. He was scared, terribly scared. He had done all that he could do. These safeguards were the best he could manage in the time he had. The worst part was knowing they were useless. The premonition had shown what would come. Nothing could change the face of reality.

Pulling out his magic wand, he gripped it tightly with both hands. Again he imagined it the double edged sword of a Crusader. He had done great and powerful things with this wand, and no one had ever defeated him while he held it. Clasping it gave him some measure of courage. He was destined to die. Let it be with honor.

He drew in one deep breath after another, forcing his racing heart to slow down. He could sense the being below moving from room to room. It was searching for him. Finally it found the stairs leading up to this chamber. He could sense it climbing the steps, foot by foot, closer and closer.

His every breath became an effort. He could not banish the pain from his mind. There was no controlling his fear now.

The lock on the door rattled, gently at first, then louder and louder. Heavy blows against the metal echoed in the room as something smashed into it out in the hallway.

In his inner sanctum, the air vibrated with the force of the attack. Jake knew that the lock would not open to any other person, but whatever hunted him was not trying to open it by normal or supernatural means. The creature was trying to smash its way in. That alone confirmed his worst fears. This was no magician, it was some terrible, elemental sending. There could be no reasoning with such a monster. Either his circle of protection and his magic wand would protect him, or it would not. For a brief instant, Jake wondered if perhaps the premonition had been brought about by the powerful psychic surge of the monster's death. Then, regretfully, he abandoned that hope. The premonition had been much too specific. The pain belonged to him.

The reinforced steel door began to buckle. Jake's eyes widened in astonishment at the sheer brute force of the attack. The wood of the portal began to crack. Already the steel beneath it showed through. Desperately, he began to chant the invocation of power from the *Grimoire of Honorius*, one of the most powerful of all books of black magic.

"Behold the Lion who is the Victor of the Tribe of Judah, the Root of David." The steel of the door screeched as it started ripping from the hinges. "I will open the Book and the seven Seals thereof." The lights flickered; somone was using magic against him and there was nothing he could do. All of his mental energy was locked on the words of power. It took all the concentration he could muster just to keep his voice steady. "I have the power to crush dragons, scorpions, and all mine enemies beneath my feet." The constant pounding on the door was like a chorus of drums that echoed his every word. The room felt insufferably warm. Sweat dripped into his eyes, soaked his clothing. Still, the words tumbled out of his mouth. "Nothing shall harm me, by Eloy, Elohim, Elohe . . ."

The light bulbs flashed and exploded, plunging the room into total and absolute darkness. Startled, Jake hesitated for an instant. With a crash, the door to his sanctum gave way. The hallway outside was dimly lit. His attacker stood fully outlined in the entrance. The thing paused there, motionless for a moment, as if caught by surprise. It filled the doorway, nearly seven feet tall. A shaggy mat of tangled hair covered its entire body. Huge muscles rippled through its arms and chest. Yellow eyes blazed at Jake. Powerful hands, hands that had knocked the steel door right off its hinges, clenched in giant fists as the creature growled low in its throat.

Jake pointed his magic wand at the beast. He had to focus all of the energy in his body in one last attack. He had gambled and lost; his magic circle would do him no good against this abomination. It was a thing of darkness, but born of Earth, not some other plane of existence. For once, a gun would have served him better than his magic wand. Still, there were spells he could use—heat and cold could stop this beast.

He raced through the necessary spell. Only a few more seconds. As if sensing Jake's purpose, the creature snarled. Its muscles tensed as it gathered in on itself for the attack. Jake raised his wand high. He needed only a few instants—

Something small and hissing came bouncing into the room, thrown from behind the monster. Looking down, Jake recognized a tear gas canister. As fumes spewed out, he mentally cursed his own stupidity. He had completely forgotten the beast's master.

The tear gas started him coughing violently. He fell back, unable to maintain his balance. A psychic attack he could have defeated, but his old body was too vulnerable on the physical plane. His unknown enemy had planned well. The first thrust, using magic, had set him up for the counterthrust using purely physical means. He had been caught by surprise.

Eyes tearing, Jake blundered about, desperately trying to regain his footing. He could sense the monster's charge, but couldn't spot it in the darkness. A fit of coughing racked his body.

"Kill him," Jake heard a voice command. He recognized the speaker. It didn't matter. His doom was upon him.

In the darkness, the creature's jaws clamped on his left shoulder with savage fury, sinking deep into his flesh. He screamed as sharp claws ripped across his back. The thing pulled him close. He felt bones crack. Blood gushed from his mouth and nostrils. The wand dropped from his useless fingers as darkness closed upon him. His last thoughts were of the screams of psychic energy spiralling back in time as a useless warning to his earlier self. The premonition had come full circle.

CHAPTER TWO

Alex Warner was edgy. For the third time that afternoon he reread the newspaper clipping on his desk. It had come yesterday in the mail, in an envelope with no return address and a post mark from Chicago. Was it mere coincidence that he had received the clipping the day before Jake Lancaster's daughter was coming to visit? He was not a strong believer in coincidence. Paranoid, his ex-wife had accused. At times, Alex had to agree with that assessment. Not this time. Jake's death was proof of that.

The clipping was an account of Jake Lancaster's murder. The body had been found by the police late on Friday, after a friend had grown worried when Jake had failed to show up for dinner. There was not much to the article other than a pretty grisly description of his friend's body. The old bookseller had been savagely mutilated by some unknown animal, according to the writeup.

The account was not what bothered Alex. He had read it when it had first appeared a week ago. By the time it ran, he had already been questioned several times at length by the police. A solid alibi, confirmed by several dozen people at a faculty party, had saved him from any real hassle. The police had no leads at all and were anxious to find a suspect.

Alex licked his lips as he reread the clipping in front of him. The mysterious sender had underlined in red ink the description of Jake's body. There was no written message, but the implied threat was clear enough. Alex wondered exactly what was going on. He was not looking for trouble, but he never liked to be pushed around.

Thirty-seven years old, Alex Warner was an enigma to most of his acquaintances. Dark black hair and gaunt features went well with black eyes that seemed to peer suspiciously at everything. A little over six feet tall, he had the lean, muscular body of a professional athlete. Nevertheless, he did not participate in any interacative sports at the university. He refused all offers to play racquetball or tennis or even join the faculty volleyball team, but it wasn't from lack of competitive spirit. Alex was a ruthless bridge player and had won nearly every duplicate bridge tournament sponsored by the University in the last ten years. He played with a calm control and deadly intensity that frightened even his partner, Sam Lewis. It was Sam, a colleague in the History Department, who had dubbed Alex "The Master Assassin," the first time he had seen Alex play bridge. The nickname had become a standard joke on campus. Only Alex and a few close friends knew how accurate that nickname really was.

A knock at his office door broke his reverie. Hastily, Alex got to his feet and looked around the office. He had spent most of the morning straightening up, but it still looked cluttered: books and papers everywhere, a few bridge trophies used as bookends, a couple of old photos hung on the wall as well as his diplomas. Sheila had sarcastically labelled it a typical professor's hideaway.

Alex hurried across the room and opened the door. The woman outside had her hand raised to knock again. They stared at each other for a second. She seemed startled, as though surprised by something, and Alex wondered if he were more unkempt than usual. Her look of surprise vanished as suddenly as it had appeared. Blue eyes locked onto his and held. The two of them stood motionless for several instants.

Finally, the young woman dropped her arm, smiling at him as she did so. "Sorry. I wasn't sure if anyone was here."

"I'm probably the only one in the building today," said Alex, his mind reeling in near shock. It was impossible for him to believe that this was Jake Lancaster's daughter. "Saturday is a day of rest even for the faculty. The students always have something better to do. And, now that the football team has a winning record, they have another excuse to keep away."

"I'm sorry." She actually did sound apologetic. "I hate imposing on you like this, but I did want to talk to you so much."

"Uh, sure. No problem." Already, he was sweating. The old Alex Warner/beautiful woman syndrome strikes again, he cried silently in despair. Be cool. Stay relaxed. "Won't you have a seat. Sorry for the mess, but it's mid-terms." That wasn't much of an explanation, he realized, but it was the best he could do.

After seating the woman so that she faced his desk, Alex hurried around to his own chair. To his astonishment, he felt incredibly aroused. He had been sexually inactive ever since his divorce. Beautiful women usually interested him, but this was insane, his body was going berserk. Safely seated, he stared at Jake Lancaster's daughter.

It was difficult to believe that she was related to his old friend. He had known Jake for nearly

six years and had fond memories of the grand-
fatherly-looking old man with shocking white
hair. Given his red cheeks and bushy eyebrows,
Jake could have easily passed for a large elf.

Valerie Lancaster definitely did not resemble
her father. She was tall. At the door, their eyes
had been on the same level. That, in itself, was a
novelty. Even subtracting the inches added by
her clunky but fashionable heeled shoes, she
had to be five nine or ten. While her figure
could not be described as full-bodied, she
definitely was quite female, and her black,
low-cut dress emphasized every attractive
curve. Willowy was the first word that came to
Alex's mind. She was the most attractive woman he had ever encountered. He could not
define exactly what it was that captivated him
so—all of her features just worked together
perfectly. It was almost like magic.

As a vague suspicion flitted through his
thoughts, his eyes kept drifting back to her
stunning legs, sheathed in black nylons. After
years of seeing every woman he knew clad in
bluejeans, it was a novelty to see real flesh
again. He vaguely remembered Jake once telling him that his daughter worked as a professional model. She definitely fit the traditional
image of one. Tall and slender, with hair so
blonde that it seemed the very color of sunlight,
and the brightest, most attractive blue eyes he
had ever seen. Eyes the color of the ocean, deep

and mysterious. Eyes that you could lose your-self in. He felt lost in them already. Her lips, half open in a bemused smile, revealed stunning white teeth. High, slender cheekbones gave her face an almost elfin look. Even with a bare minimum of makeup, she radiated warmth and sensuality.

"Hey," said Valerie, the sound of her voice, deep and husky and filled with amusement, breaking into Alex's thoughts. "You still there?"

"Sorry." The blood rushed to Alex's head and he knew he was blushing. He always did when he was embarrassed. At least he was still able to speak. Sometimes, when flustered, he became tongue-tied. "You weren't exactly what I was expecting."

Immediately, he worried that she might be insulted. Damn. He wasn't well-versed in dealing with beautiful women. He had never won an argument with his ex-wife, and she was nowhere near Valerie's league.

Fortunately, Valerie didn't seem upset. She began to laugh. It was a smooth, attractive chuckle that captivated him even more. Mentally, he tried to collar his rising desire. He was too old to be acting like this. Life was filled with too many temptations already, like worldly female students.

More important, thoughts of sex were in terrible taste. Jake's daughter was in mourning, probably still in shock. And all he could think about was getting his hands on her. He better be careful before he made an absolute fool of himself. Still, his mind argued in return, she was a knockout.

"You thought I'd be short and dumpy, with prematurely white hair, I gather?" Her eyes twinkled as she spoke. "Sort of my father but younger . . . and a woman."

Alex opened his mouth but nothing came out. Tongue-tied. "A woman," he managed to choke out, and then wished he hadn't. His face felt like it was on fire. He wondered if there was any blood left in the rest of his body. It all had to be rushing to his face—and his groin. He cleared his throat and tried to get his body under control. "I have to admit that you've caught me off guard. Most of the women I encounter are less . . . attractive." He groped for words, trying not to make things worse. Everything he said sounded foolish. "I mean, not many good-looking students take courses in Medieval Theology or the Witch Cult in Europe. I usually get radical feminists who feel dresses are manipulative." She smiled at that line and he felt a little more relaxed. Concentrate on something else, Alex mentally commanded himself. Without trying to be too obvious, he fixed his eyes on his Doctoral Diploma displayed on the wall behind Valerie's left shoulder. That helped a little. "Jake didn't have any pictures of you around, and my taste in magazines is pretty esoteric—mostly history journals. I rarely get to see *Cosmopolitan or Ladies Home Journal.*"

"Don't look at the swimsuit ads, either?" Valerie's smile broadened. It was totally captivating. "I've done more than my share of them. Not to mention some layouts in the men's magazines. The more sophisticated ones, of course." She grinned at him. Challenging him. Alex kept his eyes fastened on the diploma.

Pleasant as this all was, Alex knew it was time to change the subject. He owed that much to his murdered friend. There were things he wanted to know, but at the same time he had to be careful. Some things could not be said in haste. Jake had entrusted him with many confidences; he could not reveal them without being sure he was doing the right thing. "I was shocked when I learned of Jake's death," he said. "Hard to believe. Absolutely horrible. I had lunch with him on Thursday. Police said I was one of the last people to see him alive."

"I know. He spent most of the day at the University Library doing research, had dinner at his usual time and place, then went home. Where the killer struck." As she spoke, Valerie's voice grew softer and softer. Her face was still beautiful, but her features had hardened now. Alex recognized the look: Jake got that way when something had him angry. On

Jake it had always wanted to make Alex laugh. It made the old scholar look like a bulldog. Valerie's expression was much more threatening.

"Right. His killer. From our conversation on the phone this morning I take it you feel something more than robbery was the motive for Jake's murder."

"I know it." There was ice in Valerie's voice. "I suspect you know it, too. Listen, Alex Warner, my father told me to see you for some reason. He trusted you. The old geezer had his faults, but he was nobody's fool. Let's cut the crap. I need your help. No *ordinary* thief could kill my father. The police didn't have a clue, so they came up with the robbery story. It didn't fit the facts but it sounded a lot better than them admitting they had their fingers up their noses. You and I both know they'll never come up with the real killer. Someone else has to do it."

Alex was staring at Valerie now, the diploma forgotten. "So you intend to find him?"

"You bet your ass." She leaned forward, resting her forearms on his desk, and revealing an astonishing amount of cleavage. "Vengeance is mine."

"I shall repay," completed Alex. His voice remained calm but inside he was starting to wonder about Valerie's sanity. She had evidently been under quite a bit of strain. He did not like the direction their conversation was taking. "Most people forget that Mickey Spilane wasn't the first to make that remark. I doubt if God meant it to become a justification for murder."

"Murder, Hell." Valerie's eyes flashed brightly. Her cheeks glowed red with passion. Her voice grated harshly with barely repressed anger. "It'll be justice. Did you see what Dad looked like? Did you? I had to identify his body, and the papers didn't tell the half of it. Damn it to Hell. He was no saint, but he was my father. And, even if he wasn't, no one should die like that."

Valerie gulped several times, then dragged her upper teeth across her lower lip. Her voice grew calm though her face was still flushed. "The cops can't explain the wounds. They say the burglar must have had a dog with him. A *dog*." Valerie shuddered violently. "You find me a dog that can crush a man's ribs, claw out his eyes, and bite nearly *through* his neck. Damn it. Even the morgue attendant couldn't swallow a line like that—he told the cops they were crazy. I kept my mouth shut and played the dumb cute model, the poor bereaved daughter." Her eyes bored into his. "Are you with me?"

Alex remained silent. He didn't know what to say. Valerie's argument made sense, but he still had his doubts; she might be a very good actress. There was still that newspaper clipping on the blotter in front of him. Had she sent it? Already, he had that hunch about the lust that still gripped his body. She could be playing a much deeper game than showed on the surface.

His eyes involuntarily focused on Valerie's half revealed breasts. She was showing quite a bit of skin. Was his guess right? Did she have some of the Power? Paranoia strikes deep, he hummed to himself, remembering the lyric of his favorite rock song. He wasn't willing to commit himself just yet.

Valerie's blue eyes filled with tears. She brushed them away and muffled a sob. Alex remained silent. This was like playing cards only the stakes were different. Bid and bluff. Let your opponent make the mistakes. He had learned his lessons the hard way.

Valerie frowned for a minute and then straightened up in her chair. Her eye makeup was nearly gone and her face looked terrible. She had a hurt and disappointed look. Alex had seen that expression many times before on his ex-wife's face. It could mean a lot. Or nothing.

"I can see that I made a mistake coming here. I thought you wanted to help."

Before Alex could reply, the intercom on his desk buzzed. "That's odd," he said, actually pleased by the interruption. Give her a chance to think a little. "Damn thing hasn't worked all week. Guess they finally got someone to fix it while I was in class the other morning." Alex depressed a button. "Professor Warner here."

There was no sound on the other end of the line. Alex held the button down for a few seconds, but the connection remained silent. "Ha. So much for repairs. There must still be a few bugs in the system they didn't get." He released the switch and looked back at Valerie. She was starting to rise from her chair. Time to make a decision, he thought. He decided to trust his feelings.

"Listen," he said. "Wait a minute. Don't leave. Let's talk things out a bit. Look at it from my side. I mean, I was pretty close to your father, probably the best friend he had these past few years. I want justice too. But tracking down his killer? I'm no detective. Are you? Tough talk is cheap. Action is another story. Where would you start?"

"Well, perhaps I was a little hasty," replied Valerie, still standing. She did not seem to be in any rush to leave. "Maybe I did come on a little strong."

The intercom buzzed again. Alex ignored it. "A *little* strong?" He got up from his chair and walked around the desk. Up close Valerie was still the most desirable woman he had ever imagined. He had to clasp his hands together to keep them from reaching for her. His mind felt fuzzy. Hard to think straight. Either she was using the Power or he was losing his mind. "I'm willing to help. But let's approach this problem logically."

Again the intercom buzzed. This time it was a long, insistent hum that did not stop. "What the hell is going on?" Alex demanded angrily. Returning behind his desk, he jabbed the button. "Hello, hello."

Some *thing* answered. The voice was barely a whisper, yet it penetrated every inch of the cluttered office. It was a vile, inhuman sound unlike anything Alex had ever heard before.

"The Auction," said the voice. The words came slowly, as if the speaker was pronouncing a benediction or a prayer. "The Devil's Auction."

Alex was so surprised he released the connecting switch. The voice was cut off before it could continue. Immediately, the intercom began buzzing.

"Don't answer it," said Valerie. He wasn't sure he understood what was going on. The girl's voice was choked with fear. In a second, she was at his side, grabbing hold of his wrists. Her hands were cold and clammy. Incredible tension had the veins popped out on her forehead. Terrified eyes looked into his. He had never seen fear so clearly defined in a person's expression. "Nothing human is on the other end of that line. Don't answer. It's the sound of death. The speaker is my father's killer."

"Then shouldn't we hear what he has to say?" asked Alex. Pulling a hand free, he flipped the switch back on. "This is Professor Warner. Who are you? What do you want?"

"The Invitation." The same whispering voice answered. "It is useless to you. You have nothing for the Auction. Give me the Invitation and I will let you live."

Valerie's hands tightened as the voice made the last statement, but Alex wouldn't release the switch. He had to know more. It was an eerie sensation, having a conversation with a murderer who had to be in the same building. "Am I to understand that you admit killing Jake Lancaster? And that you are threatening me as well if I don't give you some sort of Invitation?"

"Fool." The voice was louder now, angry. "I will crack your bones for their marrow. Your blood will fill my cup. Give me that invitation or learn the true meaning of pain."

Valerie had the right idea, Alex suddenly decided. Bravery in the face of the unknown could be awfully stupid. The person on the other end of the line was obviously a psychopath. Those were not the statements of a sane person. He released the switch. For a second there was silence. Then, to his astonishment, the voice continued. The circuit was still open.

"You cannot banish me so easily." If anything, the killer's voice was louder than before. Alex stared at the intercom. What the hell was going on? The switch was off; the connection was broken. The voice grew so loud that it shook the room, his trophies rattling on their shelf, his pencils dancing on the desk. Valerie trembled with every word. *"The Invitation must be mine."*

Valerie had backed away from the desk. She was biting her knuckles to keep from screaming, eyes huge against pale white features, attention fixed on the intercom. She was still shaking.

Alex tried to reassure her though he felt no such confidence himself. "Stay calm," he said, bending beneath the desk. "Must have rigged up a toggle switch inside the box. I'll break the connection . . ." But, he saw, the wire that connected the intercom to the system hung loose. It couldn't possibly work.

He straightened up slowly. This was getting very odd.

"Who are you?" He was frightened, but he was more angry than afraid. "Who the hell are you?"

"The Invitation." The words crashed like thunder in the small office. The windows rattled. One of his trophies tipped over. Alex's ears ached from the sound. *"I must have it. My teeth will rip the flesh from your bones. I will squeeze your living heart in my hands. Give me what I want or suffer eternal pain. I must have the Invitation to the Devil's Auction!"*

"You can have it in Hell." That was Valerie, her face still white but her eyes flashing in anger. With a savage yank, she pulled the intercom off of the desk. Alex tried to grab her arms, but she slammed the intercom down on the floor. The black plastic box shattered. "In Hell," Valerie repeated, stomping one foot hard on the casing. Her thick heel smashed down again and again. The inner works of the intercom flew across the room. The strange voice had been effectively silenced.

Her eyes still blazing, Valerie swung around and jabbed a finger at Alex's chest. "Now do you believe me? You heard it. What can the police do to a thing like that? Or do you still think some petty thief killed my father?"

Alex was equally angry. The voice had shaken him more than he cared to admit. For an instant, he let his fear and anger dictate his actions. With a quick jerk, he pushed Valerie back in her chair. "Sit down and shut up."

Valerie did exactly that. She huddled in the armchair, rubbing her eyes. Carefully avoiding her stare, Alex paced back and forth the length of his office. He was annoyed with himself. It was the first time he had lost control since the War. Even with Sheila, he had never acted this way. There was still that fuzzy feeling inside him. He was not as sharp as he should be; his level of concentration was off. Already he was starting to feel guilty for manhandling her. He had always prided himself on being a true gentleman, the last cavalier in a cynical world. Alex risked a quick look at her and immediately wished he hadn't. She was smiling at him again. He felt his resolve turning to jelly.

"Three questions. I'll ask them. You'll answer them." He rushed through the statement. He had to get it out before he calmed down. Another minute and he would have been lost. "Then, and only then, will we discuss whether I give you any help. Got that?"

"Got it, chief." Valerie's voice was subdued but Alex could detect a faint note of mockery in it. For being so frightened only a few minutes before, the girl had made a remarkable recovery.

"First and foremost. Do you have *the Power*?"

"The Power?"

"Yes, the Power. Don't get cute with me. You know exactly what I mean. You couldn't be Jake Lancaster's daughter and not know about the Power. The truth, now. Lie to me and you can fight—" Alex pointed to the remains of the intercom scattered on the floor. "—the owner of that voice on your own."

Valerie's body shook as if chilled. It was a very nice shake. Alex forced himself to think of other things. "Well," he said, "I'm still waiting."

"Okay. I give up. You win. My deepest and darkest secret is out in the open. You obviously know the answer already or you wouldn't bother to ask. It's hard to for me to admit it. Yes, I possess the Power. Would be a freak if I didn't, considering that both my parents were master mages. I don't practice, but I *am* gifted. The blood of witches and warlocks flows in my veins."

"Not practicing?" Alex laughed harshly. It was time to get a few things straightened out. He had no idea why Valerie was lying to him, but it had to stop. For the first time since she had walked into the office, his mind felt clear. It was as if he had emerged from a deep fog. This farce had gone on long enough.

He was around the desk in seconds. Years of inaction had not slowed him down. This time he was in complete control of his emotions. He knew exactly what he was doing: he had learned how to effectively frighten someone during his years in Viet Nam. It was something you don't forget.

Grabbing the arms of her chair with both hands, he thrust his face only inches from hers. She cringed.

"Not practicing." Alex hardly recognized the sound of his own voice. It was part of a time long buried. "Then why has my body been in a state of constant excitement ever since you walked into this office?" Valerie's eyes blinked furiously as he continued, "I'm a normal, reasonably healthy male animal. During my life, sex has occupied my mind quite a bit. *But never all the time.* Lately, since my divorce, not very often at all. Today, I can't look at you for more than a few seconds without getting aroused. No one is that good-looking. Black magic is the only answer. Admit it. I'm sick of being played for a fool. What are you doing to me? And more important, *why*?"

Valerie made choking noises in her throat. Alex backed away, the intensity of the moment gone as suddenly as it had begun. This wasn't Viet Nam any more. He couldn't believe his own actions. No matter what the cause, he had no right to act this way. All through his divorce he had remained in complete control of his temper, hadn't raised his voice once, had kept all the rage tightly locked inside himself. Now, with a near stranger, he had gone berserk.

He was so angry with himself that it took a few seconds for him to realize what sounds he was actually hearing. Alex squinted at Valerie. So much for his macho threats. What worked in Viet Nam obviously no longer did much on the home front. The minx was having a hard time holding back laughter.

Alex growled in frustration. He threw his arms up in the air, then broke out laughing himself. It was the easiest way to admit defeat. Valerie collapsed into gales of laughter.

"I was beginning to wonder if maybe you were gay or something," she managed to get out. Tears were running down her cheeks as she continued to chuckle. "I didn't want to believe it, but you were starting to worry me. God, you have unbelievable self-control. Most men would have been chasing me around the office after five minutes."

"Going through a rather messy divorce helps," answered Alex, somewhat mollified. Ever alert, he had immediately fastened on to the one line she said that had real meaning. *She had hoped not.* To a solitary, quiet man, there was a lot of promise in that line. "I'm glad I quieted your fears. Now, do me a favor and remove the damn spell? It's difficult to maintain a serious conversation with all of my attention focused on your body. And explain to me why you felt it necessary to cast it in the first place."

"It's not that easy to explain. First things first. Come here."

Alex moved closer, cautiously. Valerie stood up. "Kiss me," she commanded.

He didn't need a second invitation. Her lips were warm and half open. The embrace lasted a long time. Valerie made no effort to break away. Her arms encircled his neck and held him close. It felt good to kiss a woman again. The tension drained out of his body. The fuzziness in his mind was back, but this time not so intense. It was hardly noticeable except for a feeling of euphoria, and much of that could be attributed to the warm, desirable woman in his arms. For one of the few times since his divorce, it felt very good to be alive.

Finally, they broke apart. Alex staggered back and leaned on his desk. There were no fireworks but he was a little dizzy. "Wow."

Valerie chuckled. It was a deep, sexy sound that sent shivers of pleasure darting down Alex's spine. "Nice to be appreciated. Take a look at me now."

She was still beautiful, but in some unidentifiable way she looked different. A little plainer. Not as desirable. He could look at her directly now without feeling any primal stirring. A vital spark was gone. "A kiss destroys the effect?"

"Not forever, but for a pretty long time. Thank God for small favors. If nothing worked, I'd have to live in a nunnery. Do you know the hassles I put up with just walking down the street? Can't ever get into an elevator. I'm lucky that kissing has become a standard form of greeting in the entertainment field."

"You mean . . ."

Valerie nodded. "Now you understand. This isn't the East Coast social scene. There was no way I could come in and immediately give you a kiss. Face it—we didn't trust each other. Neither of us was sure what my father had revealed in conversation. So, I decided to wait and see what would happen. That wasn't a lie before; I don't practice sorcery. The *glamour* has been with me for years. I have no control over it. Actually, it's the reason I left home."

Brushing her hair back in some semblance of order, Valerie seemed a different person. The fear in her was gone. She seemed perfectly at ease, more so than Alex, who was still remembering a passionate kiss. All anger between the two of them was gone.

Her voice relaxed, Valerie continued. "I never wanted to be a magician. Dad married late in life, and I was born when he was forty. He was set on me following the family tradition. I don't know how much my father told you, but there have been sorcerers in his line for hundreds of years. Usually wizards, because the Power is strongest in males, but there were more than a few witches. We fought about it all the time. Mother usually sided with me in most arguments, but she stood by Dad in that one. Bad enough that I didn't want to practice magic. Worse was that I wanted to be a fashion model.

"Mom and Dad were pretty radical thinkers. Dad posed as a rare bookdealer. He liked books and it gave him something to do when he wasn't involved in the black arts, and it let him work at home without anyone wondering about it. He could also travel, supposedly searching for rarities. It was a pretty good cover and explained lots of strange things about him. He needed that because he was pretty odd. He got involved in all sorts of causes, both on the right and the left. Dad was pretty liberal, very non-sexist. The thought of his only child earning her living by her good looks instead of her brains drove him bonkers.''

"So you tried to combine both professions?''

"Pretty sharp. You guessed it. I studied with him for a couple of years. Did a lot of research and learned some of the basic rules of the trade. Then, while looking up some information for Dad, I came across my big find. I discovered the spell for "The Glamour" in the *Grimoire of Honorius*. It sounded great. A formula that made the user irresistible to the opposite sex. To a nineteen-year-old who wanted to be a model but needed a big break, it was a temptation hard to resist. I always had a hard time with temptation." Valerie grinned at him and Alex smiled back. She was flirting now and he loved it. This was real magic. He was still enamored with her, but now it was a natural, normal attraction.

"I should have asked before I tried it. Should have, but didn't. Don't forget, I was still pretty rebellious. The Power doesn't give you maturity. That has to be learned. Well, I learned my lesson pretty quick. Until then, no one suspected how powerful Valerie Lancaster really was. The spell worked. Oh, how it worked. Honorius hadn't bothered to mention that once cast, it was irreversible.''

"Even Jake . . ."

"My father was a strong wizard. One of the best. He tried, but the spell was there to stay. I inherited the Power from two very powerful magicians. My gift was greater than either of theirs. Years later, I came to realize that was one of the reasons Dad was so disappointed with me. He was positive that if I applied myself I could easily outdistance both of them. He was probably right. I didn't do things by halves. When the spell was struck, it remained. Despite all efforts to remove it."

"And you became irresistible," Alex said.

"I was irresistible all right. But the attraction was purely physical—it worked on the most base instincts. Life became a nightmare. I couldn't walk down the street without being propositioned. Had to learn self-defense pretty fast, but I learned to adjust. Swore off magic, though. My one experiment was enough. I left home soon after, moved to New York, and became a model like I planned. Dad never entirely forgave me for abandoning the black arts. After a while, though, I think he understood. It was more a question of identity than revolt against parental authority. I had to be me, not an extension of him. After Mom died, we grew a little closer. And now he's gone." She smiled at Alex, a touch of loneliness in her face. "Hard to believe I'll never see him again. Life is terribly unfair sometimes. Never did get to say how much I really did love him.

"You wanted the truth, Alex. Well, you've got it. The whole bizarre story. What else do you want to know?"

"That can wait till later—not that the other questions matter as much. I know all I have to. That voice on the intercom was enough to convince me, although now you don't seem very disturbed about it."

"I'm not. Threats like that I can handle. Got me going for a minute, but I've been under a lot of strain lately. Should have known better. Nothing to worry about." Valerie dazzled him with another smile. "Truthfully."

That was all he wanted to hear. If she wasn't scared, then there was no reason for him to worry. He didn't think to question this sudden reversal of his usual paranoia. He was more concerned about what he wanted to say next. Suddenly he felt nervous and self-conscious. The fear of rejection had raised its ugly head. Spell or not, she was still unbelievably beautiful . . . and he was just a middle-aged college professor. Not exactly a romantic twosome.

"Did you have, uh, any plans for dinner?" he asked.

"Not really." Valerie's smile was going full force now. "Is that an invitation?"

Inwardly, Alex exalted. He tried the best he could to keep his voice calm. "Sure is. I'm starving. There's a nice Italian restaurant right off campus—nothing fancy, but the food is great."

"Best offer I've had all day."

The phone rang. They both looked at it.

"You expecting a call?" asked Valerie, her voice trembling.

"No one knows I'm here," said Alex, rising to his feet. "Come on. Let's go."

The phone continued to ring and ring and ring as they hurried out of the office. In his mind, Alex heard the bell long after they had left the building.

CHAPTER THREE

The eyes of every man in Mama Mia's Italian Heaven were on the two of them as they walked through the dining room. For the first time, Alex realized what Valerie had to endure every day of her life. It was as if she was wearing a shrieking siren around her neck. Pretending not to notice, they followed the hostess to a booth in the back of the restaurant. Several male patrons smiled suggestively at Valerie. One slightly drunk college student whistled. Valerie ignored him, and Alex followed her lead. He didn't want to embarrass her. In other circumstances, Alex would have reacted more forcibly. He had to remind himself he was a gentleman.

The silence was uncanny. Not a word was spoken the entire time they weaved their way between tables. Even the women were quiet, shocked into silence by the intruder in their midst. Alex wondered if Valerie had many female friends. He tended to think not. She was too much of a threat. While the spell would leave them unmoved, its effects were obvious. Realizing that Jake Lancaster's daughter was probably very much alone in the world, he thought her unusual behavior during the past few hours made a lot more sense. Valerie's affliction made her a loner, suspicious of everyone she met.

The booth was a private one, set off in a back corner of Mama Mia's. Alex always asked for it when he ate at the restaurant. During his short and explosive married life, he and Sheila had often dined here. It was quiet and cozy and away from the prying eyes of other patrons. Now that Valerie was no longer in view, conversation resumed at its usual low roar. The hostess lit the solitary candle in the center of the table and, with a slightly puzzled expression, gave them their menus and left.

"One of your students?" asked Valerie, using her head as a pointer.

"Sharon? How did you guess? She works here on the weekends."

"The look she gave you. I don't know if you

realize it, but your reputation as a ladies' man has just taken a huge leap forward." Valerie sounded slightly bitter. Not at him in particular, but at the world in general. "I'm always a catalyst. Everyone will be curious to know what attracted *me* to you. Word will be all over campus by tomorrow. Wait till the questions start. Friends, colleagues, even people you never met. And then the propositions from the girls. The obvious ones at first, wanting to know what secret you possess. Then, later from ones you would never suspect. No, don't protest." Valerie was smiling, but there was little humor in her expression. "I've seen it happen before. Not in the same surroundings, but in similar circumstances. You don't know. I do."

"The spell is that strong?"

"Did you forget the effect it had on you? And I can assure you from years of coping with the *glamour* that your willpower was exceptional. Most men would have been pawing at me in minutes. If you thought walking through that crowd was bad, you should hear what I have to put up with when I go out for dinner alone." More than bitterness, there was grim resignation in Valerie's voice. "A week, maybe less. Then you'll start getting the phone calls. More women than you can handle."

"They'll be wasting their time. I'm with the one lady who matters," said Alex.

He caught her by surprise with that line. She looked at him strangely. Timidly, one hand reached out and touched him lightly on the cheek. "Very nice, sir," she said, in a much different tone. "Very, very nice. Truly gallant."

"I meant it," replied Alex. He did. Valerie was someone special. There was a strange chemistry between them, much more than just physical attraction. Somehow, she just felt *right*. He had never experienced the sensation before. They sat there for a moment, the world forgotten. "You have the bluest eyes I've ever seen," said Alex, dreamily. "Ocean blue."

"Magic blue." Valerie blushed. "That's how Dad described them. Bright blue for sorcery."

The arrival of their waitress cut off further discussion. At Valerie's insistence, Alex ordered for the both of them. He didn't bother looking at the menu. "Antipasto salad for two. Baked lasagna. A bottle of the house red. And let Makoto Tsuiki know that I'm here. If he can make it out of the kitchen, there's someone here I want him to meet."

Valerie's eyebrows arched in curiosity. "Makoto Tsuiki? Japanese?"

"Third-generation American, actually," said Alex. "His grandparents came to Chicago from Tokyo in the '20s. His family has been in the restaurant business ever since. The Tsuikis own six places in the city. Mak runs this one. He's always here on Saturday night to supervise the kitchen. Among other things, he's a terrific chef. He's popular enough with his employees that they're actually glad to see him."

"There's no Mama Mia?"

"Not unless she's Japanese. Don't worry. You'll swear that Mak was born in Italy after you taste the lasagna. I've been after his secret for years, but he's your typical inscrutable Oriental born and raised in the Midwest." Alex smiled. "Fu Manchu would be proud of him. It has to be in the spices, but Mak won't divulge an ingredient. Probably some ancient family recipe."

"No doubt," Valerie said.

"Ah, rescued." Alex broke off his chatter as their waitress approached. "Here's the wine. And bread. The two necessities of life."

Their waitress opened the wine bottle and departed. No fancy service, here. Alex poured a small amount and took a sip, deciding it would do. He filled Valerie's glass and then his own. It was nice to share a bottle of wine with attractive company. Despite the strange happenings of the day, he felt good. Exceptional. The best he had felt in years, since before the trouble began with Sheila. Smiling, he raised his glass.

"A toast." He hesitated for an instant. Unbidden, a favorite snatch of verse emerged from his subconscious. It fit the mood he was in perfectly. "Ah, my beloved, fill the Cup that clears Today of past Regrets and future Fears."

"*The Rubaiyat*. I loved it when I was in high school." Valerie sipped her wine, peering over the rim of her glass at him. "Before this goes any further, I have to warn you of something."

Alex's spirits plummeted. There was a cold knot in his gut. He knew she was too good to be true; his emotions had betrayed him again. At least, he had not made much of a fool of himself. He should have known better. Women like her were not for college professors. "Warn me of something?"

"You *are* an insecure one," said Valerie. Alex had not realized how poorly he was masking his feelings. "Your ex-wife must have been a real gem."

Alex nodded glumly. "My lawyer nicknamed her 'The Dragon Lady'. Remember? From the comic, *Terry and the Pirates*?"

"Got me. You're older than I am. Anyway, wipe the doom and gloom off your face. All I was going to say was that wine makes me dizzy. And very amorous." Her right hand made funny little patterns on his hand holding the wine glass. "Especially when it comes to vulnerable but gallant gentlemen."

Alex shook his head to clear the cobwebs. If he went through many more personality shifts, he'd turn schizophrenic.

The arrival of the lasagna provided a welcome break. He needed a little time to come back down from the clouds.

Hannah Stine waited in the darkness in the back yard of the Lancaster woman's home. It had not been hard to learn the address, just a couple of phone calls to the right people. Hannah had parked the Mistress's car a few blocks away and walked to the right street. It was a quiet neighborhood. People minded their own business here. In the gathering dusk, no one questioned a solitary stroller, especially one as plain as she. In the darkness, it was easy for her to make her way behind the row of townhouses. Her inner, sharper senses identified the right unit. No one was inside. That was to be expected. Lancaster's daughter was still having dinner with that college professor. The ruse this afternoon had made the fool over-confident. She would not be expecting an attack tonight. It was as her Mistress had planned. All was going well. Hannah would wait. Just like she had waited for the father, so would she wait for the child. She was patient. Very patient.

Alex and Valerie chatted happily through dinner, with Valerie doing most of the talking. Alex enjoyed listening. Since he lectured all week long, it was nice to be quiet and let someone else ramble on. Between funny stories of her job in New York, Valerie made quick work of her dinner. She cleared her plate and devoured most of the bread as well as several glasses of wine.

"Dessert?" asked Alex. "The cannoli here are made in Heaven. Or Hell, depending on whether you're on a diet or not."

"Bite your tongue, knave," said Valerie, wiping the last bit of sauce off her plate with the remnants of a piece of bread. "Diets are for work. I'm on an extended leave-of-absence and I'll eat what I want. Bring on your sinful pleasures."

"Coffee first. Then some straight talk. Then, and only then, dessert."

Valerie stuck her tongue out at him. "You drive a hard bargain. How about dessert first, then talk."

"No way. I'm stuffed. Let the food digest for a while."

"I'll make it worthwhile," said Valerie with a grin and a wink. She leaned forward. Her dress bunched up around her breasts, revealing quite a bit of skin. Valerie glanced down and back up at Alex. "Change your mind?"

Alex raised a hand to his face. Closing his eyes, he placed his thumb and index finger on his eyelids.

"What are you doing?" asked Valerie.

"Pushing my eyeballs back into their sockets. No fair. You have me at a disadvantage, but the answer is still no. Coffee first. Talk second. Dessert last."

"Beast."

Their waitress brought the coffee. Alex told her to return with dessert in fifteen minutes. "Not an eternity," he said to Valerie after the student had departed. "You can do it."

"I guess I'll have to." Valerie's expression grew serious. "Fooling time is over. What do you want to know?"

"Everything. What's the Devil's Auction? Can you explain this business with the voice over the intercom? How does all this tie in with Jake's murder? And where do I fit into the whole picture?"

"That's more than fifteen minutes' worth of talking."

"I couldn't agree more. Luckily I've got no plans tonight. Like the wise Chinese philosopher once said, 'The longest journey begins with the first step.' You want my help? You got it. But I still want some explanations before I stick my head in a noose."

Valerie settled back in her chair. Her hair swirled about her head in golden waves as she made herself comfortable. "One condition. You want answers. Well, so do I. You haven't exactly been a wellspring of information. You know a lot about me already, but I don't know a thing about you. I'll talk, but you have to respond in kind."

"Sounds fair. I have nothing to hide."

"Everyone has something to hide," replied Valerie, giving a snort of laughter. "Everyone. Where do you want me to begin?"

"The voice on the intercom. I got the impression it affected you a lot more than me."

"That's because it did. You weren't the target. In *Grimoires* it was called the Voice of Death. Was pretty popular in the Middle Ages. Crowley devoted an entire chapter of his *Magick in Theory and Practice* to it."

Alex nodded, trying to concentrate. Wine and a beautiful woman made serious thought difficult. "I've got it now. Eliphas Levi wrote about it as well. In a magical duel, the sound of a magician's voice can be enough to kill his enemies."

"Right. But it only affects other magicians. Translate that into those with *the Power*. Like me. Whoever was on the line was trying to kill me. The sound was sufficiently distorted by the intercom to take most of the kick out of the spell. I doubt if it would have worked even in person. Like most of the things Crowley described, he never offered any hard evidence. I suspect all the spell did was get the target extremely agitated. Exactly the way you saw me react."

"But how did our mystery man get the intercom to work in the first place."

"Mental projection. A good trick, but nothing that most second-rate sorcerers can't accomplish. Dad used to tease me with it all the time when I was a kid. Talk to me on the phone while he was riding on the El. Stunts like that. When I smashed the intercom box, it destroyed the link. Our unknown enemy had to search for something else to use. Took him quite a while to latch onto the phone. That's a clue in itself. A master magician would have had the phone ringing in seconds. Jake's killer is definitely not in that class. Just as well. We'd have a hell of a fight if we had to battle a master mage."

"Hey, back up for a second. Jake and I were pretty good friends. I'd guess I was probably as close to him as anyone, even you. He wasn't one to brag, but over the course of years I got the impression he was a pretty heavy hitter. Now you tell me he was killed by someone not very powerful. That doesn't make much sense."

Valerie took a swallow of coffee and then shook her head. "You're equating apples and oranges. I've no doubts that Dad was a more powerful sorcerer than his killer. There were only a few magicians in the country of his stature. That's not the point. Dad wasn't killed by magic. He was gassed and then attacked by some beast. Police showed me a tear-gas canister. It was another angle they couldn't understand. Why would anyone use gas during a home break-in?"

"To throw your father off balance so that he couldn't use magic to defend himself. Very slick."

"It all fits," said Valerie. "Not that it does us much good. There are probably over a hundred sorcerers and black magicians practicing in the United States these days. Any one of them could be the killer." She drew in a deep breath, causing her breasts to jiggle and sending his hormones into culture shock. "We don't lack for suspects."

"Jake had friends in high places. Couldn't they help?"

"Why? He's dead. Except for those with the Power and a few normal people who have learned the truth, no one believes in the forces of black magic. Ever since the Witchcraft Trials of the Middle Ages, sorcerers have worked trying to eradicate all knowledge of their existence. By and large, they've finally succeeded. Go tell a policeman that Jake Lancaster was killed by a rival magician and we'll see who they lock up. Jake was popular when he was alive, but nobody is going to rock the boat now that he's dead. Besides, for all you know, one of Jake's friends could have been his killer."

"So we're on our own."

"You said it. My turn to ask a question?"

"Fair enough. What do you want to know?"

Their waitress had left the pot on the table. Alex freshened both their cups.

"How did you meet Dad?"

"No mystery in that. He audited one of my courses. It was in September, a little more than six years ago. My book on the Witch Cult in Europe had been published by the University a few months earlier, so the Chairman of the History Department thought it would be a good idea to offer a course on the subject. I disagreed, but it was listed anyway. So much for academic freedom. Nine people took it, one more than the minimum class size requirement, and they were all radical feminists looking for deeper meanings than I was willing to attribute to medieval witchcraft. They saw women's liberation as a motivating force throughout history. We fought all semester. Hell, did we argue.

"Your father was the only male in the class. He got permission from the Chairman to audit the course. He never said a word the entire semester, and didn't take notes either. But he was attentive, which is more than I can say for my students. One night, near the end of our session, there was a particularly bitter fight. I was accused of everything from being a male chauvinist pig to an enemy of working women. After my judge and jury left, your father came up to me and suggested we go out for a bite to eat. I was in no mood for food, but he insisted it would help calm my nerves.

"We came here—sat in this same booth, in fact. Funny. Now that I think of it, that was probably the first time I sat back here. Whatever, I'm wandering."

"Don't be silly. I enjoy listening."

"Where have you been all my life? I never had one of my students ever say that. Anyway, getting back to that night. We came here and ordered a late dinner. I don't remember what. What I do recall, like it was yesterday, was your father insisting that we not get any wine with our meal. We had a pitcher of water instead."

"I know what's coming next," said Valerie, grinning. "Dad did it every chance he got. One of his favorite tricks."

"He was a sneaky devil." Alex shook his head from side to side. "Caught me completely by surprise. Jake had a subtle sense of humor. We talked about the class for a few minutes, then, somehow the topic focused in on real magic. That old devil had a way of twisting a conversation so that it always ended where he wanted. He was curious as to whether I believed that the witchcraft I described in my book really worked. Or did I think the practitioners were merely self-deluded lunatics? He got me to admit that I was pretty much of a skeptic. It was pretty difficult for me to accept a bunch of women in the 16th century flying around on broomsticks and casting spells on people they didn't like. Jake got me quoting all the major authorities on mass delusions and self-hypnosis.

"Then, I took a drink. The spicy Italian peppers and the intense conversation had me dried out. You can imagine my reaction when the water in the pitcher turned out to be fine white wine."

Valerie giggled. "He was a pistol all right. He loved that spell. It was one of the first ones he mastered. Did he ever tell you how he used to go to a different church every Sunday to practice? According to Dad, he sat in the back row and during the Mass would change the wine from red to white. Didn't stop until he got married and Mom made him give up his pranks."

"She was Catholic?"

"Nope. Unitarian. She was afraid that sooner or later someone would realize the transformation only took place when a certain Jake Lancaster was on hand. Mom was positive they'd burn him as a witch."

It was pitch black now. Hannah's sixth sense told her that they had finished their meal. Soon her prey would be leaving the restaurant. She could sense a growing rapport between the two of them, an emotional bond forming. All the better. It would make her task all the easier. Both of them had to die. Caught in the throes of passion, they would be easy prey. The professor she would kill immediately. A friend of the old man, he was unimportant to her plans. Lancaster's daughter would live a little longer only because she knew the location of the Invitation. Hannah would make her tell where it was. Only then would she let the girl die. That had been a mistake her Mistress had made with the father. They both had assumed the old man would not be able to hide the card. Somehow he had tricked them. The daughter possessed it now, but not for long. Hannah waited patiently in the darkness. It would be time to act soon enough.

"Your dessert, I believe?"

They had been so caught up in each other that Alex had not noticed anyone approaching. The sound of another person's voice caught him completely by surprise. He swung around in the booth to face the speaker.

Five feet seven, one hundred and forty pounds stripped. Yellow skin that perfectly complimented jet black hair. Bright eyes that sparkled with good humor. Wearing a white apron embossed with a picture of Opus the Penguin holding a soup ladle. With Jake Lancaster gone, this man was his closest friend in the world.

"Can it be?" Alex said. "Mama Mia in the flesh?"

"Had to come over and say hello. Especially after Sharon told me you had brought in the foxiest woman ever to grace this humble establishment." Makoto Tsuiki bowed his head respectfully. "I see that for a change the young lady spoke the truth." His friend placed the plate of Italian pastries in front of Valerie. "Please accept this small offering as a token of appreciation for your gracing my humble eating emporium with your presence. May I join you for a moment?"

Alex couldn't believe it. This was a first for Tsuiki. Never once during all the times he had brought Sheila with him to the restaurant had Mak ever spent more than a few instants at their table; a quick hello had always been it. His extended conversations with Alex had always been when he had come with Jake or on his own to Mama Mia's. Alex could feel a slight tinge of jealousy rising within him. He had forgotten Valerie's spell. For some odd reason, he had thought Makoto would be immune to it. So much for theories.

"Valerie Lancaster, Makoto Tsuiki," said Alex, trying not to sound annoyed. "Valerie's father was Jake Lancaster."

"Aha. I thought I noticed the resemblance. I was grieved to hear of your father's death. A terrible tragedy. We were friends for many years." Makoto put an arm around Alex's shoulders. "We both tried our best to take care of Alexander."

Alex turned his head slightly and glanced at his friend. Mak wasn't trying to be funny; sarcasm had never been part of his character. Sucking in a deep breath, Alex decided he should have known better. There was no way he could be angry with Mak very long. He owed him too much from the years gone by—his life, for one thing. And, recently, since the divorce, Makoto had helped him through some pretty hard times.

"Did you?" asked Valerie. She had a funny look on her face, and Alex wondered if he was missing something.

"Sometimes yes, sometimes no," Mak said. Alex did not always listen to the wise advice of his friends."

"Yeah," said Alex, breaking in. "There was Sheila, for example. Both you and Jake tried to warn me about her."

"The Dragon Lady." Makoto loved that nickname. "But, stop. It is not polite to talk poorly about another woman when in the company of one so beautiful."

The topic turned to their dinner. Valerie raved about the food. Mak told a few funny stories about problems raised being Japanese while owning an Italian restaurant. Alex relaxed, at peace with the world. Finally, Makoto rose to his feet. "I've intruded long enough. Please, enjoy the pastries." He bowed again to Valerie. "A great pleasure meeting you. I only wish your return had been in more pleasant circumstances. I trust you will take good care of our friend." Valerie smiled and nodded. Makoto turned back to Alex. "You are in good hands. I will rest peacefully tonight. Monday afternoon at the dojo?"

"For sure. It'll take me a week to work off all the lasagna I ate tonight. Sometimes I think you cook this stuff just to slow me down."

"You are a slug already, foreign devil," said Makoto, with a laugh. "No excuses can save you."

With those words, his friend departed. Alex turned back to a somewhat bemused looking Valerie. "What was that all about?" she asked.

"Mak and I train at the same dojo. We practice together. He's an eyelash faster than me and won't let me forget it. I blame it on his cooking. He claims no westerner can ever best a Japanese in the martial arts."

"Dojo? Judo?"

"Karate. I got interested in it in Viet Nam— that was where I met Mak. We were the only Chicago boys in our Unit, and we grew pretty friendly there. He saved my life. A couple of times."

"And you did nothing for him?"

"Well, there were a few instances when I

67

repaid the favor. Let's drop the subject. The War isn't one of my favorite topics of conversation."

"Fine with me. Did you notice, by the way, that your friend wasn't affected by the *glamour*?"

"He wasn't?" Alex snorted. "You don't know him. That was definitely not normal behavior for Makoto Tsuiki."

"Nevertheless, I know my own powers. He wasn't affected. And I don't think it had anything to do with lack of sexual prowess. His mind was . . . different. I could feel it. His mind was at peace."

"Perhaps I know what you mean after all. *Tranquility*. Mak is a follower of Shinto. He's been involved in it most of his life. He tried to get me to study it more than once, but it never took. I'm too hyper. In any case, a true Shinto master becomes one with all of nature, at peace with all things. Tao."

Valerie nodded. "He's a good friend. You're lucky to have him. Not many people have someone who cares."

"I guess so; I never gave it much thought before. Mak really took a shine to you, though. He despised Sheila—tried hard to talk me out of marrying her. So did your father, for that matter."

"Jake was always meddling in other people's lives," said Valerie. She didn't elaborate and

Alex let the statement rest. Valerie was probably thinking how her father had pushed her into the world of black magic, he thought. It was time to change the mood.

"Had enough? Why don't we get going? My car is in the campus lot. I'll drive you home."

"Sounds fine to me. Not to Jake's place though; the police have that sealed. No one was sure when they'd be through. I own a townhouse on the North Shore, anyway, for when I'm in the city."

Alex left a five dollar bill for the waitress. "Mak keeps my bills on a tab. I pay him once a month and deduct it as a business expense on my taxes. For research."

A new crowd of customers had replaced those who had been in the front room when they had arrived. The result was the same: total silence as they made their way to the front, all eyes glued to Valerie. Alex was willing to swear that no one even breathed. By the time they exited, he was holding his own.

He said, "You eat out very often?"

"Hardly ever."

"I'm not surprised. Is it always like that?"

"Worse sometimes. Depends on where I go. And with whom."

Valerie looped her arm gently around his as they walked. She seemed to know instinctively what pleased him the most.

The air was cool and crisp. The wind

whipped through Valerie's hair, forming a blonde halo around her face. Her ankle-length black coat with long slits up the sides hugged her body. She was the most beautiful woman Alex had ever met, both physically and mentally. And she was with him.

They drove up Lake Shore Drive heading north. Alex put a Glenn Miller tape on the cassette player. At least he had one thing to thank his ex-wife for. She loved 1940s big-band music and he had been a willing convert. The soft strains of "In the Mood" filled the car as they made their way uptown. Valerie was quiet, huddling up close next to him. There was no need to talk. The events of earlier in the day seemed very far distant.

Valerie's townhouse was located off the La Salle street exit of the Drive, on a quiet side street a few blocks from the Park. The large brick condominium was attached to two others. Each unit had its own separate driveway. There was even a built-in garage on the lower level of the building, resting beneath the living room. Alex was no expert on real estate values, but he knew Chicago neighborhoods pretty well. Location meant a great deal in this city, and this townhouse cost more money than he would earn in all of his years as a Professor. And Valerie had implied she only used this place when she was visiting the city. Alex pulled his car into the driveway. "Door to door service."

"How about coming in for a drink?" Valerie showed no evidence of abandoning her position snuggled up close to him. "We still have lots to talk about."

"Uh, maybe tomorrow. I've got a lot of work to finish. It's been a wonderful evening, but I'd better be going."

"Going? Alex, what's bothering you? Did I say something wrong?" She moved off of his shoulder and swung around to look directly at him. "Please, tell me."

He was torn between telling her the truth and making up some excuse. She actually seemed pretty upset. The outside lights on the garage reflected off what had to be—tears in her eyes. There was no way he could lie to this woman. She deserved the truth.

"I'm sorry," he said. "You've been fine. Wonderful, actually. I've had a terrific time. You can't imagine how much I've enjoyed being with you. That's what scares me. I like you too much."

Valerie raised both her hands so that one touched each of his cheeks. Holding his head gently, she moved forward and kissed him. It was a long kiss, but not the passionate embrace of that afternoon. Instead, it was gentle and delicate, a loving kiss. "Once burned, twice cautious," whispered Valerie, when she drew back from him. "Alex, life goes on. You can't be afraid of what might happen between us, what *is* happening. I'm not your ex-wife and you aren't the same person who married her. We are who we are. Can't we leave it at that for now?"

"I guess so. I have to admit, I really wasn't that anxious to leave. Still, all your money . . ."

"Can't buy me happiness." Valerie rested a hand on his. "Or respect. Or friendship. Or love. The money I make from modeling is very nice, Alex. I won't dispute that. But I live alone. When I'm not working, I spend most of my time by myself. You can fault me for many things, but please, don't let the money I make put you off. I deserve better than that."

"You're right." He was feeling guilty now, almost wallowing in self-pity. He had been pretty casual about the way he was treating Valerie. It was not the way a gentleman acted, and he had always prided himself on acting like a gentleman. "I've been pretty dumb. Did you say something about a drink?"

"You bet. And Alex," Valerie's hand was still on his, "I don't think you've been acting dumb. Just very, very human."

They got out of the car. Holding hands, they climbed the steps leading to the door. Valerie turned her key in the lock, but before she could push the door open, Alex stepped forward.

"I don't mean to be an alarmist, but how about letting me go first? That voice over the intercom made some serious threats. And Jake's death was no joke. The two of us have been acting pretty casual about this. I mean, there *is* a killer on the loose, and according to the voice, you're next on the list."

Valerie shook her head. "I can't imagine our mysterious enemy trying anything tonight. Dad was caught by surprise. That won't happen with me. Anyway, it's okay inside. Remember, I may have been a novice sorceress, but I was raised in a family of magicians. Parents have always worried about their kids and strangers. One of the first things I learned as a child was how to sense the *feel* of my home. I'm quite sure there's no danger inside. Come on in. Nothing to be afraid of. Other," and she grinned at him, "than a predatory female."

"I'll take my chances."

Hannah smiled. They had arrived. It was early yet; let them get comfortable. Relax. Perhaps even indulge in the pleasures of the flesh. She would know when the moment had come, when all their defenses were down and they were helpless. Then, and only then, would she strike. Hannah flexed her fingers instinctively. To feel her claws rip human flesh, her fangs dig deep into living tissue. To rend and claw and tear. That was the true pleasure that no sexual experience could match. She was patient. *Soon.* Her time was coming. *Very soon now.*

CHAPTER FOUR

Valerie followed Alex into the townhouse. She flung her coat on a chair in the front foyer and he did the same. The next instant she was gone, moving from room to room, turning on lights everywhere. He followed at a more leisurely pace, looking around and trying to get a feel for the house. The place had the empty look of a model home.

"I always like lots of illumination," Valerie called from the rear of the townhouse. "Makes a house feel so much more lived in. You want something to drink?"

He found her in the kitchen, pouring herself a glass of fruit juice from a large plastic pitcher.

"A soda pop would be nice," he said. "The

wine and the company has me a little dizzy."

"There's an open bottle of Diet Pop on the kitchen counter, if you want. Otherwise, I have some big two-liter plastic bottles of Coke in the 'fridge door."

"Coke, please. I don't care for the taste of anything with the word Diet on it."

"Me neither." Valerie wrinkled up her nose. "But it's all I drink when I'm working. I'm on an extended leave-of-absence for now, but I still can't have dinners like the one tonight very often. Otherwise I'll be modeling hefty bags instead of swimsuits."

"Never," said Alex, with emphasis, and he meant it. In the bright lights of the room, Valerie looked better than ever. The harsh illumination betrayed no hidden flaws. She was tall and slender, almost angular. She moved with an economy of motion that Alex found extremely graceful.

Idly, he looked around the kitchen. It was bright and shiny and, he suspected, not used very much. As Valerie pulled some ice cube trays from the freezer, he spotted a host of low-calorie TV dinners wedged in the frozen food shelves. Two chairs rested at the breakfast bar, with one of them wedged underneath the overhang. It looked like it had been that way for a long time. A heavy wood door broke the length of the back wall.

"Where does that door go?"

"Oh, into the jungle." Valerie giggled as she poured him a glass of soda pop. "To my backyard, actually. Mr. Peterson, my neighbor, was supposed to take care of it but he was away most of the summer. Never realized how wild a yard could get if no one took care of it. The people on the other side, the Marantzes, are gone most of the time and use a service. Wish they had let me know how bad my yard had gotten. Next spring I'll have to hire a bunch of natives with machetes to cut down the growth."

Alex walked over and inspected the door. It was solidly built, made of heavy wood, with crossed beams reinforcing the bottom half. There was a narrow glass panel, 3 inches by 8 inches across, at eye level. The door was made for keeping out intruders, but only a cheap boltlock held it shut. As added protection, there was a thin sliding chainlock as well. Alex knew how little safety that guaranteed. He peered through the glass panel into the yard. It was too dark to see anything, and there was no back light. He didn't like the arrangement one bit. Grabbing one of the unused kitchen chairs, he carried it over to the rear entrance.

"Ever go out this way?"

"No." Valerie was emptying a bag of potato chips into a wicker basket. She didn't pay any attention to what he was doing until a chair leg scraped on the floor.

"Alex, what's going on?"

Without answering, he shoved the top of the chair under the knob of the door. One push and it was wedged tight, its back legs resting solidly on the kitchen tiles.

"I'm not crazy." He took the Coke from Valerie's hand and smiled at her astonished expression. "Just paranoid." Then he got serious. "Listen, Valerie. Your father was killed a little more than a week ago. The police think otherwise, but you and I both know it was done for a reason. I'm not sure what. That voice today said something about an Invitation. Hopefully you'll explain that to me now. In any case, those threats on the intercom were real. I don't care how powerful your magical senses are, and whether or not you think the killer won't strike again because you're ready for him. You can't use logic when dealing with murderers. They work by different rules than you or I.

"You admitted this afternoon that Jake was easy prey for a direct physical attack. He was in that fortress of his on the third floor of his house, and that didn't save him. What chance would you have in this place? Your front door has a nice sturdy deadbolt. This door is completely unprotected. Since you don't use it, leave this chair here. It's something at least. If someone tried to break in, it would give you a few extra seconds. That could be the difference between life and death."

"I won't argue with you," said Valerie as she walked past him carrying his drink and the basket of chips. "Though I think you *are* a little nuts. Come on into the living room. It's a lot more comfortable there."

The living room sat directly above the garage and looked down on the driveway. The furniture, like everything else in the house, appeared virtually new. Alex wondered how much time Valerie spent here. Obviously, not very much. A huge console TV and stereo system covered one wall of the room, and a bright blue couch faced it on the opposite wall; a matching loveseat stood in front of a huge picture window. Curtains kept the room isolated from the street. The coffee table and several expensive-looking end tables provided a touch of wood. Each small table held a delicate crystal lamp. To Alex, it looked terribly sterile: another indication of the emptiness in Valerie's life.

They sprawled on the huge couch that dominated the room. "Not exactly the height of sophistication." Valerie held up her glass of juice and smiled. "Fruit juice, Coca-Cola, and potato chips."

"You asked me in for a drink. This suits me fine." Alex gulped down half the glass of pop. "I can use the caffeine. Can we get back to our game of question and answer?"

"If you insist." She kicked off her heels and stretched her arms high over her head. The motion did extraordinary things to her dress and set Alex's pulse racing. "You want to know about the Devil's Auction."

It took Alex a minute before he could reply. Putting his glass down, he clasped his hands together and counted to ten. His heart was still pounding, but he was now capable of logical thought. Valerie was teasing him. It was pretty obvious by now even to someone as thick as he was. Her every motion was calculated to drive him wild. Alex had to admit that she was doing a great job. The rest of the evening was going to be interesting.

"Ever since the incident with the intercom this afternoon," he said, "I've been trying to remember where I heard that expression. I must have encountered it somewhere in my studies. Tell me what you know about it. Maybe something you say will strike the right note."

"Well, I hope you're not going to be disappointed. I don't know much. Wouldn't have remembered it at all if Dad hadn't clued me in with his phone call."

"Phone call? What phone call?"

"Sorry. Never got around to telling you. I didn't say a thing to the police about it, so it's between you and me."

"Of course. Now what are you talking about?"

"The night he died, Dad called me. I was off on assignment in Canada and my answering machine recorded the message. When the police found Dad's body on Friday, they tried to contact me but I was staying with friends in Toronto and hadn't left a number with my agency. I didn't learn of Dad's death until Saturday morning when I returned to my apartment in New York. Fortunately, before I flew to Chicago I checked the answering machine.

"I can only guess what had happened. Somehow, Dad knew he was going to be killed. I have no idea how. He was the sorcerer, not me. Why does it matter anyway? He knew. His call was meant as a warning to me. And provided a motive: the Invitation to the Devil's Auction."

"You still haven't told me what that means."

"Let me tell it my way, okay? It's the only way we'll be able to make some sense out of this mess. Believe me, we don't have much to go on. Dad's message was short and to the point. I think he was afraid someone else might hear it and didn't want to say too much."

"Not too surprising," said Alex. "Almost

anyone can get messages from an answering machine these days with a whistle and some determination."

"I can't remember his exact words. I wrote them down somewhere if you need to know. The gist of what he said was that he had received an invitation to attend a rare curio auction in upstate Illinois. He was quite certain he wasn't going to make it. Dad made sure that I understood that to attend the auction you had to have an invitation. The event was going to be held there on Halloween at an estate owned by Vassily Romanov."

"Great. We can trace . . ."

"Not so fast, handsome. It's a little more difficult than that. Vassily Romanov was one of Dad's closest friends. He had studied with him in Europe when he was a teenager. Dad told me lots of Romanov stories when I was a kid. The guy was not a great magician, but he did things with a style and flair that I think Dad envied."

Alex frowned. He had a bad feeling that he knew where Valerie was leading. "Do I get the distinct impression that Romanov is no longer with us?"

"Give the man a cigar. Vassily Romanov died thirty years ago."

It was time for the change, Hannah Stine decided. This present form was doing her little good. She had forgotten the Lancaster girl's accursed aura. At a distance it was not a problem, but close up it filled the psychic sphere with static. The wave of sensuality she exuded was so powerful it completely blocked off all of Hannah's psychic probes, leaving her with no way to tell what was going on inside the house. Still, they had been in there for quite a while and the professor showed no signs of leaving.

Hannah was no fool. She had served her Mistress for too many years not to know what was probably taking place. Disgusting, revolting joinings. The very thought of sex made Hannah feel ill. It was unclean. When her Mistress took a lover, life was unbearable. Happily, such occurrences usually ended in a quarrel. Hannah was always given the job of ending the discarded lover's worthless life. She suspected that a great deal of the excitement her Mistress derived from such sexual couplings was the knowledge that soon her lover would be screaming in pain when Hannah toyed with him. Often, her Mistress had her torture the victim for hours. Sweat formed on Hannah's brow as she remembered the last satisfying entertainment. Even with his guts ripped open, he had lasted for *such* a long time. Much better than killing old Lancaster. That had been done in a rush—no telling what the old man would have done if given the time.

Lancaster's daughter would make up for the loss. Hannah would make the girl last a long time. A very long time.

Suddenly anxious to begin, she removed her clothes. There were no labels or identifying tags inside them in case she did not have a chance to recover the garments. Her Mistress made sure she was very careful. Hannah smiled. They made a very good team. Beauty and the beast. She raised her eyes up and concentrated on the full moon. Barely moving her lips, Hannah pronounced the word of power.

The Change began.

"Maybe I'm dense, but I seem to have missed a turn somewhere. Why did Jake refer to Romanov if the man died before you were born."

"Aha." Valerie pointed a finger at him in melodramatic fashion. *"That* is the question. I asked myself the same thing a dozen times on the flight out here. It took me a while to remember, but then it hit me. Years ago, Dad told me the story of Romanov's death. It was in a fight with another magician. They were battling for possession—"

"—of an invitation to The Devil's Auction," Alex finished. "So this isn't the first time it's been held."

"Not according to Dad. Last time was on

Halloween, which, according to Dad's call, is when it is to take place again. He also told me that only a small number of invitations are sent out and you can't attend without one."

Alex was fascinated. He was positive that he had read about a similar auction in one of the books in his library, but he could not place the right one. The title was lurking in the depths of his memory. He hoped that a little more information would provide the necessary clue.

"What's auctioned off at this big affair? And who runs the show?"

"Two good questions, my dear. I wish I knew the answers. All Dad had were theories."

"Theories. What kind of theories?"

"I don't remember them very well, Alex. Remember, I was told this story years ago, long before I moved out. I've forgotten most of what Dad said. On the other hand, I gave both questions a lot of thought during this past week. It doesn't take a lot of imagination to make some good guesses. You want to try a theory or two on your own? Just based on what I've told you."

"Hmm. I think I see what you mean. Play detective using the clues we already have. Sounds simple enough. For one thing, basic logic dictates that whatever is auctioned off at this event is pretty valuable—considering at least two men have been killed by other magicians wanting their invitations."

"According to Dad, when Romanov was killed there were a lot more than murders in the scramble."

"Strengthens our line of reasoning. The actual object or objects being auctioned off aren't important to us. For all we know, no one knows what they are. In fact, I'm willing to bet none of those attending have any idea what is up for auction."

"That's a pretty big assumption."

"In the back of my head there are bells ringing. I can't pin the story down yet, but I know I've heard it before, or seen it someplace. In one of the books in my library there's a description of this auction, or one very similar. And I remember distinctly that no one knew what the valuable object being offered for sale actually *was*. There were rumors and stories, of course, and afterwards, no one admitted ever attending the auction. Nor was there any confirmation of what was sold. Or who got it. Such secrecy in magical circles points to some pretty potent stuff, since the commentaries on magic seldom leave much out. So, I think we can assume this object must be of great value to sorcerers. Otherwise, why all the killing?"

"I came up with pretty much the same answer. If we follow that line of reasoning, that leads us to one possible conclusion: It has to be a magical talisman of great power."

Alex rubbed his chin with one hand. "A talisman? A magic charm?"

"More, Alex, much more. You're an expert on the history of magical practices. You must know about objects of power."

"Of course. It's just hard for me to accept that Jake was killed by someone who wanted an invitation to an auction where some ring or necklace is going to be offered for sale."

"It has to be the reason nonetheless, Alex. Don't mock. You know that most magic involves two things. *The will and the way* is the first thing anyone trying to become a true magician learns. Only a few people possess the certain psychic gifts, what we call *the Power*, to perform real magic. That is the will. Anyone can try to use magic but the spell will work only for those with the Power.

"Theoretically, a true sorcerer should be able to do anything he wants merely by concentrating. Dad once suggested that Jesus Christ was not divine but instead the greatest of all sorcerers. Using *will* alone, Christ was able to perform miracles. Mom wouldn't speak to him for a week until he apologized. It's a fascinating thought. In any case, all of the sorcerers living today need aids to help them in their magical pursuits, paths that help them achieve the level of concentration or mental readiness, certain words that are necessary for them to focus their will in special directions. It is a very important part of the black arts. The Way. Thus you have spells, rituals, ceremonies, and yes— even talismans and charms. Many such objects have absorbed their own measure of power from long years of contact with powerful magicians. Certain talismans can retain both the will *and* the way from their users. Think of them as gigantic batteries, filled with psychic energy. These magic talismans are passed down from generation to generation. It's a give-and-take situation. A magician uses it for greater powers, and in doing so, imparts some of his magic into the talisman for a future user. Obviously, the older the talisman, assuming it has been used again and again, the greater its power. A knowledgeable adept can tap into that power and perform great acts of sorcery."

"And men will kill for these talismans?"

"Read the paper. Men kill for lots of things. Money, love, hate, you name it. A powerful talisman, an ancient symbol of power, for example, might enable a magician to raise the dead or control the weather. Didn't you ever read that occult book about the Spear of Destiny? The one supposedly used to kill Christ? Imagine the power such an object would possess. Or the Shroud of Turin." Valerie's voice had a strange ring to it. "Imagine. Do you wonder that legends grow up about such things?"

"Okay, I'm convinced. I know all the myths, too. I always considered them mere fabrications. Since sorcery exists in the world, I guess that implies magic talismans as well. Just give me a little time to adjust to the fact.

"Let's back up a bit, though. We're pretty well set so far. The auction was last held thirty years ago, and is going to be held again next week. Some mystical talisman or talismans may be offered for bid. You can only attend with an invitation, and invitations are hard to come by." Alex shook his head. "Great stuff. For every question we answer, five more are raised."

"Well, don't start yet," said Valerie, sliding over on the couch. "Time for a kiss and Coke break."

"A what?"

"Here, let me demonstrate."

Valerie's demonstration had him gasping for breath after a few minutes. Her fingers twirled across the back of his neck as they embraced, setting his hair on end. Alex could feel the warmth of her body pressed tight up against his side. Valerie definitely had other things on her mind.

"Want some more Coke?" she whispered softly in his ear, running her tongue across his ear lobe immediately afterward. "I need another glass of juice."

"Whatever you say." Alex loosened his collar.

Sweat trickled down his neck and across his chest. "Sure is hot in here."

Valerie laughed, a deep, low chuckle that sent shivers all over his body. She gathered their glasses and rose from the couch. "It'll get a lot hotter later, sweetie." She ran her tongue slowly over her upper lip. "A *lot* hotter."

CHAPTER FIVE

The pain ripped through her as it always did. It was part of the Change. Her Mistress had tried to explain the metamorphosis to her once but the words had made little sense. Hannah did not care; she needed no clarification of the alteration that overwhelmed her.

Somehow, by uttering a Word of Power, her body transformed from that of a mere human into a creature of the night. She became a thing that could kill.

Now she stood motionless in the moonlight. Her muscles stretched and grew as the Change moved down her back and into her lower body. It felt as though her muscles were pulling apart. Bones cracked as they shifted beneath her skin. A terrible itching swept through her. Thick, coarse hair covered her arms and legs. Huge teeth expanded in her jaws.

Then the Change was complete and Hannah Stine existed no longer. A huge beast stood in her place.

Her senses were much greater now. The smell of her prey filled her nostrils. They were close, very close. She could almost taste the hot blood in her mouth. No longer could she maintain the patient watch she had kept all evening. In this form, patience did not exist. Thought led to immediate action. With a silent growl, she leapt onto the wooden back porch of the Lancaster woman's home. The two humans waited inside. Only a thin piece of wood stood between her and them. No lock could hold her out.

She did not hesitate. Her massive body smashed into the porch door.

Valerie started for the kitchen, swaying her hips in an exaggerated motion. It was more silly than sexy, but it set the mood. Serious talk was past. There was a time for being a gentleman, and then there were other times. This was one of those exceptions. Valerie left no doubts about her intentions for the rest of the evening.

Alex scrambled off the sofa. With a wild giggle, Valerie dashed into the kitchen. He was quick to follow.

He caught her by the counter, where she was putting the glasses down. Reaching from behind her, he encircled her with his arms. Without hesitation, she swung around and pressed up tight against him. They kissed passionately. His body pushed hard against her, pinning her to the refrigerator door. Alex could feel the heat burning within her. Valerie's arms were locked around his neck, holding his face tight against hers. His hands slipped down across her back, pulling her forward and even tighter.

With a loud crash, the outside door shuddered violently. The heavy wood panels shook, as something huge slammed against them again and again. The chair beneath the doorknob screeched against the tile floor but held. Paranoia had triumphed. Outside, something *howled* in anger.

Alex pushed Valerie away. He had to clear his head fast. It was hard to think with his brain numbed by passion. Savagely, he bit his tongue. The pain snapped him into full awareness. Automatic defense mechanisms buried deep in his subconscious took over. It was that night in Viet Nam all over again. *Escape* commanded his mind, and his body reacted.

The door vibrated again as the thing outside smashed into it. The wood would not hold another assault. Alex pulled his car keys from his pocket and thrust them into Valerie's hands. He half lifted, half pushed her to the living room doorway. "The car. Get the car going."

"I can't leave you here, Alex!" She was trembling but otherwise in complete control.

"Get going. I know what I'm doing." He shoved her again. "Go!" Valerie hesitated only for a second, then turned and ran.

Alex whirled around and ripped open the drawer in the kitchen counter. He cursed when he saw that all it held was a fork and a smooth edged knife. He had hoped for a steak knife at least.

Behind him, the back door crashed to the floor with a hail of wood chips. There was a plastic bottle half full of Coke on the counter. Alex grabbed that. In deadly combat, anything could be a weapon. He turned to confront their attacker.

The monster stood in the rear doorway, its blazing yellow eyes narrowed from the bright lights of the kitchen. Poor vision, Alex noted. It had a gaping mouth filled with huge teeth, a muscular body covered with dark hair, and gigantic hands ending in clawed fingers. It seemed sexless. He recognized it almost immediately. He had seen pictures of such things in many books of magic: it was a servant of the darkest forces . . . a werewolf.

The creature swung its head around and spotted him. It growled, the sound rising from deep in its chest. Its body seemed to expand as it drew in its breath. It was going to attack. *Keep the enemy off guard*, his mind warned. His one hope was that a human mind resided in the beast's body. He doubted it really possessed any great fighting skills beyond its own animal strength.

Frantically, Alex put one hand over the top of the Coke bottle. He shook it hard. Then, before the werewolf could react, he released his hand and let the soda pop spray the thing in the face, splashing it in the eyes and nose.

It was a lucky shot, catching the monster completely off guard. It roared in anger. The carbonated soda pop had to sting. For a second, the creature's hands were rubbing its eyes violently.

Alex ran to the kitchen breakfast-bar. He pulled out the other chair. With a flip of the wrist, he flung it into the werewolf's legs. The chair connected with a solid *thunk*, knocking the creature back.

It roared again. Blood dripped from two gashes in its flesh. The monster was strong, but it was vulnerable. It could feel pain. He had a chance.

Alex scrambled into the living room, knowing the werewolf would follow in a second. He needed a weapon. The front door of the townhouse stood open. It tempted him for a second, but his fighting instincts warned him away. He dared not show the monster his back. When Valerie signalled, he would flee. Until then, he had to fight.

With a bestial roar, the werewolf entered the living room. From the way the thing acted, Alex suspected it had never encountered resistance before, had never actually fought anyone. It was a killer—it had to be the thing that had murdered Jake Lancaster and perhaps many others—but its every action betrayed the fact that it wasn't a fighter. Grimly, Alex stared at the powerful muscles rippling in its chest and arms. There was no way he could hold off the werewolf in a fair fight, but he had no intention of fighting fair. A fierce joy filled him. *Time to strike back.*

"Here I am, baby," he called softly.

Immediately, the creature's head swung around, looking for him. It reacted the same way it had in the kitchen, as Alex had suspected it would. The sofa pillow he launched right after speaking caught the monster full in the snout. The fabric bag did no damage, but it further enraged the monster. Keep the enemy angry and confused was another Viet Nam lesson.

The werewolf leapt forward, claws slashing down. The cushions on the sofa exploded in a flurry of feathers.

But Alex was already somewhere else. He had started moving as soon as he had launched the pillow. Circling to his left, he grabbed up a small leaded-glass lamp. As the werewolf lifted its head to find him, Alex sent the lamp flying at the monster's body.

This time it reacted faster. One arm swept out and knocked the lamp away in mid-air. Alex cursed as the werewolf came rushing right at him. For a second, gaping teeth flashed as yellow claws ripped the air.

Alex dropped to the floor. The beast crashed over him. He grabbed the creature by both ankles and heaved with all his strength. The monster slammed hard into the wall, but it was not out. Almost before Alex moved, the creature chased after him.

Then the werewolf howled in triumph. Instinctively, Alex leapt to the side and down, rolling away, his body curled in a tight ball.

The monster rushed past, blundering into the huge TV set. It hit its legs in nearly the same spot that had been damaged by the chair. Roaring in pain, it doubled up for a second. Alex grabbed hold of a heavy ottoman with both hands and shoved it at the creature. The chair struck the werewolf hard in the legs, trapping it against the TV.

From outside came the loud honking of his car horn. *Perfect timing*, Alex thought, *another lucky break*. It was like Viet Nam all over again. He rushed for the door.

The monster's howls of rage filled the room.

At the front door, Alex risked a quick look back. The werewolf had not attempted to move the chair. Instead, it was ripping the ottoman to kindling. In seconds, it would be free. Alex kept going. He slammed the door shut behind him, then took the outside steps two at a time.

Valerie was revving up his car's motor at full blast. There was no time to switch positions, so Alex swung up and over the hood. The passenger door was unlocked. Pulling it open, he flung himself inside. "Lock your door and get this thing moving. That werewolf—"

He didn't have time to finish the sentence. The picture window above and in front of the driveway shattered as the monster came charging through. It landed on all fours only a few feet in front of them. Valerie threw the car in reverse. With the motor already engaged, the auto shot backward like a bullet.

They careened into the street, tires leaving a track of rubber in the driveway. Only Valerie's quick spinning of the steering wheel saved them from crashing into the cars parked across from the townhouse. Her foot slammed down hard on the brake, bringing them to a sudden stop. Alex grabbed the door handle as he went tumbling forward. Even then, he hit the dashboard hard enough to knock the breath from his lungs.

Valerie yanked hard on the gear shaft, slamming the car into drive. She kept her foot hard on the brake. The auto shook as she gunned the motor, tires whining in protest. Face taut, Valerie peered through the front window. "Come on. Come on."

As if in answer, the werewolf came barreling down the driveway. Arms outstretched, the creature charged the car. Valerie flipped on the headlights. They caught the werewolf full on, blinding it for an instant. The beast stumbled back, arms held high to shield its eyes. Valerie released her foot from the brake. Like a wild animal, the car leapt forward, straight at the monster.

The werewolf's incredible reflexes thwarted Valerie's plans. With a perfectly-timed lunge, it leapt onto the hood of their car. Powerful fingers grabbed onto the windshield wipers' slot, digging into the steel. Alex could see the monster's cord-like muscles stand out in bold relief as it began to pull itself forward. Its jaws gaped open like the mouth of Hell.

Valerie pressed the gas pedal to the floor and they roared down the narrow street. The werewolf pulled itself closer and closer to the front window. It was hanging on now with only one hand. The other was drawn back, fingers curled into a giant fist.

"Brake!" shouted Alex. "Brake, brake!"

Valerie braked. At the speed they were going,

the car couldn't stop. Instead, it skidded sharply, lurching from side to side, shuddering and shaking.

Despite its terrible strength, the werewolf went flying off the hood. It bounced to the pavement, landed in a roll, and was on its feet in a second.

By then, they were fifty feet further down the road. Valerie needed no further coaching. Her foot slammed back down on the gas pedal and once more the car built up speed. She kept her eyes on the road ahead. Behind them, the werewolf was left standing alone in the middle of the street.

Alex released the breath he had been holding. He had not exhaled, it seemed, since he first got into the car. They had discovered the identity of Jake's murderer, he realized, and escaped without falling victim to the same fate.

"Head south on the Drive. We'll be safe in my apartment for the night. No way that creature could get up to my floor without being noticed. There are too many people about all the time. And, the powers-that-be don't allow wolves in campus apartment buildings. At least, not that kind of wolf."

CHAPTER SIX

Hannah stopped the car at the gates of the estate. She did not relish facing her Mistress. The Countess was not gracious in defeat. Her temper was terrible to behold when confronted with any disappointment. Hannah had never been thwarted before; this was the first time her quarry had escaped. The news would not sit well with her Mistress, she knew. There was too little time left to make new plans. The mysterious auction was only a few days away, and without an Invitation, they could not attend.

The sweat trickled down Hannah's back as she remembered how her Mistress had ranted and raved for hours when they had been unable to find the card at Lancaster's house. The Countess had beaten her unmercifully because she had killed the old man before they could question him. It did Hannah little good to remind her Mistress that she was the one who had ordered the magician's death. What would the Countess do when Hannah told her of this latest failure?

It did not matter much. Hannah had no other place to go: this was her home and here she belonged. There was little use in stalling. Whatever fate awaited her, it was destiny.

Grimly, she got out of the car and unlocked the gates that were the only break in the nine-foot-high wall that surrounded the vast estate. As she swung open the huge metal doors, iron grated on iron with a harsh, scraping sound. Hannah stood waiting in the entrance way. It did not take long for the noise to bring the hounds.

The two beasts came charging out of the bushes. Monstrous dogs with yellow fangs, their eyes blazed in the darkness. Each of the two weighed nearly a hundred pounds. Wolfhounds, the Mistress called them, but Hannah knew better. They were Hellhounds. The beast within her recognized the terrible souls imprisoned in animal bodies. Long ago the Countess had raised these things up from the Netherworld. They had animal form, but Hannah knew their true nature by their terrible, cold, blood-red eyes, eyes without pupils. At night, those eyes burned like coals in the darkness.

She remembered the beasts from her earliest childhood. They were the only part of her youth she still recalled with absolute clarity. Red eyes staring at her from just beyond the windows of the mansion. The hounds had always known when she was awake. They patrolled the patios outside her room. Whenever Hannah looked out, they were there, staring in at her. Glowing red eyes and huge fangs, pressed up against the glass. The beasts hungered for her flesh. Instead of frightening Hannah, that bloodlust had fueled her own obsessive hatred of the Hellhounds. That anger had only grown over the years.

Unchanging and eternal, the dogs still patrolled the grounds at night with ruthless efficiency. Not once had there ever been a complaint about them to the town police. That was because the hounds were too intelligent for mere beasts. Reckless teenagers or schoolboys on a dare, the Hellhounds merely cornered, then barked until Hannah or the Mistress came to rescue them. The thoroughly frightened children were then sent home with a stern lecture on trespassing. After being confronted with several hundred pounds of bestial fury, none of the younger generation ever made a second attempt to cross the grounds.

Nor did any other, less welcome visitors. However, the fate of solitary tramps or an occasional thief was entirely different. More than once Hannah had watched from an upstairs window as the two dogs, Gog and Magog, streaked silently across the front drive, jaws open in some silent howl of triumph. The hounds never barked when hunting. They knew better than to alert their prey. For all of their size, the two ran like the wind, their red eyes burning with a light like the very fires of Hell. Usually, a few minutes after they disappeared into the brush, a brief scream of mortal agony would indicate their hunt had again been successful. When the dogs returned to their kennel in the morning after a hunt, their jaws would be caked red with human blood. Hannah sometimes looked for their victims the day after, but she had never succeeded in finding any trace of a body. What they did with the remains Hannah never discovered.

The two hounds came to a quick halt when they saw who waited for them. They stood at the side of the dirt roadway, their mouths open, their teeth shining in the headlights of her car. Those unchanging red eyes followed her every move. Silently, the Hellhounds clenched and unclenched their teeth. They seemed to instinctively know the action put Hannah on edge.

It was quite clear to Hannah why the dogs hated her. Even when she was a child, they had sensed the difference within her. The beasts feared the wolf-form that dwelt within her. An ancient, racial hatred existed between their kind and those born of the beast. The Hellhounds lusted for her blood. They would kill her in an instant if their Mistress permitted that. But the Countess had always kept the Hounds at bay. Still, Hannah knew that only the absolute obedience to the will of their Mistress stopped the Hellhounds from attacking her. It was a frightening thought.

She spat at them in annoyance. Someday there would be an accounting. Not tonight, though. They sat guarding the entrance way as Hannah turned back to the car. She drove the auto onto the estate grounds, then locked the gate behind her. No one would dare follow her with such monsters keeping watch. Hannah wondered if tonight the Mistress might unleash the Hellhounds against her. More than once the Countess had threatened to do just that. She enjoyed making her servant squirm. Hannah knew that even in wolf form she stood little chance against the evil pair. Shivering again, she steered the car up the winding road to the mansion a quarter mile beyond. A solitary yellow light in the Library window told her that the Mistress awaited her arrival impatiently. Hannah looked for a second in the rear view mirror. She could see the blazing red eyes of the Hellhounds reflecting back at her. It was not a reassuring sight.

There were no cops around. Larry had been checking for the past fifteen minutes. The drive was clean. As he crouched down a little lower beneath the huge garbage bin where he had been hiding for the past hour, he reviewed his plan. It never hurt to be too careful: he didn't want to end up in jail for a hundred bucks.

On the street, his friends called him "Mr. Mind" because he always planned out every job to the smallest detail. Larry liked the nickname. It fit him perfectly. He did use his mind. He was one of the few dudes in the neighborhood who did. Kept him in change and off the police blotter. Which was more than most of his friends could say.

Fourteen years old, Larry Kennelly had been involved in illegal activities for nearly half his life. He started by running numbers on the southwest side when he was eight, graduating into petty thievery within a year. He had never known his real father. His mother hit the bottle quite a bit and Larry was left pretty much to himself. A short, underweight child, he possessed a natural speed and athletic ability that served him well in his criminal activities. Like the job tonight, though Larry had to admit he wasn't even sure if what he was doing was illegal. It didn't matter much. All that mattered was the money.

Squinting in the pale light of the full moon, Larry stared at the half of the hundred-dollar bill that he had been given a few hours earlier. "Half now," the old man had told him, "and the other half when the job is done." Larry shivered thinking about the strange little man. His eyes fastened on you and stayed there without blinking. The old geezer reminded Larry of the snakes he had once seen in the zoo. Spooky, the way he had known Larry's name without asking. The old man sure didn't dress like he was rich, but he kept a C-note crumpled up in his back pocket. Only crazy guys ripped a bill in half like it wasn't worth a thing.

So here he was, on the extension of Lake Shore Drive leading to Meigs Field, checking out the action, waiting for the right moment. He tightened the knots in the laces of his sneakers. His gloves were on just right. Black shoe polish all over his exposed skin, blending in with the black pants and sweatshirt he wore. No one would ever notice him.

He looked up at the statue not twenty feet away. Why the Hell anyone wanted to tape a piece of old paper to the forehead of a big piece of crap like that he had no idea—and he didn't care. If the old man was willing to pay a hundred bucks to have it done, Larry would do it. He'd done a lot worse for a lot less.

A cloud covered the moon. Larry leapt forward, darting across the street. He was up the concrete base of the statue in seconds. He scrambled higher, grabbing hold of the one leg of the horse lifted off the platform. He pulled hard, levering himself onto the actual base of the statue.

Pausing, he checked the street quickly. The moon still lay behind the clouds. There was no motion anywhere. A few cars roared by on Lake Shore Drive, but that was hundreds of feet away. With his features darkened, no one would see him. It was safe to continue.

He climbed up onto the statue, straddling the horse directly in front of the mounted man. The metal was cold and the damp breeze blowing off the lake made it wet and slippery, but Larry knew what he was doing. He had studied the figure for a long time. The rider had one arm extended holding a sword as if leading a charge, and Larry rested one hand on that arm while planting his foot on the saddle. With his teeth, he pulled the glove off his free hand. Reaching into his coat pocket, he pulled out a bottle of rubber cement with which to attach the paper to the statue's forehead. He quickly inched his way forward. Not even a minute had passed and already he was almost finished.

Next came the piece of wrinkled paper the old man had given him. It was around five inches long and an inch high: not much to look at. There were some funny looking symbols drawn on it, but Larry had never seen them before and they didn't make any difference. If the old man had wanted a beer sign hung from the statue's arm, he would have done it. He wasn't paid to ask questions.

Regular tape wouldn't work on the metal statue. But rubber cement worked fine. Larry had made sure of that earlier in the day. The old man had not specified how he was to get the paper to stay fast, only that it had to be on the figure's forehead.

Larry dabbed a wide patch across the metal, slapped on the parchment, and rubbed it down for a few seconds to make sure it wasn't going to move. Then, back into his pocket went the bottle of rubber cement. Without a wasted motion, he grabbed the statue's extended arm, swung out over the grass, and dropped to the ground, his legs only bending slightly to absorb the impact of the fall. The whole operation had taken little more than two minutes.

He ran back to the garbage dumpster. The moon was still behind the clouds. No police were about; the park was quiet. He squinted at the statue. The white paper was hard to see unless you knew it was there, pasted right on the forehead of 'Casimir Pulaski,' whoever that might have been.

He smirked in self-satisfaction. Another perfect job. Now all he had to do was find the old geezer for the rest of his money.

"I have it right here," a voice said from right beside him.

Larry spun around, startled. He would have sworn there was no one there a minute ago. Had the old man been there the whole time he had been on the statue? How did he know what he was thinking?

The wizened little man held out the half of the C-note. "Go ahead, take it. You earned it."

Larry reached for the bill eagerly. Damn right, he had earned it. Did a good job. No reason to be spooked over some crazy old man. So what if he didn't make any noise when walking? He had just caught him by surprise. That was all.

"A *smart* man," said the old guy, making it perfectly clear who he meant by that remark, "would not talk about his work tonight. Not even if he read something in the paper or saw something on TV that made him want to brag a little. Isn't that so, Mr. Mind?"

Larry nodded his agreement. Then he turned and ran into the shadows, heading for home. It wasn't until he was out of the park that he realized the old man had called him by his nickname. Damn, that dude was weird. No question about it. Wouldn't hurt to keep his lip zipped. Wouldn't be a bad idea at all.

Hannah shivered in fear. Her Mistress was very quiet. Too quiet. She had listened to Hannah's account of the failed attack without once interrupting. The Countess's eyes had remained locked onto hers the entire time like a snake eying its prey. Hannah would have preferred the Mistress to scream and shout like she sometimes did when her will was thwarted. Rage she could live with. She did not mind the beatings or the pain that the Mistress dealt out so efficiently. Such was a servant's lot. Mistakes were paid for and then forgiven. It was these silent times that worried Hannah much more. For all of her own bestial powers, Hannah was terribly frightened of her Lady. The monster within her was purely animal in nature. It hungered for human flesh and life—that was the nature of the beast. Not so with her Mistress. There were depths of depravity within the sorceress that made Hannah's bloodlust seem like child's play. To the Lady, torture and pain were arts that were raised to the highest levels. Hannah felt cold as she waited in silence.

"Your failure is noted," the Countess Marie Lamont said finally, after nearly twenty minutes of thought. She waved one slender hand, dismissing the incident. "The mistake was mine, not yours. You are blameless, my servant."

Hannah nodded slowly, wondering what her Mistress meant. It was not her place to speak. A wrong word, a foolish gesture, and she still could bring on the anger she knew lurked beneath that calm exterior. Still, she remained attentive. The Countess would explain when she was ready. She always did. Then it would be Hannah's job to listen and obey.

"Yes. I see it now. My plan was a good one. We had to wait until today, could not attack the girl until the police left her alone. Trying to scare the professor with that clipping was a waste of time . . . not that it mattered. The main thrust of our scheme was unharmed. Using *the Voice* made the girl overconfident. I knew she could manage that without any problem. It caused *her* to underestimate us. Then, after enough time to lull her suspicions, attacking her in her own home should have worked. But it didn't. Even with them totally unprepared for your assault." The Countess frowned in annoyance. "They did not suspect anything? You caught them completely by surprise?"

"I thought I did, My Lady. They were embracing in the kitchen. I could see them through the window. I could sense their passion. They had no idea I was outside. No idea at all."

"Why are you hesitating, Hannah? Tell me."

"The back door. It was a thin one. I should have smashed it in an instant. But the professor had reinforced it with a chair. That was what gave the girl time to flee. They were not aware of me. I am sure of that. But the door was barricaded. An unlucky coincidence that saved them."

"And through that luck they escaped." The Countess frowned. "I seem to have made a serious tactical error, one that will be difficult to correct. I underestimated my opponents. I knew the girl, being Lancaster's daughter, had the Power. I never suspected that her companion possessed the gift as well."

Hannah growled deep in her throat. She couldn't help it. The beast within her stirred angrily. "The professor? He was lucky, nothing more than that. No magic in his fighting. When I meet him again, I will tear his guts out."

The Countess laughed, a harsh, high pitched barking that was anything but ladylike. "Perhaps, my fine servant, perhaps. But you would be wise to remember that there is no such thing as luck. Coincidence, yes. But luck the way most people think of it does not exist. It is another strong manifestation of the Power. Uncontrolled, but dangerous.

"No human should be able to stand up to you in your beast form. Your powers are that of ten. Yet, this professor not only battled you to a standstill, but he escaped as well. Merely lucky, you claim. I know better. To me, it indicates that he has the gift. A very strong measure of the Power, I suspect. I should have checked into his background. What else could have led Lancaster and that accursed Tsuiki to him? This miscalculation may cost us dearly."

"The Invitation?" asked Hannah, and then she wished she hadn't. Her Mistress was obsessed with the Devil's Auction, and now her one possible chance to attend seemed further away than ever.

"I will have that Invitation," said the Countess, measuring each word distinctly. "We still have three days. I will not be left out!"

Hannah wondered what was so important about the Invitation. The Countess had never said why she had to attend the Auction, nor was it Hannah's place to ask. Still, rarely had the Mistress been so set on something as she was in this pursuit of the Invitation. The attack on old Lancaster had been an act of sheer desperation. Normally, the Countess would never have challenged a magician of such power. That they had succeeded had not fooled even Hannah. The old man had hardly struggled. It was as though he were resigned to dying. Even then, if they had delayed a few seconds more he would have killed them both.

Now they pursued the daughter. Hannah did not like this scheme. If an attack failed, abandon the quarry—that was her way of thinking. She was cautious. Usually, that was the way the Countess also worked.

Hannah was not used to fighting. Usually her victims fled before her. The professor had not been afraid; she had sensed that from the first second of their encounter. In some way, he seemed to rejoice in their combat. He was a breed apart. He was dangerous.

Her fingers flexed in almost subconscious fury. The man had hurt her. Her knees still ached. All the more reason to abandon the chase.

Hannah knew she was not invulnerable. Great strength would not stop a bullet. Or even a well-placed knife. A vague feeling of uneasiness haunted her. Things were not as they seemed; this man could be her doom.

Her Mistress rose from the ornate chair that dominated the sitting room. Restlessly, the Countess paced back and forth, her head down, eyes focused on the carpet, hands locked behind her back.

Hannah stared at her Mistress with dull eyes. She had seen her Lady do this a thousand times. The Countess was planning a new trap.

The front doorbell rang. The Countess raised her head in astonishment. No one came to their estate except when asked, and Hannah knew no one was expected tonight.

A brief tremble shook the Countess's body.

She licked her lips. "Gog and Magog," she asked, her voice low and worried, "they were there this evening when you came back?"

"Of course."

"Can you sense them now?"

Hannah started to protest then thought better of it. The Countess knew how much she hated the Hellhounds; mental contact with them repulsed her. Tonight was not a good time to argue. And, she had to admit, the Hounds might be needed.

Hannah reached out with the sixth sense that resided deep within her. The beast buried in her soul searched and searched but came up with nothing. The Hellhounds were nowhere to be found.

"They do not respond, Mistress. I cannot sense them. And," Hannah continued, knowing what the next question would be before it was asked, "I cannot sense anything about the one at the door. Whoever rang the bell is a total blank."

"Can the dead return?" asked the Countess. She seemed to shrink, draw in on herself, and the blood drained from her face, leaving her cheeks pale white. She looked at Hannah and smiled faintly. "Now is your chance to make up for your failure earlier this evening. Go. Answer the door. See who it is . . . or *what* it is."

* * *

Sid Levine kept one eye fastened on his side-view mirror as he directed his truck off I-55 onto Lake Shore Drive. Only cars were allowed on the Drive, and he'd get a ticket for sure if there were any cops about. That wasn't usually the case after midnight, but you could never be too sure.

He opened the throttle on the truck. Getting a ticket didn't worry him much. He'd collected plenty of them and had never paid one yet. The way Chicago worked, it would take years before the cops caught up with him. Unlike most big cities, the patrol cars here didn't maintain a computer network with Headquarters. Long before they got the equipment, he planned to move to another location. His main concern was that if he was pulled over, he'd be late for the job. That weird old bird had given him half the money in advance, and Sid wanted the rest.

He grinned at the thought. Half, all right, he decided, patting his coat pocket to reassure himself the bills were still there. Crazy. Ripping five one-hundred-dollar bills in two and giving him half. Other half when the job was done. Old guy had a few rocks loose upstairs. But the money was green and that was all that Sid cared about.

The turnoff for the Observatory and Meigs Field came up in only a few minutes. Not a cop in sight anywhere. Sid nosed the truck down

the drive and slowed it to a crawl. The old man
had said he would be waiting by the statue of
Casimir Pulaski. There was the green hunk
and, sure as Hell, there was the little guy
standing right at the base.

He was a weird old character, all dried up
and wrinkled; he couldn't weigh more than a
hundred pounds. But he was tough. Sid shook
his head in annoyance as he stopped the truck
in the street right past the statue. He didn't like
to admit being scared of anyone, but somehow
that old man frightened him. Couldn't put his
finger on exactly what it was. Maybe it was the
funny way he seemed to just pop out of nowhere. Or the polite way he talked. Maybe it
was the way he focused those unblinking eyes
on you. The old man hadn't done anything
special, but Sid was convinced. A stick of
dynamite didn't have to explode to prove they
were dangerous. The old man was the same
way, primed and ready to blow. Sid was real
polite in dealing with him.

"You have the map?" the old man asked Sid a
few minutes later, when they both stood behind the truck. The back doors of the van stood
open, revealing an empty interior.

"Got it memorized. Nothing to it. It'll take
me a few hours to get there once we get out of
the city."

The old man nodded sagely. "I have the rest
of your money with me. You will be paid once

we make our delivery. Are you ready to leave?"

"Tank's full of gas. You need a hand back here?"

"Thank you, no. Wait for me in the cab."

Sid moved forward.

"One more thing," continued the old man. "You would be wise to keep your eyes off that which does not concern you. Quite wise."

"Sure," answered Sid. "Sure."

He was not sure at all. When he took the job, Sid had figured the old man was smuggling something across the border into Wisconsin. Now, thinking about it, that idea didn't make much sense. Not for the amount of money. And why meet here? Maybe something flown in to Meigs field? Sid climbed into the cab shaking his head. The money was good, but he wished he knew what was going on.

Metal grated on metal, as if two slabs of steel were pulling apart from each other. Sid resisted the temptation to look outside. He was quite positive that he didn't want to know what was happening. He had never heard a sound exactly like that before. It stopped after only a few seconds. Nothing happened for a minute or so, then his truck groaned in protest. Somehow, something heavy was being loaded into the back.

Sid kept his eyes fixed on the Observatory at the end of the road. He knew better than to ask questions. Curious people in his business

ended up dead. That damned old guy was a
crook all right. Or a nut. Either way, Sid knew
what he was doing: stealing the statue. It had
been done before. Last year in Grant Park,
somebody had taken two statues in one night.
Maybe this was the same gang. The old man
was probably fronting the job. What the Hell
they needed statues *for* he had no idea. Maybe
the gang provided them to millionaires who
wanted unique lawn decorations. He only
briefly wondered how they moved the figures.
Who cared? Sid relaxed. Everything made
sense now.

"I believe you have been looking for one of
these," said Makoto Tsuiki. The sorcerer held
up a gray square of paper.

Hannah could not believe her eyes. From the
description pounded into her by The Mistress,
that could only be an Invitation to the Devil's
Auction. How had that accursed Tsuiki ob-
tained such a card? And why had he brought it
here tonight, to the home of his greatest enemy?

Evidently, the Countess was wondering the
same thing. Her eyes focused on her enemy for
the first time since he had entered the room.
She had studiously avoided staring at the Oriental ever since Hannah had announced from
the hallway who it was at the door. Years ago,
when in a talkative mood, the Countess had

confided to Hannah that Tsuiki was possibly the most powerful sorcerer in the Midwest, if not the entire country. She hated him, but dared not confront him. Now he was sitting here, relaxed, in her innermost sanctum. And Hannah knew that the Countess was afraid to do anything. She could sense the hatred smoldering within her Mistress. But that hatred was nothing compared to the overwhelming fear that held the Countess motionless in its grip. Despite that fear, the Countess's eyes were riveted on the Invitation in Tsuiki's grip.

"What do you want for it?" The Countess's voice was a harsh, intense whisper. "Name your price."

Hannah again wondered what made the auction so important to her Mistress. What secret did it hold? It was inconceivable that the Countess would deal with Tsuiki. And yet, that was exactly what she was attempting to do.

The Oriental smiled. "I thought so. I was not sure but I did have my suspicions. Your greed betrays you, Marie. You," and then Tsuiki turned for a second and looked at Hannah standing near the window, "or to be perfectly correct, your servant, killed my friend, Jacob Lancaster. Thank you for that confirmation. I dislike mysteries."

"You still have not answered my question," said the Countess, ignoring Tsuiki's comments. "What do you want for the Invitation?"

"Want for this?" Tsuiki laughed in the Countess's face.

Hannah growled deep in her throat. He mocked them. She did not fear this man even if he worried her Mistress. He was only flesh and blood. He could die easily enough. Then she remembered the missing hounds. Tsuiki had been waiting for her at the doorway alone, and unharmed. Even though he projected no aura, the Hellhounds should have attacked him. The anger mounting within her died as swiftly as it had risen.

Tsuiki laid the gray card on the desk. "You can *have* this Invitation, Marie. With my compliments. It was sent to me. I am happy to give it to you. Too bad I did not know you wanted it so badly. Perhaps, if I had known, Jake would still be alive today. An unhappy twist of fate. Karma."

The Countess grabbed the Invitation with both hands. She pulled it close and studied it cautiously. "It is the real thing," she finally whispered, keeping a tight grip on the card. She seemed to fear that it would suddenly vanish. "Why are you doing this? You and I have rarely seen eye to eye. You are not one to do me favors."

Tsuiki rose from his chair. "Freely given by me. Freely taken of your own free will by you." He seemed to be reciting a formula. "Your fate is your own." The Oriental shook his head slowly. "Favors? You think I am doing you a favor? You know something about these events. I know full well why you so desperately want to attend. Have you ever looked into how many ever *return* from the auction when the bidding is complete? The odds do not appeal to me. You are welcome to take my place. Goodbye, Countess. I don't think we shall be seeing each other ever again."

Tsuiki walked to the door of the Library. Hannah could not restrain herself any longer. She had to know. "The Hounds? What happened to them? Why did they not stop you?"

The Oriental glanced at her. "The Hounds? Evidently, they did not see me," he replied. He reached into his coat pocket. "Here. I believe these should explain everything."

Hannah found she could not control her own body. Her arm moved without volition. She reached out and took what Tsuiki handed her. Then, nodding politely to her, the Oriental left.

Her hand was still open. Hannah stared at the grisly remains in her palm. Now she fully understood the meaning of Tsuiki's remarks.

There were four bloody hunks of animal tissue in her palm. They were still glowing. Four red eyes.

CHAPTER SEVEN

Valerie stepped through the doorway into the apartment. She looked around in astonishment as Alex flashed a wan sort of smile and waved sheepishly.

"I wasn't expecting visitors," he said.

"I'll say you weren't," she answered, not trying to sound too critical. No sense getting him upset, she reasoned to herself, especially since he saved your life less than an hour ago. She moved forward into the apartment, closing the door behind her. "Been doing a little reading?"

"I've always had a hard time passing up a good book. Seems to have gotten out of hand lately."

"Out of hand?" She laughed. Alex stared at her for a minute and then started laughing too. Valerie relaxed. She could sense that he was still a little intimidated by her. There was nothing she could do to lessen the tension between them other than to continue to play up to him. It was all part of the courting ritual. She didn't feel that she was really deceiving him— no worse than any other woman when she was after a man. She did care for Alex quite a bit already, and she was pretty sure he was falling hard for her. He had better. Though he didn't know it, Mr. Alex Warner's future was already signed, sealed, and delivered.

There were books everywhere. Huge bookcases filled the walls from floor to ceiling. All were crammed with books. There were books on top of books, squeezed into the shelves so that there was not a trace of panelling showing. Paperbacks were stacked in piles so that not even the spines were visible. And there were plenty of books not on the shelves. They had taken over the two small end-tables in the living room as well as most of the space on the coffeetable. Stacks of books balanced on the top of a small TV tucked in one corner; more paperbacks crowded the long window casing to the rear of the room. All were in neat stacks, and Valerie noted that the room seemed pretty clean. Alex might be obsessive in some respects, but at least he was neat. "Well, at least you don't have them on the floor," she said.

"You haven't seen the spare bedroom," said Alex uncomfortably.

Valerie grinned. She reached out and pinched him on the cheek. "You're cute, kid. But I think I'm starting to get a line on why your ex-wife left."

Alex sprawled onto a sofa that had seen better days. He pushed a stack of magazines off the cushions onto the floor and beckoned to her with his free hand. "You wouldn't dare say that up close to me," he said, in a mock-menacing tone.

"You bet your life," she replied, kicking off her shoes. It felt good to be barefoot again. Then, measuring with her eye the amount of space available on the couch, she pounced.

It caught Alex completely by surprise. He had been waiting for her to sit down. Never did he suspect she'd jump him. Before he could react, she had his hands pinned beneath him, with her body pressed across him like a blanket. Their faces were only inches apart.

"As I said," she stated with a giggle, "I'm starting to get a line on why your ex-wife left."

"You treat all the men you meet this way?" Alex asked. He had not moved since she had launched herself at him. His hands and arms remained pinned beneath him, though she knew that he could easily get free if he tried.

"Not all of them. Just the ones who save my life."

Alex groaned. "You mean that your life has been in danger before? What am I getting myself into?"

Valerie laughed again. A particularly lewd image crossed her mind as soon as he spoke. The same thought must have crossed Alex's mind as well since his eyes widened at her laughter. His arms came out from under him. They wrapped around her back, pulling her tight against him. In this position, there was no escape. She was not looking to get away.

Jim Calvin was feeling pretty good. It was four A.M., the highway was clear of cars, and he was tooling along at seventy without a cop in sight. He had the fuzz-buster going just in case. Thank God he had a Dad who knew what to give for a practical birthday gift. Even though it was only in the forties outside, Jim had all the windows open. He had chugged more than a few brews during the course of the evening and the cold air had a mildly sobering effect on him. At nineteen, he was underage in Illinois. But not in Wisconsin.

It had been a great party. Lots of good-looking women and lots of beer. Got a few good phone numbers. If he didn't have to get back to campus for the Sunday morning frat game, he'd probably be spending the night with one of the Madison honeys instead. And having a lot better time. He couldn't keep his mind off the girls he had met. God, they were a horny bunch. That one girl, Marcie, the blonde, really seemed hot for his body. He whistled aloud in appreciation. She was something else. Not too bright, but her other assets made up for that. She was first on the list to call next weekend. Damn. Dumb shit fraternity football league. Why the Hell they ever scheduled games on a Sunday morning . . . well, at least this was the last one of the season. Starting in November, it would be fun, fun, fun for Jimmy C.

He turned the car radio up loud. Now that he was back in Illinois, should be able to get some of the Chicago rock stations at least. Not much you could get on FM, but WLS on AM had a signal you could get just about anywhere. Jimmy had a feeling that you could probably pick up the radio station on the moon if the air was clear and you had a big enough antenna.

The pulsating sound of rock filled the car. He pounded the top of the steering wheel as he sang along with the Rolling Stones. What a great night. It was good to be alive.

Quietly, Valerie got up out of bed. Alex murmured something in his sleep but otherwise didn't stir. They had adjourned to his bedroom when things got beyond control on the living room couch. Their clothes were scattered in disarray in both rooms.

Valerie didn't bother looking for anything to put on. It felt good to be naked. It had been a long time between lovers; she had forgotten how wonderful sex could be. A smile crossed her lips. She felt like a cat who had just swallowed a canary. Poor, sweet Alex. He didn't know his future had been determined the minute she walked into his office. Well, he could do a lot worse. Valerie let her hands caress her hips. She had to be a better bargain than his ex-wife. Sheila sounded like a real bitch.

Idly, she wondered how her father had managed to break up that marriage. More to the point, how her Dad had allowed it to take place in the first place. Tsuiki must know the answers. He always knew. She would get all the dirt from him sooner or later. He had never been able to keep anything from her when he was studying with Dad.

Tiptoeing, so not to wake up Alex, she crossed the floor and exited to the living room. She gently closed the connecting door. They had left the lights on in the front room, too carried away by passion to worry about the electric bill.

Valerie drew in a deep breath. She had never given much thought to settling down before. Now that she was faced with the immediate prospect of doing so, the choice didn't seem so terrible. Even knowing that it had been planned didn't faze her.

Jake Lancaster had been a good father except for one bad habit: he wanted to run everyone's life. It had driven her crazy the last few years at home; and more than anything else, her father's constant manipulating had finally driven her to leave. It wasn't that he didn't try to make her happy. He just never realized she might want different things out of life than he imagined.

Most other people could do very little to stop her father's meddling. With the Power at his command, he usually did what he wanted without anyone being the wiser. Among his many talents, Jake Lancaster had been a world-class chess player. He had a skill for planning attacks many moves in advance. He applied the same techniques in his personal relationships.

His only problem had been that she was wise to all his tricks and equally devious with her own. The only difference between the two of them was that she had learned things from the other half of her family as well. Her Mom had been the true master of manipulation in the marriage. She had always let Dad think he was getting his way by sly trickery. In most cases, she was actually maneuvering Dad into doing what she wanted by letting him think it was his idea. Plot and counterplot. It had always been part of her life.

Alex had been completely unaware of her father's scheming. She intended to leave it that way. There was a strong suspicious streak in her future husband, and it would be a major blow for him to learn that his best friend had been playing matchmaker behind his back. It might raise some questions that she'd have a hard time answering.

The kitchen was small but well stocked. Alex kept the refrigerator better provided than she did. Lots of goodies nestled in the various compartments. Eggs, bacon, and cheese all appealed to her. They would go perfectly with the nice loaf of unsliced rye in the breadbox. She would surprise Alex in the morning with breakfast in bed. That should put the definitive touch on their relationship, put a little domestic cheer into a rather passionate relationship. She was determined that theirs would be a permanent arrangement. Anything she could do to further that goal was worth trying. Like father, like daughter, she concluded cheerfully. There was a bag of Chips-Ahoy cookies on the kitchen counter. Grabbing them, she headed back to the living room.

She settled down on the sofa, her legs curled up beneath her. It was only five in the morning. Alex looked good for hours more sleep, and that was fine with her. She needed time alone to think. Ever since she had walked into his office, she had been planning on the go, always trying to keep one step ahead of him. It was a pretty dangerous way to operate, as the attack at her condo proved. If it weren't for Alex's luck, that would have been a disaster. She had gotten him a little too fuzzy, a little too over-anxious. Now was the time to get her priorities straight.

For openers, she decided, her modelling days were over. The job had been getting pretty boring anyway the last few years. The world of black magic was a lot more interesting; and with Alex, things should be quite lively. And she was sick of dieting all the time. One decision made, she reasoned with a nod of satisfaction. The Chips-Ahoy bag was already open. She approved of Alex's taste in snacks. Munching happily on the cookies, she continued to sort out her future.

Jimmy cursed in annoyance. He had to take a leak. He'd gone to the john before leaving Madison, but the long ride home was too much. The steady rhythm of the tires on the highway had gotten to him. More specifically, to his bladder. Damn, he was uncomfortable as Hell. The night didn't seem so friendly now. He had rolled up the car window an hour ago. It was cold out there. For a second, Jimmy debated pulling off onto the shoulder and taking a quick hike into the woods. He immediately rejected the idea. It would be his luck to have the state police cruise by right while he was relieving himself. It had happened to his fraternity brother, Paul Sorenson, last year. Cops had thought it was a riot. Didn't stop them from arresting Paul for public indecency. Cost him a bundle to get the charges dropped.

He kept on driving. There had to be a restaurant or a gas station somewhere up ahead. That was the trouble with this part of the state—the exits were so damned far apart. He had been driving for a Hell of a long time without a break. Great scenery. Trees and rocks all around. Not even any billboards to break the monotony.

He was going so fast, that he almost missed the green information sign on the side of the road. *Rest Stop—One Mile*. Jimmy hugged his legs tightly together. Talk about in the nick of time. Another few minutes and he would've had a puddle on the floor.

He steered his Chevy onto the ramp and braked hard. The road curved behind a small glade of trees that effectively sheltered the clearing from the highway. Yellow paint lines outlined a dozen parking spaces in a hundred-foot stretch. An old pick-up truck sat parked at the far end of the row. The only light came from the solitary wood building in the middle of the clearing. Jimmy spotted a cluster of old picnic tables scattered about near the cabin. No one seemed to be about, not even any teenagers in a van having fun. Deserted. He eased his car into a parking spot right in front of the building. Jimmy suddenly wished he had not gone to so many mad-slasher movies in the past few years. It looked awfully dark out there.

"Stupid shit," he said aloud, instinctively trying to build up his nerve. "Those dumb flicks were made to scare people. They're not real life. No loonie birds floating around here with butcher knives."

He opened the door of his car. It was deathly silent; nothing moved. "No one around," Jimmy decided, talking more now to break the silence than for any other reason. He quickly entered the restroom.

Everything inside was perfectly normal. Just to be on the safe side, he bent down and checked to see if anyone was in any of the stalls in the men's room. No legs showed. Still spooked, he popped open the door of each booth. As he worked, he stood ready to sprint for the exit. It was crazy, Jimmy knew, but still he did it. Wasn't going to be the first victim of some escaped lunatic who killed men while they were taking a pee. Finally, satisfied he was alone, Jimmy emptied his bladder. He never realized before how long it took. There was no way he could hurry. Especially feeling so nervous. The whole time he stood urinating, he watched the door to the bathroom. What he would do if some nut case burst through the door swinging a butcher knife at him Jimmy had no idea. But he watched anyway.

He left the men's room feeling much better. Still, he kept an eye out as he left the station. It wasn't until he reached his car that Jimmy realized that he locked the door when he left the auto. He stared unhappily at his keys dangling from the ignition switch. A narrow opening at the top of the window taunted him. He was locked out.

Several loud screams of rage didn't help him feel any better. Nor did kicking the side of his car. Limping slightly, he made his way back to the rest station. Forgotten now were the lurking hordes of mad slashers. He was locked out. How the Hell was he going to get back into the car? He didn't want to break the window. It would cost money to get that fixed, and with his luck, he'd probably cut his hand and bleed to death.

Anxiously, he looked around the station. That small opening at the top of the window might save the day, he thought. If he could find a hanger or a piece of wire, he could snake it down and pull up the knob. He'd done it before when he had locked himself out at school. But getting a hanger had only taken a few seconds there. In the restroom here he found nothing he could possibly use.

Frustrated, he stomped outside. He felt like a jerk. He could just see himself explaining to his fraternity brothers why he was hours late to the game. Locked the keys in the car when he went to take a leak. He should have stayed in Madison.

He scrounged around in the parking lot. Usually there was all sorts of garbage on the concrete, but not tonight. He swore in annoyance.

Sitting on the hood of his car, dangling his legs over the front grillwork, he remembered the old truck at the end of the lot. From here, it looked empty and abandoned. There might be something in it he could use to pry open the window. Wire and junk accumulated in old wrecks.

He decided to take a look. Anything was better than spending the night stuck here in the middle of nowhere. *Anything*.

The Countess paced back and forth in the library like a caged animal. Her face was flushed and both her hands beat a rhythmic tattoo against her sides. Hannah had never seen her Mistress so excited before. Even Tsuiki's slaughter of the two Hellhounds was forgotten. All the Countess could talk about was the Invitation.

"The Oriental is a fool," said the Countess. She laughed harshly. "He thinks to worry me with rumors and lies. As if it mattered what happened before. I shall triumph. The secret shall be mine. I will have it, Hannah. I will have it."

Hannah remained quiet. It was rare that her Mistress ever disclosed anything of importance. For a change, Hannah wanted to know exactly what was going on. The Lady was acting very strangely lately. Hannah was loyal without question, but she was not a fool. There were some sacrifices she was not willing to make without a very good reason. Perhaps she might learn some of the truth tonight.

"We will need something to offer. I've known that all along." The Countess was talking half to herself and half to Hannah. "After all, it is an auction. Payment has to be made in kind. What would be worth the most? Hannah, don't just sit there. Get up. Help me look."

"Look for what, Mistress?"

The Countess came back to earth for the first time since Tsuiki had left. She stopped in the middle of the floor and frowned. Her eyes narrowed. She bit her lower lip with her teeth, her head held at an odd angle, deep in thought. It was as though she were torn apart by some inner conflict. She stood silently for minutes. Only her head moved, back and forth, as she mentally raised and discarded one argument after another. Finally the mental debate came to an end. The Countess had decided.

"You have labored in the dark too long, my faithful servant. You deserve the truth. And, if I succeed, that success will be yours as well."

Hannah nodded politely. She had known the Mistress too long to believe any of her promises. Too often, those wild claims were forgotten once the sought-after prize was claimed. Hannah was willing to listen but she was not naïve enough to believe any mention of rewards.

"You know something of the story already. An Auction is going to be held on All Hallows Eve in northern Illinois. Only a half-dozen, powerful black magicians are invited. There they bid for a unique prize, offering both money and magical rarities of their own. *I mean to be the high bidder*, no matter what the cost."

"I don't understand. Who holds this auction? And why?"

"As to why, I have no idea. No one knows. They just take place once a generation. Perhaps he runs them for his own amusement."

"*Who* does?"

"A powerful sorcerer."

"More powerful than you?" interrupted Hannah.

"Yes," said the Countess, her voice almost a hiss of fear. "Perhaps the most powerful magician in the world today. He calls himself Ashmedai, after the king of Hebrew demons. No one knows much about him. He remains in isolation on his estate, except for rare trips abroad to certain mystic ruins. I have tried for years to meet him, but with no success. His estate is unapproachable except for the day of the auction, and only then with an Invitation. His trips overseas are always made in secret. All my investigations lead nowhere. All of what I know about him is based on second- or third-hand information. But even that is enough.

"These auctions have been taking place for nearly a hundred years. This will be the fourth since 1895. That much I have been able to learn by searching the records gathered by my father. They are always held at that same estate in upstate Illinois. And always by a man named Ashmedai."

"The same man?" asked Hannah.

"I suspect so, though no one knows for sure. As I told you, this Ashmedai is a mysterious figure. The auctioneer could be the same man each time. Or it could be the descendent of the original Ashmedai. There could even be a secret group with all of the members using the same name for some sinister purpose. Anything is possible. Nowhere in any of the stories about the four auctions is there a description of the appearance of the man who conducted the bidding. In each case, he is a complete unknown."

"But surely those who attended the auctions . . ."

The Countess shook her head in annoyance. "That is what scared off Tsuiki. But I am positive it is not as he suspects. There has to be another answer."

Hannah had no idea what her Mistress was talking about. Her face must have reflected that puzzlement.

"They were never heard from again." The Countess almost shouted the answer. "They vanished from the face of the Earth. Gone. None of the magicians who attended any of the three earlier auctions ever returned to their normal life. The stories of the event were told by ones who did not actually attend. All their information was second hand. The fate of the guests was a mystery.

"That was what Tsuiki feared. It was why he gave me the Invitation, and why he made sure that I accepted of my own free will. So that he could not be held accountable on the psychic plane for luring me to my doom." The Countess' voice sank to a whisper. "In one of the accounts of the Auction, the author claimed that Ashmedai actually *was* the king of demons, maintaining a way station on Earth. And that he held these events to recruit new slaves to serve him for all eternity . . . *in Hell*."

Chocolate chip cookies, Valerie decided as she bit into her fifth one, were addictive. Two weeks ago she would have been consumed by guilt after eating just one cookie. Tonight, this binge capped the first day of her independence from the modeling rat race. Scarfing down junk food seemed as dynamic a statement as she could make. She giggled. If sitting nude on the living room sofa at five in the morning in a man's apartment eating chocolate chip cookies wasn't a serious statement about life, nothing was.

Alex's flat was on the twentieth floor of the University Apartment Complex for professors and graduate students. Before sitting down, Valerie had opened the drawn curtains from the huge picture window in the living room. The view of Lake Michigan from this height was awe-inspiring. Alex had commented on the beauty of it at dinner. Valerie was glad she had risen early and caught the last stars shining down on the water. It was a sight not to be missed.

This apartment was one of the most desirable locations in the entire building. Usually, such plums were reserved for senior faculty members. Through an odd set of circumstances, he got it without any effort. The day he applied for housing, this place was being entered on the computer. Alex's name was matched up with the flat before anyone knew what was going on. Alex had laughed when he told her the story. A lucky break he had called it. Valerie knew different.

There was no such thing as luck. Not consistent luck. From time to time chance dictated some fortunate break for a person. Lottery-ticket winners usually won through coincidence—by some freak chance, when they picked the right numbers. One-time happenings were random couplings of fate. But people who were always lucky were not merely favorites of chance. Instead, they were unconscious manipulators of *the Power*. The only difference between them and the black magicians who practiced in secret throughout the world was conscious control of the process. The lucky ones didn't realize that they arranged the events taking place about them. Alex Warner had questioned Valerie about her power. He had no knowledge that his own psychic gifts were greater than hers.

Valerie had recognized that fact the minute Alex opened the door to his office that afternoon. Alex burned with unharnessed psychic energy, uncontrollable power. Close up, his psychic aura was overwhelming. But he had no knowledge or control over his gift. After a few seconds of initial bewilderment, Valerie had quickly revised her course of action. Originally, she had come to Alex only to ask for his help in finding her father's killer. Once she had met him, she knew he had to be hers. All of her actions since then had been directed toward both of those goals.

It wasn't till the encounter with Makoto Tsuiki at the restaurant that Valerie realized how she had been manipulated by her father. Even from beyond the grave, Dad had the last laugh. That final telephone call, instructing her to find Alex, was typical of him. Faced with death, he was still plotting his daughter's future. Dad must have known she was bored with modelling. He had told her many times that sooner or later her heritage would be too great. And he had been right.

If Dad were still alive, she probably would've been less ready to admit the error of her ways. With him dead, it was easy to concede the point. Her modelling career had been the final rebellion of youthful independence, in a sense, her growing pains. It was fun, but it was empty of any real meaning—at least when compared to practicing sorcery. Magic was in her blood. She was born and bred to be a sorceress, and she had reached that conclusion months ago. She had been planning to return to Chicago to resume her studies even before her father's murder. His death had not changed her mind. Her father, she knew, would have been pleased.

As would be his most prized pupil, Makoto Tsuiki. Poor Alex. He had no idea of the forces that were manipulating his life. What seemed like coincidences to him were anything but that. Valerie had no doubts that Tsuiki was Alex's best friend. She had sensed the bond between them at dinner. She also had no doubts that the Oriental had been keeping a close watch on Alex for years. Whether he was doing that at the request of her father or for plans of his own, she did not know, though she intended to find out. In the unseen world of black magic, nothing was as it seemed on the surface.

Valerie felt a small stirring of pride within her. She had been nimble on her feet today. The truth had been stretched, bent and broken on numerous occasions throughout the afternoon and evening. She hadn't dared tell Alex that the Voice had been aimed specifically at her and that it was a much more dangerous spell than he suspected. If she had, she was sure their romance would have stopped cold right then; he would have felt too worried and guilty to ask her out for dinner. Nor did she dare reveal that she had known Makoto Tsuiki for most of her life. Makoto had been her father's brightest pupil, and he too, came from a long line of sorcerers. And she definitely did not want to tell him about the charms she had been weaving about his subconscious mind, binding him to her with ties that romance and sex only strengthened. The spells that had taken the edge off his suspicious nature. Love was wonderful but awfully erratic. Valerie did not believe in leaving anything to chance.

Her eyes swept across the room. It *had* been

an exciting day. Abandoning her career, finding her husband-to-be, and battling a werewolf. It sounded like the script of a grade-B horror movie. Tomorrow should be a little less hectic, though. Alex had already promised her before drifting off to sleep that they would search for those references to the Auction in his books on magic. Valerie shook her head. Considering the number of books in this place, that should keep them busy for most of the afternoon.

She stretched her arms high over her head, feeling the skin across her body tighten with the movement. A pleasant tingling sensation crossed her breasts. Maybe they wouldn't spend *all* day looking through books. The more she thought about it, the more sure she became.

The truck was in pretty bad shape. The closer Jimmy got, the more confident he grew. There was nothing to be scared of in this old wreck. Must have been here for years. Funny that the highway department or some junkyard hadn't towed it away. It had to be worth something, even if just for spare parts. He hoped that it hadn't been gutted by someone else earlier. Under the hood there should be some loose wire he could rip out and use to get his car door open.

It was awfully quiet around here. Back by his car, the forest was alive with noises. He had spotted an owl and several curious eyes peering at him from the trees. Not here. Around the truck the forest was deathly still, the darkness more threatening. He could barely see where he was going. The high trees blocked out most of the starlight. The spotlight in front of the rest station barely reached this far. Beyond the truck, it was pitch black.

Twenty feet from the vehicle, a large chunk of metal rested on the gravel path. Jimmy approached it cautiously. Suddenly the same feeling he had had in the men's room returned. He cleared his throat, swallowed hard. It was as if he were living out a scene in a mad-slasher movie. Cautiously, he bent down on one knee and examined the wreckage. It seemed perfectly harmless, just twisted metal . . . the remains of a door. A truck door. It was pretty much still intact; only the hinges were smashed and bent out of shape.

It took him a few seconds to make the connection. His eyes darted up and confirmed his suspicions. The cab of the truck ahead was missing the door on the driver's side. He gulped down several deep breaths. It seemed awfully odd that this door would be on the ground if that truck had been here for a long time. *Very* odd.

He moved closer to the truck, inching one foot forward a little at a time. He was turned sideways now, ready to run the other direction if anything threatened. His eyes darted from place to place. His earlier thoughts had been mistaken. This truck wasn't some old abandoned junk. It was a fairly recent model. Banged up pretty good though. Big dents in the sides and the body. *Very* big dents, like it had been hit with a gigantic hammer. He wondered what made marks like that.

Now that he stood close to the cab, he noted that both doors were gone. The front hood appeared smashed down right onto the motor. What could batter metal with such force? It had to take a wrecking ball to make marks like that.

Maybe the truck had been in an accident earlier, towed here by the police and left until the owner could make a claim. Jimmy grabbed hold of the door-frame and pulled himself up to the cab. The glass was gone from the windshield, but otherwise the inside of the cabin looked okay. Nothing much was damaged. The steering wheel was fine, all the dials intact. Even the keys were still in the ignition.

Jimmy froze. No one left keys in a wreck. There was something strange going on here.

Quickly, he scrambled out of the cab. He darted back away from the truck, onto the roadway. He felt safer here. No one could creep up on him unawares. He glanced back at his car. The light by the restrooms called to him. But, despite the queasy feeling in his gut, he couldn't leave yet. He was still locked out of his car. He was determined to find something to open that window. Maybe in the back of the truck?

Caution battled annoyance. Annoyance won. Jimmy knew he was acting like a jerk. Mad-slasher movies were exactly that. Movies. They didn't happen in real life. Homicidal maniacs didn't wander around the countryside killing teenagers. That was the stuff of paperbacks and horror films. In real life, people got killed in the cities, not out in the middle of the country.

It was the darkness that was getting to him, he decided, playing Hell with his imagination. An abandoned truck was not that bizarre. In daylight it would seem perfectly ordinary. His theory about an accident was probably the right one, keys or no keys. They must have been left by the cops who towed it off the highway. If he didn't keep looking, he'd be stuck here until someone stopped. That might not be until sometime tomorrow. If then.

That last thought got him moving. He could see himself explaining to his frat brothers how he had spent the night in a bathroom because he had been too scared to investigate an abandoned truck. He knew how long it would take for that story to spread all over campus. He'd be laughed right out of school. Even a madman with a knife couldn't be any worse than that.

Nervously, he made his way back towards

the truck. Keeping well clear of the cab, he circled until he was at the rear of the vehicle. He stood on the grass, about ten feet back, and tried to peer inside. The roll-up door was gone without a trace. As Jimmy's eyes adjusted to the deeper darkness in the rear of the truck, he could see that there was hardly anything inside. Only a large pile of rags pushed up against one wall. Nothing else. Definitely no mad slashers.

Feeling a bit more confident, he walked forward. Nothing moved. It was safe. He grabbed onto the rear floor and pulled himself up onto the truck. The metal was awfully sticky. It felt like glue or something had been spilled all over the floor. It was still tacky, not completely dry. He got it all over his hands, all over his pants legs and his shoes. Messy as Hell. Made walking difficult. Jimmy wiped his hands on his pants, trying to get them clean. They still felt sticky. Stuff didn't come off easily.

He'd have to wash off in the bathroom later. First, he wanted to sort through that pile of rags. There might be a piece of wire mixed among them.

In the near-total darkness, it was impossible to figure out where the sticky stuff came from. No big drums or containers around. Maybe they had fallen out during the accident. Jimmy looked closer. Whatever it was seemed to be on the inside walls of the truck as well. Dark and messy. Dripping in little drops, forming small pools on the floor. Curiously, he held one hand up to his nose and sniffed.

Jimmy gagged. It smelled like . . . blood. Suddenly, he felt violently ill. His stomach churned and he vomited all over the floor. Involuntarily, he reached out to the nearby wall to steady himself. Then he gasped as his fingers brushed across the sticky, wet surface.

"Blood," he screamed shrilly. "Blood everywhere. Where's it all from?"

It was then that he realized that the jumble of rags in the corner wasn't a jumble of rags at all.

CHAPTER EIGHT

Alex and Valerie drove back to Valerie's townhouse after breakfast.

"Shouldn't be anything to worry about this time of the day," said Valerie. "That werewolf is a creature of the night. It can't function in daylight. We can just gather up my things and be back at your place before anyone's the wiser."

Alex was a little more skeptical. "Assuming that no one's watching your place. We'll have to make sure we aren't followed. This is starting to take on aspects of a spy novel. And what about the police?"

"What about them? Even if my neighbors called the cops last night, there isn't much they could have done. I'm sure that monster didn't wait around to answer questions. All the police would have was a broken glass window and some major damage to a townhouse. Without a complaint being filed, they wouldn't have much to go on. We could talk our way out of it. Doubt if we'll have to. Knowing what big city life is like, I'm willing to bet that no one reported a thing. Place probably looks just the way we left it."

She had hit upon the truth. The townhouse was undisturbed. The remains of the smashed window still covered the driveway. Even though Valerie assured him that no one was in the condo, Alex insisted on making a quick check of all the rooms before he would let her enter. She had to remain in the locked car with the motor running. While complaining aloud, Valerie was secretly pleased with the concern Alex showed. It felt good to be protected.

Her clothes and belongings were untouched. Valerie quickly packed several suitcases. "I can call someone tomorrow to get the window repaired and have something done about the wrecked furniture. We can decide what we want to do with this place later."

"*We* can decide?" Alex asked with a curious look.

"We."

Alex remained silent the rest of the time she packed. Valerie wasn't too worried. When she sneaked a look at him a little later, he was trying too hard to appear unaware of what her statement implied. But there was a smug look on his face that he couldn't hide. So much for not wanting to get emotionally involved.

"One last stop," said Valerie as they descended with her suitcases to the living room. She walked over to the front coat closet. She reached into the inner box. It was amazing how blind some people could be. They evidently still had not deduced how Jake had outwitted them. Valerie pulled the envelope out and held it out to Alex. "The Invitation."

"You kept it in the mailbox?"

"Why not? It worked for Dad. Evidently the werewolf never considered such a possibility. Must not be familiar with such arrangements. If it worked for him, I figured I'd try it too. Better than a safe."

"Let's get going. I want a closer look at this thing. And we still have those books to go through."

"Sounds like an exciting day. Lead on, Macduff."

And Alex added with a grin, "And be he damned who first cries, 'enough'."

They didn't find the reference to the Devil's Auction until nearly seven that evening. Actually, it only took several hours of searching to find what they wanted. Their plans were sidetracked by an innocent little hug that developed quickly into something much more intense. They finally began serious work when they were so physically exhausted from more pleasurable activities that all they *could* do was to thumb through page after page of esoteric books of occult lore.

Huge stacks surrounded both of them. They were awash in a sea of old musty volumes. Foot by foot, they built forts of occult knowledge as they skimmed one book after another. In the background, the Dorsey Brothers kept the silence at bay.

"Alex," said Valerie, breaking a long silent spell. "How about some dinner? Is that Italian place open? We could order a pizza or something."

Alex didn't answer. Valerie raised her eyes from Crowley's *Magick in Theory and Practice* and looked across the room at her lover. He had an open book balanced on his lap and was quickly thumbing through another, thick volume as if looking for something. Valerie watched, fascinated, as Alex turned page after page, scanning each one quickly. Finally, he seemed to find the one he wanted. His lips moved silently as his eyes swept down the page. She could almost hear the words he was subvocalizing. This was the first time he had done something like this. She was sure he had found something. She could sense a subtle building of tension in the air.

As if sensing her eyes on him, Alex looked up. He grinned when he saw her. He winked and nodded cheerfully. Valerie was positive now that he had found the reference he had remembered. She hoped that whatever he found had all the facts they needed.

"Did you say something about ordering a pizza? Sounds great to me. I'm famished. Want me to call?"

"Alex Warner." Valerie's voice was a notch louder than before. "You tell me what you learned from that book in your lap right now. Food can wait till later."

Standing up and stretching, he laughed happily. "Not what I heard last night. Wow, women sure change their tune fast."

"Sex does that," Valerie replied with a grin. "Now talk."

"Let me order that pizza first. It'll take an hour to get it delivered. This book isn't going anywhere. One minute for the phone call."

Valerie didn't bother to argue. While he dialed, she got up and walked over to where he had left the two books. The thick volume was old and dusty and rested on top of the other. It was still open to the page that Alex had been studying. Now she understood why he had been moving his lips as he read. The book was in French. He had been translating as he read. Valerie sighed in annoyance. She couldn't understand a word of it.

"Want me to tell you what it says?" Alex had come up behind her silently. It was spooky the way he could move so quietly—another thing to ask Makoto Tsuiki about before they left for the auction, she decided. She was glad they were on her side. How could a University Professor in Medieval History fight a werewolf to a stand-still? Be skilled both in foreign languages and karate? Somehow she knew that it all tied in with Alex's subconscious manipulation of the Power. Tsuiki would know the truth. He always did.

"Sit." Alex gently pushed her to the sofa. Holding the French book under one arm, he took to the floor in front of her. "Let me tell this my way. I'm most comfortable if I'm lecturing. Ask all the questions you want, though I can't promise to know all the answers. This isn't the whole story. But I think it gives us a good place to start."

"Whatever you say, boss. Lecture away."

"This is not the passage I was searching for. I found this reference entirely by accident, which leads to all sorts of interesting conclusions, since I'm positive that I've read about this auction in another book. My memory doesn't play tricks on me like that. So, we are talking about at least two different events in history. With the two recent ones, that makes four we are aware of. Who knows how many more have been held over a period of hundreds of years? Our two puzzlers are back with us. This time the questions are a little different. What is there that can be offered again and again for bid? That will always be in demand? I have a theory on that, which ties in directly with the other query: who's running these auctions?

"Whatever, let me tell you what I've discovered. This old thing is *The Fourth Book*, by Henry Cornelius. You might know him better by the name he later adopted, Cornelius Agrippa. He was one of the great occult philosophers of the sixteenth century, and most students of black magic consider this his masterpiece. This edition is nearly a hundred years old. I bought it while I was in Europe doing research on my witchcraft paper. I got the French edition because all of the English translations were severely abridged. The book hasn't been published in any language for over fifty years, but there's no mystery as to why. It's pretty dull stuff.

"Agrippa wrote one of the major studies of occult lore, *Occult Philosophy*, around 1510; but it was not published until 1531. That book details Agrippa's theories of magic and the occult. Surprisingly enough, he did not believe that sorcery had anything to do with the devil or supernatural beings. Agrippa felt magic was strictly a physical manifestation of the spirit. He even states that *imagination has a ruling power over the passions of the soul*. In other words, what you think directly influences the way you feel. Not bad for the sixteenth century. But I'm straying off the subject.

"The *Fourth Book* was published some years after Agrippa's death. There were some doubts raised whether Agrippa had actually written it, but I'm convinced he did. It contains a number of anecdotes and histories of some of his more intriguing experiments. I had no intention of going through the book until I stumbled across a passage in another volume. It's David Hoffman's *Chronicles of Cartaphilus, the Wandering Jew*. There's a brief mention about that famous character's meeting with Agrippa in 1526. It sounded intriguing enough that I pulled out the *Fourth Book*. Agrippa devoted an entire chapter to the episode."

"But what does that have to do with us?"

"Plenty. At the time, Agrippa was famous throughout Europe. He and Paracelsus were considered the two greatest occultists of the age, not that it helped him very much financially. From 1524 till 1526, he served as the physician to the queen mother of France, Louise of Savoy. Unfortunately, she refused to pay him for his services and kept him confined to Lyons without any salary until he finally managed to escape to Florence. There he set up an alchemical laboratory. Late that year, Agrippa claimed to invent a magic mirror. According to the magician, the glass would show any past event in the life of the user. It was his greatest accomplishment. Agrippa, never very wealthy, figured he finally had something that would make him rich."

Valerie tapped her fingers impatiently on the sofa cushions. This was interesting enough, but she wondered what it had to do with the Auction. At least, she was getting to observe Alex in action. He was not a bad teacher. He got caught up in his subject, that was for sure.

"Now, here comes the relevant part of the story. On All-Hallows Eve, 1526, a stranger came to Agrippa's laboratory. He said he wanted to use the magic mirror. Agrippa refused. He had just written to Charles V in hopes that the monarch would become his patron. In the letter, Agrippa mentioned the magic glass and promised it as a gift to the king. The stranger insisted. Agrippa refused again. Finally, the stranger promised the magician that if the mirror really worked he would give Agrippa *something in trade* much more valuable than the king's patronage. Not exactly an auction, but close enough. Curious, in spite of himself, Agrippa agreed."

Now Valerie understood what had caught Alex's attention. He continued to tell the story.

"The stranger looked into the mirror. In most cases, it took hours of concentration to get the device to work. The user had to focus all of his will on the event he wanted to see. Few people could do that without great mental effort. As Agrippa told it, the glass clouded over *immediately*. And stayed that way for minutes. Usually, it only took a few seconds to find the scene in time. When it cleared, Agrippa was horrified to see what was unmistakably the crucifixion of Christ. Terribly frightened by what that implied, he fainted.

"When he revived, the mirror and the stranger were both gone. Faced with no other explanation, Agrippa decided that he had been visited by the Wandering Jew. The magic mirror needed special elements that he could no longer obtain. Thus, its secret was lost forever.

"Agrippa made excuses to Charles V, who became Agrippa's patron anyway. End of episode. Or, at least, all that Agrippa wanted to reveal in the *Fourth Book*."

"So our mysterious auctioneer is The Wandering Jew?"

"Maybe. I'm not entirely convinced that Agrippa revealed the whole story. Some of it doesn't ring true. Along with practicing sorcery, Agrippa was an adventurer most of his life. He had some pretty hair-raising encounters which have been fully documented. It's hard for me to believe that he would have fainted by a picture in a mirror. And why did he let the stranger use the mirror in the first place? I'm convinced there are some elements of truth in the story, but I wonder how much is fact and how much fable to enhance Agrippa's reputation."

The downstairs buzzer sounded, putting an end to the discussion. "I'll go down to the lobby and get the pizza," said Alex. "No way I'm letting anyone into the building without seeing them. How about opening some soda pop. We can talk more after dinner."

Alex handled the Invitation as if it would burst into flame at any instant. Gingerly, he set it down on the kitchen table.

They had finished the pizza a short while ago. The only overhead light in the apartment was located here. It was the logical place to study the card that had led to Jake's death.

"You are cordially invited to an Auction," Alex read carefully, "to be held on All-Hallows Eve, at my estate in upstate Illinois. An item of unique interest will be offered to the highest bidder. Offers in kind. Overnight accommodations provided for all those in Attendance."

Alex shook his head. "I've seen some pretty ambiguous documents, but this sure takes the cake. Whoever is running this affair, he doesn't believe in giving much away. No name, no actual address, no mention what actually is being auctioned. I like that line, *Offers in kind*. He makes the assumption that you know what is being offered in the sale."

"No," said Valerie, raising the card and looking at it closely. "Not exactly, Alex. It's like we discussed at my apartment. Anyone receiving one of these invitations knows exactly what the auctioneer means. It is only ambiguous to someone who is not a master magician. Saves any embarrassment if the card falls into the wrong hands."

"Somehow," Alex said slowly, "I have a feeling that these cards are always delivered to the right people. Don't think that any of them are delayed or destroyed by the post office."

"I know what you mean. You aren't sensitive. I am. You were joking just now. I'm not. Holding this invitation, I can feel a trace of the Power. An actual trace. Do you realize how very powerful the one who sent this Invitation is? That story about the Wandering Jew doesn't seem so outlandish now that I'm holding this."

Alex got up from his chair and began to pace. "A two-thousand-year-old witness to the Crucifixion holding auctions every thirty years? Stealing Agrippa's magic mirror? Trading magic talismans with sorcerers? It doesn't make sense."

"Does it have to?" asked Valerie. "We're only seeing a small part of the total picture. Who can understand the motives of a man over twenty centuries old?"

"Yeah. You have a point there. Maybe he's bored. This whole thing might be some elaborate game he's dreamed up to entertain himself."

"Possibly." Valerie shifted her head, shaking her blonde hair so that it swirled about her face. "Though I don't think so. Don't ask me why; I can't explain it. I just have a feeling that there's something deeper here than an immortal's *game*. We're missing something."

He frowned. "Perhaps." Then he wondered whether they should actually go, considering how little they knew.

"Well, not to change the subject . . ." Valerie held up a hand like a stop sign. "The answer is yes."

"I haven't even asked the question?" Alex had stopped in his tracks and was staring at her suspiciously. "Can you read my mind?"

"Nope. But I *am* sharp. Don't ever think that just because I'm a model I don't have brains."

"Never. I swear it. You're the smartest sex-object I've ever met."

"Good enough. I'll settle for that. In any case, it's been on my mind too. Do we attend the auction or not? Assuming that my father's killer doesn't get the Invitation from us, we can attend. Should we? I say yes."

"Fine with me." Alex pulled Valerie up from her chair. He held her at arm's length and looked her directly in the eyes. "I thought that would be your answer, but I'm not going to rant and rave about the danger. You're a big girl. Even without your Invitation, I suspect Jake's murderer will still make it there. And who knows how many other sorcerers."

"All intent on obtaining the talisman offered," continued Valerie. "And not too worried how they obtain it. Even if that means killing off all the competition."

"You got it. We'll be at a distinct disadvantage there. You have the Power, but not the training. I don't even have that. I'm not interested in being the winning bidder. But it would be nice to return in one piece. Now that I've found you, I don't want to lose you so fast."

Valerie pulled Alex close. She hugged him hard so he couldn't see the tears that had suddenly formed in her eyes. "Not to worry, sweetie," she finally managed to say. "Anyone who can handle a werewolf in a one-on-one isn't going to be a pushover. And I have a few tricks up my sleeve. Not a lot, but Dad wouldn't let his only child go out into the harsh cruel world without teaching me how to defend myself, whether or not I wanted to become a sorceress. We'll manage."

"Good enough. Now to the sixty-four-dollar question. Maybe we won't win this auction. But it would be nice to be able to bid at least."

"Well, we don't have Dad's book collection. If we did, I think we'd be in good shape. He assembled one of the finest collection of grimoires in the world. I know that for a fact. Oops, I forgot. You're an expert on stuff like that. Dad probably told you about his books."

Alex grinned. "We shared a common mania. An obsessive desire to own every book on magic that existed. It was a standing joke between the two of us. Jake had all the rare and expensive ones. I owned all the rest."

"The cops sealed his house. Sooner or later, they'll drop the case and let me take possession. But I doubt if it will be soon enough for us. I could ask for permission to remove some books, but that might not be wise. Might raise a few suspicions among the police, especially if they discovered how much those things cost. Let's leave the library as a last resort." She snapped her fingers. "I do have one thing! Remember that last phone call from my father I told you about? Dad said something about needing a hand. I thought he was talking about getting help from you, but I should have known better. He would never use language like that without a reason. He was referring to the gift he gave me before I left for New York. For my protection, he said. Actually, it was a pretty practical thing. Using it, you never have to worry about rapists waiting in ambush in your apartment or, for that matter, locking yourself out. Only trouble was its appearance. Kind of awkward explaining why you were keeping a mummified hand with a candle held between its fingers in your purse."

"A glory hand?" Alex said. "That's a real find. They're a powerful magical tool. There can't be many in existence, not any more. Only time I ever saw one was in the permanent exhibit on witchcraft in the British Museum. It dated from the eighteenth century. Where did Jake get one?"

"You got me. Dad always seemed to have a surprise or two up his sleeve. No pun intended. When I left for New York, he gave me a jewelry box. Told me the contents would keep me safe. I thought it was some magic ring or something. You can imagine my reaction when I opened it and saw a severed hand resting on a black satin cloth. Almost tossed up my cookies."

"He sure didn't make it," said Alex. "Jake knew what he was doing, but the formula for creating such things has been lost for hundreds of years. Only one book ever described all the steps medieval sorcerers used making a Glory Hand. According to *The Marvelous Secrets of the Natural and Cabalistic Magic of Little Albert*, you had to cut the hand off a corpse who was just killed by hanging. After squeezing all the blood out of it, you pickled it for fifteen days using peppercorns, saltpeter, pounded salt, and something called *zimat*. Little Albert's secret died with him. No one knew what *zimat* was. So no more Hands of Glory. The rest of the formula was pretty easy. You dry the hand during the dog-days, when Sirius the Dog Star rises and sets with the sun, save all the human fat that came out of it, and mix *that* to make a candle, which you wedge between the dead hand's fingers."

"I know what you do next. Dad gave me a card with instructions for its use. You light the candle," said Valerie, "repeating three times *All locks are open. All visitors are still.*"

"The knock of a dead man opens any lock," continued Alex. "The lifelessness of the hand reaches all in any room through the light of the candle, striking them as motionless and silent as the dead."

"Perfect companion for a single girl in Manhattan," said Valerie, laughing. "Better than a can of mace or a tear-gas sprayer. Can't you see me whipping out this mummified hand and a pack of matches?"

"You have it with you?"

"No way, Jose. It wasn't exactly what I'd call a sentimental keepsake. It's in my apartment in New York, still in its velvet lined-box. Tomorrow morning, I'll call my office. Candy, my secretary, has a duplicate set of keys to my place. I'll have her send it to us by messenger. We'll have it by supper time. The Auction isn't till Tuesday."

"Sounds good. Guess it's my turn."

Valerie squinted at him. *"Your turn?"*

Alex disappeared into the other room. Valerie could hear him rummaging about for a few minutes. A stack of books crashed to the floor. Another followed. Then, Alex was back, proudly displaying a large, leather-bound volume.

"Protective coloration," he said. "Learned it in Viet Nam. Easiest way to protect something valuable was to leave it in plain sight. Don't make any fuss about it and make sure that it blended in with the scenery."

"So you leave your most valuable books in the living room bookcase, right next to your mystery paperbacks."

"You got it. Here. Take a look at this."

The book was the size of an encyclopedia volume. It was bound in black leather. Even without opening it, Valerie could see the pages were thick and untrimmed. It was heavier than it looked and she had to hold it with both hands. It gave off an odd, pungent smell that she couldn't immediately identify. Inhaling deeply, she ventured a guess. "Graveyard mold?"

"Mothballs. Previous owner was an oddball

book collector who lived on the South Side. Protected all of his rare books from bugs by packing them in plastic bags filled with mothballs. It worked. Not a wormhole to be found. Got to wear noseplugs if you want to do any serious reading, though. Here. Put it down on the table and open it up to any page."

Valerie immediately saw why the book was so thick. It was not printed but entirely handwritten. The print was small and cramped, filling each page right to the margins. The words were inscribed in black ink, with certain sections underlined in red. Strangely enough, it was in English. "What *is* this thing?"

"Early magicians believed that for a grimoire to be of real worth, it has to be written in a magician's own hand, told in his own words," said Alex. "Thus the book becomes the sorcerer's own magical instrument. That is why there are so many variations of the most famous magical textbook, *The Key of Solomon*. Different magicians, translating from a language not their own, gave you variant texts. When modern printing was invented, the practice all but died out. Still, from time to time, I've come across books done the old way. This has to be one of the most unusual ever written."

Alex flipped the heavy pages until he came to the front of the book. "Take a look. You'll never see another copy of this edition. It's *The Secrets of the Hanged Man* by Justin Geoffrey. His one attempt at non-fiction. According to the National Register, there's a copy at Yale, and another at Miskatonic University. And this one. No others are known to exist of the original thirteen copies Geoffrey had privately bound in 1922. Each one was written in Geoffrey's own hand and all of them are different. I checked the other two copies on trips to the East Coast. The text, while similar, was not exactly the same. There was a regular hardcover edition published in 1930 by the Golden Goblin Press, but that text was severely abridged. It was little more than a feeble attempt to cash in on Geoffrey's already fading notoriety."

"I recognized Geoffrey's name," said Valerie. "I always thought he was a poet, not a magician. Dad had an autographed copy of his *People of the Monolith*. Cost him a mint."

"Fortunately, I didn't have to pay a lot for this treasure. Never could have afforded it on my salary. I got it on a lucky break. A guy I knew before I went into the Army sold it to me for a song. He told me it was mixed in with a big lot of books he bought at an estate sale. Thought it was a horror novel. When he saw it wasn't, he contacted me. I guess I was born under a lucky star."

"You ever read it?"

"I tried," answered Alex, making a face. "It's

filled with the most obtuse meandering imaginable. The Hanged Man is the most obscure figure in the tarot deck. There have been speculations on the true meaning of the card for hundreds of years. Everyone from Eliphas Levi to A.E. Waite has written something about it. No two authors ever agreed on its actual significance, and Geoffrey's theories were as clear as mud. It's not surprising, when you remember he died in an asylum in 1924, two years after completing the book. But it doesn't matter if the thing makes any sense. Lots of books of magic are so obscure that only a lunatic can understand them. Reading the *Kaballah* gives me a headache after fifteen minutes. The language alone is enough to drive me up the wall. And then, trying to discover the meaning hidden *behind* the words. Jake said the same thing about the *Lemegeton*. No one disputes that they are both extremely important books of magic. They're just written in a deliberately paradoxical style.

"The same argument holds true for *The Secrets of the Hanged Man*. Geoffrey might have actually discovered the significance of the Hanged Man. He spent most of his life investigating the dark corners of the world . . . and the human mind. It is equally possible that the book is no more than the ramblings of a famous madman. Lunacy or not, it was written by the most important poet of occult verse since Poe. If the Wandering Jew is collecting rarities, he'll want this book."

"What's this mean?" asked Valerie, pointing to a line written in red ink, just beneath the title. "This isn't English."

"It's Latin. Comes from the Vulgate translation of Isaiah. It's a very famous quote. *'Percurrimus foedus cum morte et cum inferno fecimus pactum.'*" Alex said each word slowly, letting them roll off his tongue. "'We have signed a treaty with death and with Hell we have made a pact.'" Alex shuddered and raised his eyes from the book. "Hopefully, not a prophetic statement."

After a second, he continued on a lighter note. "So we have two items. Might not be enough to be top bidder, but should at least put us in the running."

Valerie yawned. She stretched high up on her toes. "Enough for one night. How about some TV and then to bed."

"You getting sleepy?"

"Sleep?" She grinned. "I didn't say anything about *sleep*."

"Alex. You still awake?"

"Barely. Whatcha want?"

"Remember earlier when you told me about Agrippa and the Wandering Jew."

"Sure. Make it quick, Val. I'm awfully tired."

"Just one second more. When you first started telling me about Agrippa, you said you had a theory about what was offered at the auction, something to do with the identity of the auctioneer."

"Okay." Yawning, Alex shifted around in the bed. He raised his head and folded one arm underneath for support. "It makes sense if the auctioneer is the Wandering Jew. But I'm still not convinced he is."

"What makes sense?"

"Look at the clues. It can't be a talisman like we originally thought. Not if it's been offered again and again. We now know that is the case from the number of auctions that have been held. How many talismans can there be? It has to be something else.

"The prize involves magic. We figured that out pretty easily ourselves. And it obviously has to be something very desirable. Not wealth. Agrippa wouldn't have been willing to trade his mirror for gold, not with Charles V already on the horizon. The way I see it, the only thing left is knowledge. It has to be some kind of magic formula, one that magicians would kill for. A secret only the auctioneer possessed. I put all the facts together. Came up with what had to be the answer. All based on the assumption that our guess about the Wandering Jew is correct."

Valerie's eyes widened. "You don't think . . . you don't really think . . . ?"

"Sure I do. What else can it be? What can't all the money or power in the world get you. One more second of time. The prize of the Devil's Auction has to be the secret of eternal life."

CHAPTER NINE

It was pouring rain when they awoke Monday morning. Valerie stood at the window and watched the gray clouds swirl about the apartment building as Alex wolfed down the last of his breakfast. During her years in New York, she had forgotten how gloomy autumn was in Chicago. Once summer was over, the city seemed to go into a long period of hibernation until spring. The sky was gray more often than not, and cold, dreary rain was an integral part of October and November. She had been extremely lucky this trip. This was the first major rainstorm since she had been back. Valerie wondered if it heralded things to come. The Auction was tomorrow night. The thought of attending the gathering suddenly depressed her. Now that she had found Alex, revenge didn't matter so much. He was more important than finding her father's killer. Now her main concern was their returning from the Auction alive.

Alex came walking into the living room. Immediately, he must have sensed how gloomy she felt. "Hey, good looking," he said with a smile, "don't let the weather get you down. This is Chicago, remember. The only city where you can have all four seasons in one week. It'll get better by afternoon. I've got classes this morning and a faculty meeting right after lunch, and I can't miss either. I'll find someone to take over for the next few days. So you're on your own for most of the day. We'll go out for dinner. In the meantime, cheer up. Can't have you sitting around in a funk all day long. Do something. Think of the possibilities. We might be talking to a two-thousand-year-old man tomorrow."

"Do you really think it's possible?"

"What? That we'll get a chance to talk to him? I certainly hope so."

"No, silly." In the short time they had been together, she had discovered that Alex had a habit of doing that. He answered the most obvious question raised, often when she meant something entirely different. She wasn't sure if he was teasing her or was just very literal minded. It was probably a combination of both. The literal part came from years of having to answer student's dumb questions. And the other half of the time, she suspected, he enjoyed teasing her. "Could he really be two thousand years old?"

Alex went back to the kitchen for another piece of toast. He returned in a minute. "Before I met your father, I would have laughed at the idea. Not anymore. If sorcerers exist, not to mention werewolves, why can't the Wandering Jew be real? There are lots of reported encounters with him in my books. He sounds like an interesting character."

Breakfast finished, Alex donned a raincoat and grabbed a big black umbrella from the hall closet. "I'll be back around three o'clock. You shouldn't have any problems. Our *friends* seem to have given up trying to get your Invitation. And even if they haven't, they won't try anything in the daytime. See you later."

The first thing Valerie did was call her office in New York. With the hour time difference, her secretary was already there. A few minutes of patient explaining took care of everything. The Hand of Glory would be on the way within hours and should arrive late in the day.

That done, Valerie settled down and watched cartoons on TV for a half an hour.

When she was positive Alex would not be back, she picked up the phone and dialed a well-remembered number.

"Mak? It's me, Valerie."

"Val. I had hoped to hear from you. How are you and Alex getting along?"

"I'm staying with him at his apartment, if that's what you mean." She laughed. "As if you didn't know. Do you have some time free to talk? In person? I don't trust phones."

"Very wise. I had a feeling you might call today, so left my morning free. I'll be by in fifteen minutes. Will buzz you with the old signal. Come down when you hear it. And only if it's the old signal."

"You really think that codes are necessary?"

Makoto's tone was grim. "With the Countess involved, you never can tell. She might be listening to us right now."

For Valerie, the world suddenly stopped moving. Everything clicked into place. She *knew*. Old memories came flooding back. In her mind's eye she saw a beautiful woman clad entirely in black. And, hovering nearby, a hulking, brutish woman companion. Beauty and the Beast, her father had called them. The Countess Marie Lamont and her ever-present servant. What was her name? Hannah? That was it. Hannah Stine.

"Val? Val?" Tsuiki sounded worried. "You still there?"

"The Countess," Valerie managed to get out. "She killed him, didn't she? She always hated Dad. I should have known she did it. Or that servant of hers, Hannah."

"We can talk when we're together. Remember, wait for my signal. I'll be there as soon as I can."

One long ring, then two short. That was Mak's signal. They had come up with it a long time ago, when she was still a kid living at home and he was her father's best pupil. It had been a game then, a secret code between the two of them. Only now it was deadly serious.

Across 57th Street, on Lake Shore Drive, a small finger of rock jutted out into the lake. It was a favorite spot for students and Hyde Park residents to go fishing. The city had even provided a small lot for automobile parking. From your car, you could look directly out into Lake Michigan. On days like today, that lot was deserted. Mak parked his car in a spot facing the gray waves and turned to Valerie.

"Seems like old times."

"A little. But Mom and Dad are both gone. And the two of us are a bit older."

Mak chuckled. He had a pleasant laugh, low and vibrant, almost dignified-sounding. It fit him. Everything about Mak was in harmony. He was the most balanced person Valerie had ever known. Her father had put it best a long time ago: "Others strive to find inner peace," he had told her. "Mak never lost it."

"Unlike most of us," Mak stated with a smile, "growing older has agreed with you. The last time we were together, you were an attractive girl. Now you are a beautiful woman." Mak hesitated for an instant. "It is good to see you again, Val. Even if it is under such unfortunate circumstances."

"Tell me about it. I don't think I'll ever accept the fact that Dad is gone. Every time the phone rings, I pick it up half expecting it to be him on the line, telling me that it was all a mistake, another one of his elaborate tricks. I keep waiting for him to come through the door. But he never does. Maybe someday the realization will finally sink in. Not yet."

"It never does." Mak's face was solemn. "It is part of the human condition. We cannot accept such loses. In time the wound heals. But the pain is never gone. It lingers there forever, hidden beneath the surface, perhaps, but always there. Such links with the past are what make us what we are."

"Hmmm. That's an interesting thought." Valerie straightened up in the seat and smoothed her hair away from her face. Her dark mood seemed to flow out of her. Alex was right. Life was too exciting at the moment to be depressed. "Think of what an immortal man might experience over the course of two thousand years. How much pain and anguish and loss can a man stand? No matter what his powers, he could not prevent death after death. Friendship and love would always lead to pain. In time, he would avoid those emotions at all cost. No wonder such a man might become a wanderer. And, when such a life no longer was possible, he'd become a recluse."

Mak pursed his lips together. "Living away from people, except for once every thirty years. I see that Alex has been up to his usual mental gymnastics trying to puzzle out the Auction. Have you come up with any reason for our mysterious hermit to interrupt his solitude?"

"Not yet. The only idea so far has been that the Wandering Jew does it for his amusement. Or a love of rare magical relics. Neither explanation satisfies Alex."

"Nor should they. I doubt if they are correct."

"You know the answer, don't you, Mak? You always know the answers."

"Your confidence in me is most flattering, Valerie; but in this case, I am afraid, misplaced. I know little more than you or Alex. There is one thing, however, that you might want to consider before attending this Auction tomorrow."

"And that is?"

"No one who participated in the Devil's Auction has ever returned from it. No one living

admits to have ever received an invitation. That can mean but one thing. Those who did attend never returned. They disappear from sight. That is why so little is known about the event. There is no one to ask what took place at it. That is why your father thought Romanov foolish for keeping the Invitation. And why I gave my Invitation away."

"You had an Invitation?"

"Of course. They are always sent to the most powerful practicing magicians in the country. I do have a little pride, my dear Valerie. You have to agree I satisfied the requirement."

"And . . . and . . . you gave it *away*." Valerie couldn't believe what Mak was saying. "Weren't you the least bit curious?"

"Of course. But not *that* curious. I enjoy living too much to allow my existence to be terminated because of curiosity. You might be interested in knowing to whom I gave the Invitation. I delivered it in person to the Countess."

Valerie stared at Tsuiki in astonishment. "Mak. How could you? You practically admitted to me she was the one who killed my father. The motive had to be his Invitation. Now you're telling me you gave her exactly what she wanted. Are you crazy?"

Mak gave her the *look*. It was an expression of his, a combination of "If only you knew," and "Someday you will understand." She'd hated it as a teenager, and it didn't sit much better with her now.

"Think about what I told you for a minute, Val, before getting so hot under the collar. *No one* ever returns from these Auctions. I can't make it any clearer than that. Marie Lamont is set on going. She'll attend and that will be the end of her. Jake's death will be avenged. Nice, neat, and with no loose ends. What could be simpler."

"Maybe for you, but not for me. For one thing, everything we know about this Auction has been rumor or legend. No actual facts. What if you aren't right? Maybe, just maybe, you guessed wrong. And, in doing so," said Valerie, with a trace of bitterness, "gave the Countess a chance at immortality."

"It might not be as simple as that."

"She killed my father without hesitation, looking for his Invitation, and she tried to kill Alex and me!"

"I didn't know that. How?"

Briefly, Valerie summarized the events of the last day. When she got to the fight with the werewolf, Mak interrupted with a wave of a hand.

"Definitely Hannah. The Countess found her in an orphanage years ago and taught her the correct words of power. She is not very smart, but possesses an animal cunning. Be warned. Hannah is a dangerous customer despite the way Alex handled her. She is a killer—has killed many men. And she is slavishly loyal to her Mistress."

"The Countess Marie Lamont." To Valerie, it was like pronouncing a curse. "The most notorious sadist to practice magic in this century. Dad used to scare me as a child with stories about her. The infamous Countess. How many men has *she* killed, Mak? Wouldn't she love to be immortal. She's not getting any younger. Must be around fifty now." Valerie smacked her hands together in frustration. "The Countess always managed to have her own way before. What makes you think she'll let anyone stop her now?"

"Ashmedai."

"Huh?"

"The master of the Auction. He calls himself Ashmedai. That much is known about him. He's the most powerful magician in the world. No one knows any more than that. He lives on an isolated estate somewhere upstate. No one knows where. If, as you suspect, Ashmedai is in reality the Wandering Jew, he has managed to achieve the isolation he wants. He guards the location of his retreat jealously. Do you have any directions to the auction?"

"Never gave it much thought; but now that you mention it, no."

"Don't worry about it. I'm sure you'll get them when you need them. Not until then. And somehow, I suspect, they will be worthless without an Invitation. A small demonstration of his power. This is the point I was trying to make. Marie Lamont is a vile woman. We both know what she is—a sadistic maniac who has used her powers to further her excesses for decades. The Countess exemplifies the worst aspect of those with the Power. Unfortunately, her kind is too typical of the few who practice the Black Arts. Those with a sense of morality are a small minority. Power corrupts. I think Ashmedai tries in his own way to balance the scales."

"Sort of paying back for his sins." Valerie chewed on her lower lip as she consider Mak's argument. "I see what you mean. It presents a possible motive behind the Auction. You think they are really a trap for the wicked, a one way ticket to Hell. Ashmedai invites the most powerful mages to attend, promising them immortality . . ."

". . . and then giving them the justice they deserve," finished Mak. "Exactly. That is why I say, let the Countess attend. Her fate will be of her own making."

Valerie shook her head in disagreement. "It doesn't ring true, Mak. For one thing, Dad was no evil sorcerer, and he got an Invitation. So did you. You're not evil. A little weird, perhaps, but not evil. More importantly, you're giving your fellow adepts too little credit. They might

be greedy, but they are also a pretty suspicious
bunch. Do you really think this Ashmedai
could fool them for generation after generation
with the same scheme? There has to be some
thread of truth to the Auction. Otherwise, no
one would attend. If no one ever returned, like
you claim, then there shouldn't be anything
known. And yet there is. Listen to this idea:
maybe the people attending do disappear. Maybe not. It might all be part of an elaborate
coverup. After all, if I was one of the losers at
such an event, I wouldn't want anyone to know
I even attended. A fact like that could perma-
nently damage your reputation. You know how
vain most sorcerers are. Think about it for a
minute. Couldn't that be the *real* explanation of
these disappearances? They might not be disappearances at all. Instead, the losers might
vanish through the simple method of never
admitting they attended in the first place. Since
it only lasts one night, all they had to do was
come up with an alibi for the evening, then
keep quiet about the event ever after."

Mak didn't say anything for several minutes.
Valerie was secretly quite pleased. Even if he
didn't agree with her, Mak was at least giving
her arguments some consideration.

Finally, Tsuiki shrugged and made a vague
gesture with both hands. "Much as I hate to
admit it, you could be right. It *is* hard to believe
that anyone would attend these Auctions if

certain death was the only reward. As you point out, it would account for all the legends that have grown up about the Auction over the years. A slip of the tongue here or there by a disgruntled loser, and a story is born.

"Valerie, you have your father's gift for intrigue. It never was one of my strong points. I don't know what to say. It looks like I misjudged the whole situation . . . though I still think that Ashmedai is more than a match for the Countess and her schemes."

"I hope you're right. In any case, Alex and I are going to attend. We would go even if you hadn't told me about the Countess. It has gone far beyond avenging my father. This whole thing intrigues me. I *have* to go, and Alex feels the same way."

"Not to change the subject, but it seems that you and Alex have hit it off pretty well."

Valerie grinned. "I'd say so. We make a good pair."

Mak nodded, his expression serious. "You do. A very good pair. I'm sure you realized that Jake had a hand in all this."

"Right away. A few years ago, I would have resented it. Not any more. Maybe if Alex had been an ogre my feelings would be different, but he's not. If anything, he's better than I deserve. My father, the matchmaker. I assume from your friendship with Alex that you were involved in arranging this as well?"

"Not guilty. In fact, I never once mentioned Alex to your father the entire time I studied at your home. I had my own plans for him. Your family isn't the only one with good bloodlines, you know. There have been sorcerers in the Tsuiki family for over five hundred years. From the day I met Alex, I was scheming to add him to my family. His genes mixed with ours would have produced a very powerful adept. My father and grandfather both agreed that he was a perfect match for my younger sister, Rushi."

Mak's voice trailed off and for a moment, his eyes were filled with sadness. Valerie's subconscious came to her rescue. "I remember now. She was killed in an auto accident soon after I left for New York. Mom told me over the phone. So all your plans were for naught."

Mak nodded, sighing heavily. "Man plans and God laughs. It's an old Yiddish proverb. Pretty much sums it all up. Rushi never even met Alex. She had just turned eighteen. I wanted to wait another year or two before introducing them. Kismet."

"When did Dad enter the picture?"

"With Rushi gone, I saw no reason to keep Alex hidden from your father. You had been gone a few months. Your mother was busy with work of her own. I was no longer Jake's student. Not much was happening in magic, and Jake was bored silly. So I told him about Alex." Mak held up both hands in mock defense.

"Never once occurred to me that Jake would want to set the two of you together. You were gone and that was it. I wanted your Dad to meet Alex for other reasons."

"No need to apologize. I'm not complaining."

"Thank you. I'm happy for the both of you. Alex deserves the best. Especially after his first wife, Sheila."

"The Dragon Lady? How did she come in to the picture, Mak? That doesn't sound like one of Dad's tricks. Unless my old man was a lot more subtle than I ever knew."

"No. Sheila was an unexpected complication." Mak made a face. "She was a minor sorceress taking some courses at the University. She registered for one of Alex's classes on witchcraft. Sheila was not very smart, but she had enough brains to immediately recognize Alex for what he was. She caught your Dad and me completely unawares. Before we knew anything was going on, Alex told us he was thinking of getting married. Did we feel like two jerks! She hooked him right under our noses."

"You couldn't stop her?"

"She used a fairly potent love charm and there wasn't much we could do about it. As you heard at the restaurant, we tried to talk Alex out of the marriage, but that was a futile gesture. It wasn't till after their wedding that Jake was able to go to work. She never stood a chance against your Dad. When he wanted, Jake could be diabolical.''

"I don't know if I want to hear any more. At the moment, my opinion of my Dad is pretty high. I'd hate to have it go to Hell so quickly.''

"On the contrary,'' said Mak. "He was on the side of the angels. If Alex had been truly happy, there wouldn't have been much Jake could have done. He was only a catalyst. Their marriage would have been in trouble sooner or later even without Jake's prodding. Sheila could captivate Alex, but she could never hold him. Alex was miserable with her. She wanted his luck, not him. There was no real emotion in that match.''

Valerie squirmed a little bit at what Mak was saying. It hit a little too close to home. She couldn't help wondering if she was any better than Alex's first wife. There was a certain sting in Mak's words.

"Getting you worried, Val? Don't be upset. *True* love is stronger than any spell. It's what's happening between the two of you now. Aha, you are blushing. I still can read your thoughts even without telepathy. I can assure you that you are not like Sheila at all. I knew that you would start wondering if you weren't the same sort of creature as the Dragon Lady. You don't have to worry. You love Alex already—I can see it in your eyes every time you mention his name. This is one area in which **I** am the master. There is a bond between the two of you that is already stronger than any magic. You might think of yourself as cold and calculating—a rather dramatic and adolescent fantasy you have maintained. I know you better. You don't have the follow-through. You are not your father. If Alex hadn't appealed to you on an emotional level, Power or not, you would never have made a play for him. Nor would you have chased him so hard until he caught you."

"Stop it, Mak." Valerie could feel her cheeks burning. "You're embarrassing me."

"No one ever died of embarrassment. I am sure you will survive as well. The point I'm making is an important one. Please don't think I'm raising it for no reason. You may have used a few shortcuts to bring the two of you together, but that is no terrible sin. Women have used one type of magic or another for thousands of years. You were just a little more direct than most."

"Enough, enough." Valerie glanced at the clock. "It's getting late and I have a million other things I want to ask you about Alex."

Mak shook his head. "I have to get to the restaurant. One of my cooks is sick and I have to fill in. Monday is a busy day for us. Most commuting students aren't ready to face cafeteria food after a weekend without it. I should have been there a half-hour ago."

"But I have so many questions."

Mak started up the car. "Don't look at me for the answers. The less you know about Alex's past the better. You can't accidentally mention something you had no way of knowing. Let life take its course. Learn about him from him. You already know all you need to know. Everything else will just round out the picture."

"But, but, but, . . ."

Mak laughed as he steered the car out into traffic. "Looks like the sun is trying to push its way through the clouds. Maybe we'll have a break in the rain after all." He looked over at Valerie. "Don't pout at me, young lady. Magician or not, you sometimes have to live by the same rules as anyone else. This is one of those times."

They rode back to Alex's apartment building in silence, Valerie pondering what Mak had said. After a few minutes, she had to conclude that her friend was right. If she knew too much about Alex, a wrong word could lead to difficulties. Her future husband didn't seem the type to talk about himself. She would have to change that. A little prying linked with some flattery should work well enough. . . .

The rain had stopped by the time Mak steered his car to the front entrance of the apartment complex. Putting the gear shift in neutral, Mak turned and grinned at Valerie.

"Alex is a quiet man, but I am sure you can get around that. From what I saw at my restaurant the other night, you already have him enthralled. Consider it a challenge."

Valerie had to grin back. Mak knew her better than anyone. It was impossible to be mad at him very long. Impulsively, she reached out and touched him on the arm. "I hope this isn't goodbye for the last time."

"Worried about the Auction? Can't say I blame you. Even if your theory is correct, it still will be very dangerous. Maybe fatal. You don't *have* to go, you know. You could just rip up the Invitation. Or not attend."

"No." Valerie shook her head. "I have to go. If I didn't, I'd spend the rest of my life wondering what I missed. I'm sure Alex feels the same way. The Auction is in our blood. It's calling to us. There is no way we can't answer."

"Well, good luck to the both of you. Since I gave away my Invitation, you can tell me all about it when you get back. Call me and let me know what I missed."

"I'll do that. For sure, I'll do exactly that."

They were watching the Nine O'Clock news that evening when the phone rang. Alex picked it up. He listened for a few seconds, then turned to Valerie, an odd look on his face. He put one hand over the speaker before saying anything.

"It's for you. Man says you were expecting his call. His name is Ashmedai."

Valerie swallowed hard and nodded. "The directions," she managed to gulp out, "to the Auction. From the one sponsoring the affair."

Wordlessly, Alex handed her the phone.

"Hello. This is Valerie Lancaster."

The voice on the phone was deep and pleasant. Almost soothing. Valerie was not sure what she had been expecting, but this was not it. The speaker sounded like a radio disc jockey on one of the elevator-music stations.

"Good evening, Miss Lancaster. Sorry to call at this hour, but it has been a busy day. Several of the other guests have been difficult to reach. You are the last on my list."

"The last? How many others are attending, if I might ask?"

"Why not?" The man on the other end of the line laughed. "The real question is never if you can ask. All people control their own actions. What the *response* will be is another question. However, I see no reason for you not to know. There will be six other bidders at the Auction. As you already know, one of them will be the Countess Lamont."

Valerie sucked in her breath. Ashmedai was somehow aware of her interest in the Countess. And of her conversation with Mak that morning. "Fine. I am looking forward to seeing her."

"Dinner will be served at eight. Cocktails

first. I would appreciate it if you and Professor Warner would be here before then. Early evening would be best. Informal dress, of course. The Auction will take place after our meal. Since it might go on for some time, the two of you will be welcome to spend the night here."

"Sounds delightful. Where is *here* though?"

"My home is easy enough to find. Take the Toll Road north to upstate Illinois. Take the Oak Grove exit going west. You will cross over the highway. Around a hundred feet further, there is a turnoff onto an unpaved dirt road. Watch carefully, as there is no sign. Follow that road for several miles and you will arrive at my door. It should take between two or three hours from downtown Chicago, depending on the traffic. Oh, one last thing. Make sure your Invitation is with you on the trip. Otherwise, you will have a difficult time finding your way. Is everything clear? Wonderful. I look forward to meeting the two of you. Good night."

Hanging up the phone, Valerie dropped onto the sofa next to Alex. "Why do I have a feeling that I was on the line with a talk show host? Damn, that man had a pleasant voice." She quickly told Alex everything that Ashmedai had said. "He was so . . .," she searched for the right word, ". . . *civilized*."

"This Countess. You never mentioned her before."

"I spent some time today going over possible

suspects in Dad's murder. She fit the bill. There have been rumors about her for years—nothing proven of course. She has a big estate up on the North Shore and lives there with a big hulk of a servant named Hannah. Her full name is the Countess Marie Lamont. She inherited a lot of money from her father, who was also a powerful sorcerer. When I was young, there was a lot of dirt going around about her. She is definitely a sadist, and very likely a homicidal maniac. Uses her magic to keep the crimes secret. No one could ever prove anything, but suspicions are enough for most magicians. I don't remember anyone in the Black Arts willing to deal with her. From what I remember, she is a very vain woman. Beautiful in a very cold way—you know what I mean. Black leather and whips and all that stuff. I'm sure she is panic-stricken, growing older. Have no doubts at all: she would kill for the secret of eternal life."

"Seeing that Ashmedai specifically mentioned she was attending seems to confirm your suspicions." Alex's face was grim. "We'll have to be prepared. I've dealt with people like this Countess before. I can't imagine she would be a good loser. She might not follow the rules for bidding, either. In any case, we have to be ready for the worst."

A stray word from the TV news caught Valerie's attention. "Alex. Listen to this."

". . . has police in that small northern Illinois community baffled. The dead man has been tentatively identified as Sid Levine, a smalltime hoodlum from Chicago. Hindering the investigation is the condition of the body." The newscaster paused dramatically before continuing. "Few details have been released to the press, but unnamed sources in the Oak Grove police department have told us that Levine's body looked like it had been run over by a steam roller. In a written statement, Chief Gustafson of Oak Grove hints that the murder might be drug-related. Supporting that claim is the fact that five one-hundred-dollar bills, all neatly ripped in half, were found in the dead man's pockets. No further information is available at this time.

"Now, turning to local news. In Chicago's own baffling mystery, there are still no clues to the whereabouts of the statue of Casimir Pulaski that disappeared from . . ."

Alex got up and shut off the television. "Looks like the Countess might not be the only thing we have to worry about. Oak Grove sounds like it's going to be a lively place tomorrow evening. Lively, or very deadly."

CHAPTER TEN

Valerie woke to the sound of Alex on the phone. He was just hanging up when she wandered into the living room.

"Sorry," he said. "Didn't mean to wake you up."

"It's okay." Valerie yawned and stretched. "Kind of early to be making calls, isn't it? Who's awake at seven in the morning?"

"The guy I was talking to never sleeps. Or so he claims. You want some breakfast, or are you going to get some more rest?"

"Food sounds good. I don't think I can sleep anymore."

Alex nodded. "I know what you mean. Only caught a few hours myself. I never was very good at waiting. I'll be glad when we are on our way."

Valerie went into the kitchen and started making coffee. Alex joined her a few seconds later. He pulled out the carton of eggs from the refrigerator. "You want some bacon and eggs?"

"Fine. I'll make some toast. God, I don't know how I'm going to fit into all my clothes. I'm eating like a pig. I've probably gained five pounds since I met you."

"No problem. On you, it doesn't show."

"You're no judge. But I appreciate the kind words none the less. You have a nice way of saying the right thing, honey."

"No trick to that. I say what I mean."

Valerie popped the toast out of the toaster. She turned to Alex, who was busy with the frying pan on the stove. "Alex. I love you very much."

"And I love you too, Valerie." He pulled the pan off the fire and gave her a peck on the cheek as he went looking for a spatula. "Want to get some plates out? Bacon should be ready in another minute or two."

"Alex. Put down that food for an instant. Didn't you hear what I said. I *love* you."

"I heard. And I love you too. I intend to continue to love you for the next fifty or so years. That's assuming that we survive this trip today. With all that time, I think we can eat our breakfast while it's still hot."

Valerie stuck out her tongue. "So much for romance. Here I confess my innermost feelings and do you care? All you can think about is your stomach."

"There is a time and place for everything, Valerie. Confessions of true love are best *after* breakfast. I function better on a full stomach. Sit and eat. Romance later."

"Promise?"

"I promise." Alex put down the dishes and encircled her with his arms. "You rescued me from myself. I swore one try at love was enough. Almost convinced myself of that before you came into my life." He nuzzled her on her neck, sending shivers running up and down her spine. "I love you more than you can ever imagine."

Their kiss was long and sweet. Valerie could feel herself growing aroused. Alex was reacting the same way. It was clear that she was going to have to start wearing a nightgown. Sleeping nude was fun but too distracting. "Breakfast," she said, pulling away from him. "Otherwise we'll never get going."

"Breakfast," said Alex, with a trace of regret in his voice. "Do me a favor, though? Put on some clothes first. I don't think I can make it if I have to stare at your naked body across the table. My blood is boiling already."

"One nightshirt coming up." As she slipped

it on, Valerie remembered what had awakened her. "Alex, who was that on the phone?"

"An old friend from my Army days. Calls himself the Brick. He owes me a few favors and I'm collecting one now."

"What kind of favor?"

"The people attending this auction are playing for keeps. That news report last night was no joke. I don't care how pleasant this Ashmedai sounds on the phone. He might not have our best interests at heart. The other bidders surely don't. We need to even up the odds a little bit. Brick deals in weapons, all sorts of weapons. If I'm going to drive into a trap, I intend to have enough firepower to blow my way out of it."

"You sound like you've done things like this before, Alex."

"Not for a long time. Some skills you never forget. Let's hope that I don't have to use them. Better to be prepared, though, than the alternative."

"The alternative?"

"Dead."

It was well after two o'clock and dark clouds were gathering over Lake Michigan when Alex and Valerie came down to the car. Valerie wore jeans and a floral-print top, with her hair tied back behind her head. In a large overnight bag, she had a nicer outfit to change into once they reached the Auction.

Alex was dressed entirely in black: black slacks, black pullover shirt, and dark black windbreaker. He even had a black beret that he wore pulled down tight over his forehead. "Let's just say it matches my suspicions," he said to Valerie when she questioned his lack of colors. "I've got a change of outfit in my bag as well."

The two rarities were securely wrapped and packed away at the bottom of Alex's suitcase. After breakfast, he had dug up an old plastic drop sheet which the two of them had attacked with scissors and tape. The book and jewelry case were both embedded in several layers of heavy translucent plastic for protection. It wasn't fancy, but it was practical and quick.

Alex dropped both bags in the back seat of the car. A large airline shoulder bag already rested on the floor: a gift from the Brick. Valerie also knew that Alex had a sheath knife strapped to his calf. And several pieces of metal in his windbreaker pocket rattled against each other softly every time he moved. Alex was armed and dangerous.

To Valerie, the real weapon was Alex himself. He seemed the personification of death. She could sense the coldness within him. Alex Warner, Professor of History, no longer existed. He had reverted back to his wartime personality; the part of him that had battled the werewolf now controlled his body. He seemed to flow from place to place, never making a sound. His head darted from side to side, his eyes taking in everything, though acknowledging nothing. Now she saw the Alex Warner who suspected everyone and everything, almost to the verge of paranoia. All the black magic in the world could not stop a man like this. Valerie felt glad he was on her side.

"Let's go," said Alex. His voice sounded harsh and cold, tight with suppressed excitement. "Time to get moving."

They climbed into the car. Alex started the engine then gently eased the auto out of the parking lot. As he drove, his body seemed to relax slightly. Valerie turned on the tape deck, and the gentle sound of Benny Goodman filled the car. After a few minutes, Alex began to tap his fingers on the steering wheel in time with the music. A few minutes more, and off came the black beret. Valerie relaxed.

It was in the low forties outside, so they kept the car windows closed as they headed north. Dark clouds filled the sky. Traffic was light and they made good time. As Alex paid the first toll at the O'Hare interchange, the first drops of rain dotted the windshield. A gray mist descended as the rain fell in a steady drizzle. The car tires rolled out the miles. The Benny Goodman tape came to an end, and Glenn Miller took its place.

Neither of them spoke. It was enough that

they were finally on their way. Valerie caught herself dozing off more than once. The gray skies, the steady drone of the tires, and the soft patter of the rain had a soothing effect. She had offered to drive earlier. As expected, Alex had turned her down. He was too tense to let anyone else behind the steering wheel. It was probably just as well. With his luck, Alex would never be involved in a major accident.

"Another toll," said Alex wearily. "Have forty cents in change left, Valerie?"

"Nope. Sorry. Break a dollar."

As Alex handed the bill to the toll collector, he asked, "How much further to the Oak Grove west exit?"

"About twenty minutes," answered the man in the booth. Then, he looked at Alex oddly. "Did you say Oak Grove *west*?"

"You got it. West."

"Funny. You're the second one today to make the same mistake. There's only one Oak Grove exit, and that goes east. Hooks up with Oak Grove Road after a mile. Maybe that's what you're thinking of."

"Maybe," said Alex, and he directed his car out into traffic.

Alex turned to Valerie, a frown on his face. "Time to put the Invitation on the dashboard. This should be some trick if Ashmedai can pull it off." Then his mood changed, as he continued. "We were the second ones to ask about that exit. Looks like we won't be first to arrive."

"Fashionably late," said Valerie in agreement. "It will help keep my image as a high-price fashion-model intact."

Together, they counted down the miles. Alex kept the car at a steady sixty. Forgotten now was the tape player. Nor did Valerie feel the least bit sleepy. They were close, and each minute brought them a mile closer.

"Over there." She pointed across the highway ten minutes later. "The rest stop where that body was found. Not very far at all from the Auction."

"Means that someone knew where this thing was scheduled to take place." Alex pumped the gas pedal a little harder, sending his car surging forward. "Nine miles to go."

At two miles to the exit, Valerie spotted a green highway sign announcing **Oak Grove— Oak Grove Road—Two Miles**. There was no mention on the sign of an east or west branch. Her fingers curled into fists in anticipation. She could see Alex's hands tighten on the steering wheel in a death grip.

A second sign proclaimed that it was only a mile to the exit. Then, in thirty seconds, they were on the exit ramp. Alex slowed the car down to twenty. After speeding along at three times that speed, it felt like they were crawling. Along with the steady rain, there was a low curtain of fog covering the road; it was difficult to see very far ahead. Alex immediately switched on the lights. They caught the flash of a metal sign a few hundred feet ahead. They coasted up to it as Alex braked the car to a slow roll. **Oak Grove-West. Next Left.**

"So much for that toll collector," said Valerie, with almost a sigh of relief. "He must have been thinking of another exit."

"I don't know," said Alex, as he gave the engine a little gas. The branch in the exit was only a few hundred feet further. A perfectly normal overpass crossed the highway. Alex directed his car onto the bridge. In seconds, they were on the other side of the road. The fog was a heavy white curtain that was barely cut by the headlights.

"It's hard to believe that guy would make the same mistake twice in one day. And this fog seems to have come up awfully sudden . . . the road has a funny feel to it, too." Alex shook his head. "Not that it really matters, as long as we get there. Here comes that dirt road. He told you a few miles on that, right? We should be there in ten minutes or so. I'm taking it nice and slow; dirt roads aren't made for regular tires."

The car groaned in protest as Alex turned onto the unpaved road. It was little more than a rough track hewed out of thick forest; it twisted and turned through the ancient wood. Huge old trees lined both sides of the pathway. Dense shrubbery packed up against the road, forming a nearly impenetrable wall. Alex had barely enough room to maneuver. The ground was not leveled and the car bounced and crashed as he fought with the steering wheel to keep them from crashing into the undergrowth. The fog got worse as the trees shielded what little light still remained. It was impossible to see more than twenty feet ahead.

Alex watched the road intently. The fog lights were little good in this gloom. His hands were locked on the steering wheel and he was using one foot on the gas and the other on the brake. Sweat covered his forehead. His lips were tightly pressed together in concentration.

Valerie sat braced with her arms up against the dashboard. Every bump rattled her jaw. Her head was ringing from the constant jolting. The seat belt did little good on a road like this. Her hands ached from pressing against the dashboard. She stared out the front window, trying to make out shapes in the fog. The mist was not natural. She could sense dark magic in its origin. Some primitive fear stirred in her mind. There was something terribly wrong in the forest.

"I see something up ahead," said Alex. Without taking his eyes off the road, he reached into the back seat with one arm and grabbed hold of the mysterious airline bag. Cords of muscle stood out in his arm as he pulled the bag into the front. "Grab everything," he commanded. "This might be the end of the road."

Valerie did as she was told. There was no time for questions; Alex knew what he was doing. She gathered the two overnight bags on her lap. The headlights fastened on the object only a hundred feet away—another car, stopped in the road. There was no way around it.

Alex let their car roll up close to the other one. Twenty feet away, he switched the bright lights on. The strong beams didn't go very far in the dense fog. Valerie rolled down her window a crack, but there was nothing to hear. The forest remained silent. Thin tendrils of mist crept into the car. The air felt damp and cold. The drizzling rain beat a steady tattoo on the roof.

"I don't like the looks of this," said Alex. "No reason for anyone to be stopped here, with no house in sight. We've got no choice. We'll have to see what's going on."

He reached into the flight bag and pulled out a hand gun. To Valerie, the pistol looked as big as a cannon. Alex held it in his right hand and checked to see that it was loaded. Next, he swung it around, moving his hand back and forth, up and down. "Getting used to the feel of it," he said to Valerie. "You never should handle a weapon until it feels right."

Alex pulled several clips of ammunition from

the bag. "Better prepared than not." His eyes locked with Valerie's. "The two of us will go out there together. I think it would be a good idea for us not to split up. Ever. If something happens, drop the bags and run. We can always get more clothes. You ready?"

"As ready as I'll ever be. I don't like this very much, Alex."

"Tell me about it. Nothing much else we can do. No time for chatting. Let's go."

By the time Valerie had opened her door and pulled the two bags out, Alex was around the car and at her side. He used his left hand to steady her, while keeping a constant watch on the nearby forest. His right hand, the one with the gun, moved back and forth as if it had a life of its own.

"Seems quiet enough," said Alex. He stepped forward, gently tugging Valerie with him. Cautiously, his head weaving from side to side, he made his way to the other car. She kept close behind him. It was only ten feet away, but in the dense fog, the auto was a vague, indistinct mass of dark metal. She shivered as they drew nearer. She could sense death close by.

The car was a black Cadillac limousine. "Must be an airport rental," said Alex. "Looks like the type you see up there. Has to be one of the other bidder's."

Squinting in the mist, Valerie could make out a bulky piece of steel at the edge of the road. She edged over closer to the wreckage. It was a door to the Cadillac. Valerie noted that the lock on the door was still pressed down and the window still rolled shut. At the right and left sides, the metal was crumpled and broken. The edges of the breaks were all pointing inward. It was as if some terrible hand had ripped into the steel and pulled the door right off its hinges. Valerie shuddered. What creature could do this?

Alex was by her side for a moment, then moved forward. She hurried up behind him, just as he reached the side of the Cadillac. "Don't look inside the car," he warned, but it was too late. Valerie turned away, suddenly feeling very sick.

The thing on the back seat had once been a man. Now it was a smashed ruin, crushed to a pulp. Blood pooled on the floor and soaked the seat through and through. Chunks of flesh and bone were everywhere. It was impossible to make out the features of the victim. If the person hadn't been in a business suit, there would have been no way to tell if it had been a man or woman. Nothing human could have caused that damage.

Alex's words were clipped and full of ice. "Take a few deep breaths. There's no time for panic. Whatever killed that truck driver has been here too. It ripped the door off the car to get at the passenger. Now it's probably out in the woods somewhere, waiting for more victims. Us."

Gulping, Valerie reached out. Alex took her hand and guided her forward. They stepped quickly in front of the Cadillac. Valerie glanced ahead and froze for a second. A fallen tree blocked the road. A number of branches were gone from the trunk and there were huge gouges gone from the bark, showing the wood beneath. The mud in front of the tree was a gooey mess. There was blood everywhere. This time, there was not even a body.

Alex darted forward. He quickly examined the site. Then, he scanned the area beyond the barrier. In seconds, he was back beside Valerie.

"Two sets of footprints. One was that of a normal man—probably the driver. The other prints are massive, too big to be that of a man. And deep. The killer must be heavier than hell. The way I see it, our unknown murderer blocked the road with the tree, then settled down to wait. A car came along. The driver got out to investigate. When he got close, it attacked. The driver must have been killed immediately. The bidder, still in the car, saw what happened and locked the doors. Not enough with this monster. It ripped open the car and finished the job."

"What rips doors off cars?" asked Valerie, trying to control the shakes sweeping through her body. "What smashes men to pulp?"

"I have no desire to find out. Whoever, or whatever, it isn't here at the moment. No telling when it will be back. We have to get going. From the directions you got, we should only be a half-mile or so from Ashmedai's estate. We'll hoof it. Give me one of those bags. Let's move."

Alex helped her over the fallen tree. The rain was getting pretty heavy now, and darkness had fallen. It was muddy, slow going. Valerie sniffled in disgust. Her hair was plastered down flat against her head and her clothes felt like wet rags on her body. Fortunately, she had been wearing flats. Heels would not have lasted a second in this mud. Her feet squished with each step. A small pebble had gotten into one shoe and rubbed against her heel. There was no time to stop and remove it.

They made slow but steady progress for the first few minutes. Alex set a comfortable pace and they stayed to the center of the road. It was muddy, but flat. Alex seemed to intuitively know how fast Valerie could move and held their speed to that level.

It was rough going, and soon it got rougher. The underbrush crept closer and closer to the road, the trees pressed in on both sides, and the dense fog clung like a blanket around them, muffling their vision beyond a few feet. Rain continued to drizzle in a ceaseless, depressing onslaught; the air was thick with moisture and each breath became an effort. Throughout it all the dark forest remained completely silent.

By unspoken command, they remained silent as well. From time to time, leaves swirled down at them from the rain-soaked trees. The odor of decaying vegetation served as a constant reminder of the death close by.

Alex stopped and looked around. He shook his head in annoyance. Coming up beside him, Valerie followed his line of sight with her eyes. She almost burst into tears. There were trees up ahead of them. The forest formed an impenetrable barrier on three sides. The only open path led back to the cars. Alex looked at her, his face shaded by doubt. "This can't be right. We followed the directions. Road never split. Yet, there's no way to go on. We're at a dead end."

Suddenly, Valerie realized what was wrong. "Alex, we have to go back."

"Why? What's wrong?"

"The Invitation—we need it with us. It's the key. You guessed it earlier; this road isn't real. This stretch of highway only exists through Ashmedai's sorcery. The Invitation opens the gate. Once we get beyond the influence of the Invitation in the car, the road ceases to exist. We have to have it with us to get to the end."

Nodding unhappily, Alex turned around. "Let's make it fast. I have a hunch our time is running out. Even my luck has its limits."

They sloshed through the mud and rain as fast as they could. Alex half-carried, half-dragged her along. A cold wind was blowing now, whipping through their clothes. Valerie never imagined she could feel so wet and cold. The constant fight to move her feet through the thick mud had her ankles aching. Each breath was an effort. Damp, cold air swirled down into her lungs, chilling her inside as well as out.

Up over the fallen tree. Past the Cadillac with its grisly cargo. Back to their car. The bright lights glared as strong as ever. It seemed like hours since they had left the auto. Valerie checked her watch. They had been walking for less than thirty minutes. The wind howled as they pulled open the car doors. Rain lashed them like shotgun pellets. The storm was growing worse.

Exhausted, Valerie dropped onto her seat. The Invitation was where she had left it on the dashboard. She shook her head, trying to get some of the wet out of her hair. There was a box of Kleenex tissues on the seat. She pulled out a bunch and wiped off her face.

Alex remained standing outside, his eyes constantly searching the woods for some sign of motion. Valerie took the Invitation and stuffed it inside her shirt. She sighed. It felt good to be out of the rain, even if it was only temporary. A few minutes more and she might feel almost human. "Be ready in a few seconds.

You want to use some Kleenex to dry off?"

With a shrug, Alex reached for the box. His hand half-way there, he froze. He swung around, the hand with the gun straight out in front of him. "Out of the car. Quick."

Valerie didn't need any urging. She could hear branches snapping as something big and bulky made its way through the dense forest. The killer was returning to the scene of the crime. The gun in Alex's hand suddenly seemed terribly inadequate.

The crashing in the woods came closer. Alex grabbed her by the hand. All thoughts of rest were gone. They had to run for their lives. In seconds, they were past the Cadillac and up over the tree trunk. No time to pause for breath; the roar of the wind drowned out the sound of their running. They wasted no time trying to hide their trail. There was only one way to go. There was no time for deception.

Now the road stretched on into darkness. Where there had been trees a short while ago, the mud and gravel continued along in an unbroken path. Valerie had no explanation for the change. It was magic. Panting, she struggled through the fog and rain. She kept her eyes glued to the road ahead. Somewhere there had to be a break. Ashmedai's mansion couldn't be much farther.

Alex trailed behind her, keeping a watch both on the road ahead and the trail behind.

His face was grim. The gun in his hand was steady, held in a grip of iron.

Metal screeched on metal. The noise rang through the forest like some ancient Chinese gong. There was a thud, then a loud clanging. Metal screamed again. "Found our car," said Alex. "Now it knows we're out here. It'll be coming after us."

Valerie didn't say a thing. She just kept on moving. Every step was an effort, but she couldn't give up now. Alex moved up beside her and hooked his free arm around her back, his hand reaching and holding her beneath her shoulder. She sagged against him as they struggled forward. The wind was blowing directly against them, sending the rain splashing into their faces. Between the heavy forest and the dense fog it was impossible to see more than a dozen feet in any direction. It was an unending nightmare. With a curse, she forced herself to stand up straight. They had to keep moving.

Thump. Thump. Thump. Each step was like the roll of a drum. The ground didn't shake, but it could have. Something heavy was pounding along the road. It was getting closer fast. Valerie knew it was a monster that could pound a man to a pulp. The thing was after them now. Relentless. Untiring. She knew they would never escape.

With a growl, Alex stopped moving. He

turned and planted his feet the best he could in the mud. With a steady hand, he raised his gun in the direction of the noises, bracing his wrist with his other hand. "Keep going," he said. "I'll catch up in a second."

Valerie reacted without thinking. She dropped the two bags onto the ground. In seconds, she ripped open Alex's suitcase. Out came the book and the jewelry box. "You can't stay behind, Alex. The forest will close in on you if I take the Invitation ahead. You'll never find your way."

"Go on without me, then. I'll delay this thing. I know I can. Better you get away than the both of us getting killed."

For a second, tears threatened to overwhelm her. Then, instead, anger came surging forward. With a wild cry, Valerie grabbed Alex by an arm. "No way," she screamed, wrenching him around, forcing him to face her. "You told me we shouldn't split up, ever. Those were your exact words. Damn you, Alex. I won't let you be a martyr. Both of us keep going, or neither of us. Come on. We're in this *together*. One way or another."

Thump, thump. The very air seemed to echo with the heavy footsteps. Wordlessly, Alex stared at Valerie for a second. She still held his arm with both hands. His eyes searched her face as if looking for an answer.

Thump. Thump. Their pursuer was only

yards away. She could almost make it out in the fog. Something not human, but humanoid, a monster walking erect. Manlike, over seven feet tall, dark as the night itself, its feet pounded the earth like two triphammers.

Alex shoved the gun in his waistband and dropped the flight bag to the ground. Growling deep in his chest, he pulled himself free of Valerie's grasp. Surging forward, he caught her around the waist. Up went his arms, throwing her over his shoulder. Then, he was off.

Momentarily stunned, Valerie was barely able to hang onto their two treasures. Alex held her over his shoulder like a slab of meat. He staggered and stumbled as he ran, but somehow he kept his balance. In seconds, he was huffing and puffing. Valerie could feel his heart pounding as he struggled to keep moving. It was a wild, ungainly effort, a mad, desperate sprint. Slowly they pulled away from the thing that followed.

The ground became firmer and he found better purchase on the roadway. The distance between them and the killer grew greater and greater. The forest thinned out. The darkness around them no longer seemed as deep. They had to be getting close to Ashmedai's home.

One final burst of speed and they broke out into a large clearing. As if fearful of the light, the creature fell back into the fog. The night swallowed it up. Valerie was sure she saw a flash of metallic green in the mist, and then it was gone. The giant footsteps faded as well.

Alex continued to stagger on for several more seconds. Only gradually did it sink in that they had escaped. Finally, he sensed that they were safe. With a gasp of sheer exhaustion, he dropped Valerie unceremoniously to the ground. "After this," he managed to wheeze out, sucking in deep mouthfuls of air, "no more desserts for you for a long time. Better start drinking diet pop, too. Definitely no pasta dinners."

Valerie scrambled to her feet. She took Alex by his shoulders and shook him unmercifully. "Agreed. As long as I don't hear any more crap about me going on without you. Understand, stupid? I've been alone too long to give you up that easy. *Comprende*?"

Alex nodded wearily. Valerie grabbed him close and hugged him very tight. "Very noble of you," she continued in a much more subdued tone. "But also very very dumb."

After a minute, she let him go and pointed at the building only a hundred feet distant. "Looks like we made it after all. That has to be Ashmedai's hovel."

Away from the forest, the fog lifted. The rain still came down, but it had turned into a steady drizzle. Ahead of them stood a mansion right out of a gothic romance novel. The huge wooden building stretched two stories high, with long arms of rooms extending east and west. Light spilled out into the night from rows of high windows. All in white, the mansion looked like it had been painted yesterday. A long, blacktopped driveway circled around the front of the building, passing through rows of short hedges trimmed in geometric shapes. Two columns flanked the huge front doors.

"Well," said Alex, "one thing is for certain. Ashmedai's not running this auction because he needs the money."

"You never can tell," replied Valerie with a faint smile. "Can you imagine the heating bill for a place like that? Building that size must need a nuclear power plant to keep it warm in the winter. Come on, I want to meet this mysterious character. And I want out of these wet clothes."

Together, they made their way to the front door. Alex was still wheezing. Valerie's feet felt numb. She knew she had to look like a witch, but it no longer mattered. All she could think about was a hot bath and something very potent to drink. Without a moment's hesitation, she lifted the ornate door knocker and let it fall.

Almost instantly, the door opened. A short, stocky man stood in the entrance way. The first thing Valerie noticed about him was his dark glasses, which completely hid his eyes. His face, otherwise, made a strong impression. Deep angular features appeared to be carved out of stone. A dark black beard covered most of his lower jaw. Equally dark eyebrows clustered thick over his glasses. His nose jutted forward like the beak of some bird of prey.

He looked at the two of them, his head held at a slight angle. Almost immediately he called out in a clear, pleasant voice to someone inside. "Claude. A bottle of brandy and some glasses. Quickly."

With a smile, the dark man stepped forward and linked his arms with each of them. Still smiling, he gently propelled them forward, the perfect host escorting guests into his home. As they walked into the bright hallway, he nodded pleasantly at each of them in turn.

"Please accept the hospitality of this house, my friends. You must be Valerie Lancaster. And your companion is, of course, Dr. Warner. I was starting to worry about you. I am your humble servant for this evening's entertainment. And your host. Men call me . . . Ashmedai."

CHAPTER ELEVEN

Alex let the icy water splash across his body. The cold shower invigorated. He felt almost back to full strength after that wild dash through the forest. He hoped a similar shower worked the same miracle for Valerie. He would check on her in a few minutes.

After giving them each a drink of brandy, Ashmedai had insisted they retire to their rooms and freshen up. He had waved aside their attempts to tell what had happened in the woods. He seemed neither surprised nor worried, and Alex had been in no mood to argue. Valerie had remained noticeably silent. Their two rarities were given to a silently waiting servant to be put in Ashmedai's safe. Their host discreetly did not ask them what was sealed inside the plastic wrappings.

They had adjoining rooms in the west wing of the mansion on the second floor. A discreetly closed but unlocked connecting door between the two suites made it clear that Ashmedai knew of the relationship between them.

Claude, the butler who had escorted them to the chambers, assured them that there would be suitable clothes provided to replace their ruined ones. With that promise, Valerie had immediately started to disrobe. "I am taking the hottest shower possible," she had declared, quickly ripping off her bluejeans as the servant made a hasty though discreet exit. "I'll be out when every bit of dirt and grime is off my body. And not until then."

Alex found little to argue with her on that. A shower sounded awfully good. The last few hours had been a tremendous strain. Fortunately, he was in terrific shape, the result of years of constant training. He was tired, but untapped reserves of energy remained dormant within him. Somehow, he knew he would need them all before the night was over. He left for his room as Valerie fiddled with the hot water in the shower.

Upon re-entering his room, he first checked the door to the hallway. To his pleasure, he discovered a heavy bolt lock almost hidden in the ornate carving. He clicked it shut. He didn't expect trouble, but eternal vigilance never hurt in strange surroundings. What easier way to dispose of a rival in the Auction than murder him in the bathroom? Alfred Hitchcock, Alex reasoned, wouldn't have thought it such an unusual idea.

Minutes later, he let himself relax under the cold caress of a needle-fine shower. The highly pressurized cold water almost stunned him with its intense spray. When he couldn't take the cold any longer, he switched the water onto hot. Steam rose as the water hit the chilled tiles. The contrast between the two temperatures made him gasp. He let the hot water cook him for a few minutes, then again switched back to cold. An old but reliable method of treatment, the constant switching of temperature shocked his system back to full efficiency. Unfortunately, he felt like a lobster dinner before his body responded.

Alex became so engrossed in his shower that he didn't notice the shadow on the shower-curtain until a woman spoke from only a few feet away. "Do you need your towel, now, sir?"

"Uh, sure. That would be fine."

A woman's hand reached around the curtain, holding a thick, plush bath towel. As he grabbed the terry-cloth sheet, Alex noted that the limb holding it was well muscled and tanned to a golden brown. Not the hand of a young woman, he decided, even though her fingernails glowed bright from a red gloss polish. The skin quality revealed age more than most people realized. He quickly dried himself and wrapped the bath towel around his waist. Cautiously, he pulled the curtain back.

His guess had been right on target. The woman who stood before him clad in a black-and-white maid's uniform was darkly tanned and very attractive, extremely well built. But she was no youngster. If anything, she was a little *too* good-looking just to be a maid. Her large breasts strained against the thin material of her tight white blouse. Her jet black hair fell in long waves down to her shoulders. Red nails matched equally red lips. She wore a short, black, skirt, revealing very nice legs sexily clad in black-seamed nylons. She wore high spiked heels—not very practical servants' attire. Her dark eyes watched him with frank interest as he stepped from the bath tub. She smiled wickedly. "Anything else you need, sir? Anything . . . at all?"

Alex clutched the towel even tighter around his waist. First Valerie and now this woman. He was not used to predatory females, nor was he quite sure that he trusted this one. Women in outfits like the one she was wearing usually starred in X-Rated movies. This whole scene was a little too contrived for his taste. Plus, there was a certain look in her eyes that he didn't like. Alarm bells were ringing inside his head. Ashmedai had nothing to gain from a scene like this. Alex wondered what was behind the sexual overtones.

"The butler, Claude, said something about clothes?"

"Yes sir," the maid replied, still smiling. "I've *laid* out your outfit on the bed. When I heard the water shut off, thought you might have difficulty with your towel. I know how *hard* it sometimes is."

Alex cleared his throat and quickly stepped past the maid into the large bedroom. A dark gray pinstripe suit rested on the bed. A folded blue silk shirt, matching tie, and even matching socks sat in a pile by the suit. At the foot of the bed was a pair of black shoes. "No underwear," said Alex.

"Oh, I forgot," answered the maid, following him into the room. "There must be some in one of the dressers."

She casually walked to the bed and sat down on the edge, crossing her legs. Her skirt rode high up on her thighs. "I never wear any myself." She breathed deeply, doing interesting things to her blouse. "I like my body to feel free and natural. Do you know what I mean?"

"Sure, free and . . . natural." Alex started searching through the bedroom furniture for some undergarments. He kept the large bath towel clutched around his waist. "You always this friendly with visitors here?"

"Friendly?" The woman laughed. Somehow she managed to make it sound vaguely obscene. "This isn't anything. I'd like to show you what friendly really means. Why don't you give me that towel. Then I'll be very, *very* friendly."

"Sure. I'll bet you would." In one of the drawers, Alex found several pairs of shorts and undershirts. Surprisingly, they were cotton; he had half-expected silk. "Would you mind leaving while I get dressed?"

The woman frowned. For an instant, her face seemed a good deal older than he had imagined. She was definitely not a youngster. "What's wrong? Not *up* to a little company?" Her voice had a nasty ring to it. "I thought you were a man. Perhaps I was wrong."

"Perhaps you were," said Alex.

He returned to the bathroom with the shorts. It only took a second to slip them on and return to the bedroom. The maid was already half-way to the door. She turned and sneered at him. "Since you obviously aren't capable of satisfying a woman, I'll leave now. If you need anything, don't bother to ring. It won't do you any good."

She sauntered toward the door, wiggling her hips in an exaggerated motion that caused her tight black skirt to rise up even higher on her thighs. It also made it quite clear she hadn't been lying about not wearing anything underneath her outfit.

Alex snorted in disgust. He found it hard to believe a real maid would wear clothes like those. Her outfit was right out of an S&M catalog, complete with the black skirt and spike heels. All she needed, Alex decided, was a leather whip.

Everything suddenly fell into place and the whole incident no longer seemed to crazy. That last thought had served as the catalyst. The door had been locked when he had entered the shower. No real maid would have entered an occupied room locked from the inside. The entire deception became terribly clear.

He couldn't find his gun, but his bowie knife sat on the dresser where he had left it. He whipped it out of its sheath as the maid lunged for the door. He whirled after her, the blade's naked steel glistening in the lights.

"Hannah!" cried the woman, as she grabbed the doorknob. "Now is the time. Quickly!"

The door burst open with a crash, sending the maid sprawling back. Alex was at her side before she could recover. His left hand encircled her neck, catching her chin in the crook of his elbow. The knife in his right hand flashed up. He let the cold metal of the blade rest on the side of her nose, directly in front of her right eye. Only then did Alex dare look at what stood in the doorway.

The werewolf seemed less menacing this time. Perhaps it was because he held the upper hand. The huge beast stood there, its mouth half open, its yellow teeth flashing, its hands gripping the side panels of the doorway. It remained frozen in place. Its gaze was fastened on the knife in Alex's hand and stayed there.

"One move and they'll be calling your boss One-Eyed Charlie," said Alex in a mildly bantering tone. His grip on the Countess did not lessen in the least, nor did the knife blade flicker a hair. "Edge away from that door. Now."

The beast did not move. It growled softly, the sound rising up from deep in its throat. Alex could see the muscles in its arms tightening. It was preparing to spring.

"Call your little girl off, Countess. I'm not bluffing."

To emphasis his point, Alex let the edge of the knife dig into the flesh of her nose. The woman stiffened. Alex shifted his weight, bringing his body around so that she was tight up against his left hip. "If wolf-girl attacks, you won't live to see her arrive. I'm no amateur."

"Hannah," said the Countess, her voice muffled by his arm around her neck. "Do nothing. Stay back."

The werewolf hesitated, but the muscles in its arms and shoulders did not relax. It rocked back and forth on the balls of its feet. Alex could almost feel the hatred the thing was radiating. He was not bluffing. There was no way he would battle two enemies. The Countess would die the instant the werewolf charged. Then, he would face the beast one-on-one.

He must have tensed his own muscles in preparation, sending a message in body language to his prisoner. Panic stricken, the Countess's voice cracked like a whip. "Hannah. *Obey me*. Go back to our quarters. *Now*."

The beast stiffened, and then seemed to shrink in on itself like some huge balloon suddenly deflating. Its gaping jaws closed shut. The glow disappeared from its eyes as its muscles went slack. With a last forlorn look of defiance, the werewolf turned and disappeared into the hallway.

"Very wise move," said Alex. He did not release his hold on the Countess. If anything, this woman was much more dangerous than her servant. Without looking, Alex flipped the bowie knife up in the air, back behind him. It hit the floor with a solid thunk where it remained quivering straight up in a sea of white carpet.

As soon as his hand was free, Alex pulled up hard with the arm that encircled the Countess's neck. The woman was forced up onto her toes by the powerful jerk of his elbow. She gagged reflexively and her arms flailed about wildly—exactly what Alex had expected and wanted. His right hand fastened on her wrist. With an expert twist, he bent her right arm up and around while at the same time releasing the hold on her neck. He had freed the Countess from the elbow lock to place her in a hammer lock instead.

Savagely, he shoved the Countess's wrist high up her back. She yelped from the sharp pain, but Alex didn't care. He had no mercy for this woman. Valerie had stated the case against her too well: she had killed Jake and would have killed them as well, if able. This whole episode was yet another attempt at murder. The sorceress whimpered in shock as he shoved her forward to the door.

"You'll pay for this." Her voice was ragged and full of pain. "No one humiliates me so."

Alex laughed harshly. "Really? Then you shouldn't be wearing this kind of outfit. Gives the impression you enjoy being pushed around."

He shoved hard, releasing his grip. The Countess stumbled out the doorway and crashed to the carpeted floor of the hall. In an instant, she had spun around onto her hands and knees. She glared at him fiercely. The skin of her face was taut, her teeth clenched together in a near skeletal snarl of pure hatred.

"Hannah will flay you alive for this insult. And then tear you to pieces one joint at a time."

She was gone, half-running, half-crawling down the hallway, before Alex could react to her threats. Shaking his head in disgust, he closed the door. For the first time since he had been surprised in the bathroom, he thought of Valerie. Had they attacked her first? Alex rushed to the connecting door. He was in the other suite in an instant. He could hear water cascading in the shower. "Valerie. You okay in there?"

"Sure," she called back. "Time to get dressed?"

"Getting there. Finish up."

Breathing a sigh of relief, he returned to his own room. The Countess had gone after him first for some reason. He shuddered thinking what would have happened if he had yielded to the woman's lust. Valerie had hinted that the Countess had pretty bizarre tastes. Alex had no doubts about his intended fate. Being slashed to death by a werewolf at the peak of sexual union with her mistress was a particularly gruesome way to die. The Countess was like a human black-widow spider. She was enough to make a man swear to celibacy.

He carefully put on his clothes, checking each garment before dressing. It was doubtful that the Countess would resort to poisoned needles—tricks like that were commonplace in Viet Nam—but he was not in a trusting mood. This undeclared war was little different from the combat he remembered.

As he pulled on his trousers, Alex reflected for a moment on his actions the last few minutes. There had been no hesitation. He had fought with the same cold intensity as the days back in Viet Nam. Pretty much as he had always suspected, the killer within him had not disappeared, even after all these years. That part of his personality had only been resting, lying beneath the surface of his mind waiting for the right event to trigger it back into action. It seemed only fitting that the Countess, who controlled one terrible beast of the night, should let loose another. Alex felt no remorse. Sometime the only answer to savagery was retaliation in kind.

He walked over and retrieved his bowie knife. He found his gun in the bottom of one of the drawers of the dresser. It didn't surprise him to find all the bullets gone.

The Countess had been quite emphatic in her threats, but words meant little. The most dangerous killers never wasted time on threats. They just acted. In Nam, his buddies had called him 'The Silent One.' He did what he had to do, with no wild talk or crude bragging. Now he was at it again. "Shakespeare had it right," Alex whispered, his thoughts far away in times past. "Cry havoc, and let slip the Dogs of War."

"What did you say?" asked Valerie, standing in the doorway between the two rooms, an odd look on her face. Her hair was still pretty wet and all she wore was a large bath towel wrapped around her body.

"Nothing. Nothing important," replied Alex, sheathing the knife. There was no way to hide it from her so he treated it as if it was not important. He casually fastened it beneath his armpit as he continued to talk.

"Had a visitor. Couple of them, for that matter. Surprised that they came to see me first, but it was just as well. I convinced them that we didn't have much to talk about."

Valerie turned pale. "The Countess. And Hannah Stine. What did they want?"

Alex summarized the events of the past half-hour as he dressed. He didn't hide anything; it was better that Valerie knew the full story. One forgotten fact could be deadly in a dangerous game like this.

"So, after the Countess was gone, I checked your room. Guess they thought I'd be the easier one to eliminate . . ."

"No," said Valerie, twisting an edge of the towel around one finger. "You were the one they wanted." Her voice was soft and somewhat hesitant. Alex could sense the nervousness in her. "It's time you know the truth. The whole truth."

"Sounds ominous," said Alex, trying to remain calm. "Want to explain what you mean? Why me? You're the sorceress. I'm just the flunky boyfriend."

Valerie giggled, sending shock-waves rippling through her towel. Carefully, she sat down on his bed, pulling her legs up beneath her. Alex dropped down close beside her. "She wants the prize of the Auction. Desperately. And she knows that unless you're out of the picture, she doesn't stand a chance of winning. Somehow, some way, your luck will win it for us."

"My luck? Are you nuts?"

The towel was half off Valerie's body, but she was so intense that she didn't seem to notice. "No. Just full of regrets. I know telling you this isn't going to do much for our relationship, but you've got to know. I can't go on deceiving you.

"You have the Power, Alex. A great deal of it. The only difference between you and me is that I consciously control it. Yours is a function of your subconscious mind. Through my mastery of the Power, I perform feats of magic. Through your subconscious control of that same force, you experience unbelievable luck."

Alex shook his head in disbelief. "I'm lucky. I'll agree to that. But not *that* lucky—take Sheila for example."

"Not that simple, my love. You have to be in a situation where chance comes into play. You weren't looking for a woman. If you were, I doubt you would have come up with Sheila. She was after you. Think about it. Luck, bad or good, never had a thing to do with it."

Alex stayed silent for a few minutes, digesting what Valerie had said. He needed time to grasp all of the implications of this revelation. Her earlier statement about deceiving him finally registered. Valerie sat nude on the bed next to him, but thoughts of sex never entered his mind. She had her eyes fixed on him. Small tears started to roll down her cheeks.

"So, I'm like a giant rabbit's foot or horseshoe that really works," he said with a smile. "Making me a rather desirable company for a sorcerer . . . or sorceress."

Valerie nodded, not saying anything, her teeth dragging across her lower lip.

"I can understand that. From what I learned from you and Jake both, magic is a pretty iffy operation at best, without much room for error. One false step and that demon you raised has you for a snack. Having your own powerful lucky charm would be a major asset."

Valerie nodded again. The tears fell in a constant stream now, making her eyes look red and puffy. Gently, Alex reached out and brushed the teardrops away with a finger.

"So you schemed and plotted to make me yours. And now that I know, you think I'm going to walk out of here in a huff and never speak to you again."

With a sniff, Valerie regained her voice. "Aren't you?"

Alex let his fingers curl through the wet hair bunching across the nape of her neck. "Why should I?" he asked, a reflective tone in his voice. "All I've discovered is that the paranoid suspicions I've lived with for years are actually true. In a way, I'm pretty relieved."

"You're kidding."

"No reason for me to lie. I always wondered why Jake popped up in my class out of the blue and what attracted Sheila to me." He half closed his eyes for a second. "Don't tell me. I can guess already: Mak too. He has all the makings of a magician. That's the nice thing about paranoia. You're suspicious of everyone. I had my doubts about him for a long time, the way he and Jake got along so well right from the first, that little scene in his restaurant the other night. Him too?"

Valerie just nodded her head in agreement. Alex laughed at her confused look. "You don't understand. It doesn't matter, it really doesn't."

"You're just saying that."

Alex stood up and stretched. "Not at all. Hopefully, it's the difference between being suspicious of people and being crazy. Years in Viet Nam made me cautious. It was a desperate time and I learned not to trust anyone. Lots of men came back with an edge, and I was one of them. I kept my emotions in pretty tight control. But there is a big jump from being extremely careful and thinking the world is out to get you. Sure, I resent learning that I've been manipulated and deceived for years and years. But to what end? The army did the same to most of us. The government sure as hell does. I resent that, but I still pay my taxes. Jake never took advantage of me; he was a good friend. Mak saved my life again and again in Viet Nam. So what if my luck helped him sometime? That's not enough of a reason for me to hate him—or to think any less of Jake."

"What about me?" asked Valerie in a very soft voice.

"Ah, a fate worse than death. Tricked into marrying a beautiful fashion model, with lots of brains, incredibly sexy, and loaded with money. Horrible. So manipulative that she can't hide the truth from me after knowing me less than a week. Somehow, some way, I think I can survive the disappointment."

Valerie looked him straight in the eye. "How can you ever trust me knowing that I deceived you."

"Simple. You could have abandoned me when the werewolf attacked us at your place . . . not to mention during our encounter with the thing in the forest. I seem to remember something about both of us or none of us. I might not be the greatest judge of character in the world, but I'll settle for that."

Valerie stood up. Alex suddenly felt very sweaty. Nude, she was the most desirable woman he had ever seen. "Uh, we have a dinner downstairs to attend. In a few minutes."

Valerie wrapped her arms around his neck. "A few minutes," she agreed. "Amazing the things you can get done in a few minutes." She drew his mouth down onto hers.

CHAPTER TWELVE

Alex and Valerie missed the cocktail hour entirely. The other guests were sitting waiting for them when they hurriedly made their way into the dining room. It was an elaborately decorated place, filled with gold and silver—elegance that matched the rest of the mansion. Outside, the night winds howled and the renewed rain beat heavily on huge full-length windows. The two of them brought to thirteen the number of people at the table. To Alex, the number seemed a sinister coincidence.

As they walked across the room, Alex couldn't help but notice the other guests watching them intently. Sizing up the competition, he decided. Valerie got most of the attention. She looked stunning. Her black-and-white dress, black heels and crystal earrings were magnificent, the height of fashion. The clothes provided by their host seemed tailored specifically for her and her alone. Another casual demonstration of Ashmedai's power.

Their mysterious host sat at the head of the long table. He wore the same gray pin-striped business suit as when he met them at the door. Only the dark-lensed glasses he wore distinguished him from an insurance agent. He smiled in welcome as they came forward, their shoes beating a staccato rhythm on the polished hardwood floor. He waved them to the last two place-settings on the right-hand side of the dining table.

Alex had only a few seconds to take in the other guests, but he didn't need any more time. In the war, he had learned to absorb vast amounts of information with one quick glance. Six people sat to each side of Ashmedai, facing each other across a long, wide table. To their host's right, an elderly gray-haired woman peered at the two of them with undisguised hostility. Next to her was a much younger looking woman, wearing, from what Alex could see of it, a very tight leather pants suit.

Next to the girl in leather, two thin men with pinched features and sallow skin whispered in low voices. The resemblance between the two of them had to be more than coincidence. Brothers, perhaps even twins. They had the look of typical business executives. After them came Alex and Valerie's chairs, the last two in the row.

On Ashmedai's left a little wizened old man faced the gray-haired woman. His eyes appeared half closed, as though near sleep. He was dwarfed by the huge ugly woman next to him. Third in that row, the Countess looked quite elegant wearing a designer dress and long string of pearls. Next to her sat a slender, very dark black man. Alex immediately spotted him for a professional soldier. A near-identical-looking companion matched him in the last seat. Between the two of them sat a very fat, nearly bald black man wearing a rumpled white suit. He reminded Alex of a black Sidney Greenstreet.

Valerie sat down across from the fat man. Alex dropped into the chair at the end of the table, facing one of the man's two bodyguards. As he took his seat, he again considered the number of guests at the table. Was this to be their Last Supper? The dark surface of Ashmedai's glasses seemed to hide a multitude of secrets.

As soon as they sat, an unobtrusive servant began filling the water glasses. At the same time, Ashmedai started to speak.

"I am pleased to welcome you all here. Our gathering is complete. One other was to be here tonight, but I regret to report that he will not be able to make it. We will proceed without him, since I know you are anxious to get on with the business of the evening. But first, we shall have our dinner."

All eyes were fixed on Ashmedai. All except Alex's. He watched the guests, looking for some flicker of emotion. No one seemed very disturbed by the news. Alex felt no surprise. These people learned early how to hide their feelings. Deceit and subterfuge filled their lives. Even Ashmedai might have arranged the thing in the forest for some reason of his own. Nothing visible indicated that there had been another setting at the table for the murdered guest.

"One less bidder," rumbled the big, fat black man, directly across from Valerie. "His misfortune. Our gain." The two slender blacks on each side of the fat man nodded.

"Survival of the fittest," said the Countess. Looking at her, Alex found it hard to believe the woman's age. She wore a demure blue dress that could not hide her lush figure. Gold earrings, encrusted with pearls, matched her long-pearl necklace. Her eyeliner perfectly complimented her dress. She wore no lipstick. Alex had to admit that she was a remarkably good-looking woman. Even the fact that she had tried to kill him less than an hour before didn't negate that fact.

"Put your eyes back in your head," whispered Valerie, leaning close to him. "She gobbles up little boys like you for breakfast."

"I can believe it," said Alex. "Literally."

The arrival of the first course interrupted their conversation. "My chef is one of the finest in the Midwest, if not the country," said Ashmedai. "I hope you will enjoy the meal. We will have wine with the main course. Please, no business until we have finished dessert. After the dishes have been cleared away, we will talk."

"*Gratin de Langoustines à la Mangue et au Poivre Vert*," announced Claude, standing behind Ashmedai's chair. A pair of young women entered the room, each bearing a tray loaded with plates of the delicacy. "This is a combination of scampi and slices of mango glazed in a vermouth sauce sharpened with green peppercorns. An excellent beginning for any meal."

The food *was* excellent. Between bites, Alex and Valerie carried on a whispered conversation. Each of the guests seemed sunk in his or her own thoughts. Those who had come with companions talked to them. Those on their own remained silent.

"The big ugly woman, next to the Countess, is Hannah, our friendly werewolf?"

"Right. I haven't seen her in years, but she hasn't changed a bit. Face that could stop a clock."

As if sensing they were talking about her, the thick-boned woman turned her head and stared at them. Her eyes locked with Alex's. Then her eyebrows sank down as her mouth opened in a half-snarl. There was a great deal of the beast in her even when human. Alex grinned at her and winked. Hannah growled angrily.

The Countess looked up from her food and whispered a few words to her servant. Hannah nodded and concentrated on her plate. The Countess glanced across the table at Alex. She nodded pleasantly. "Remember my promise," she said as if discussing the weather. "Hannah is eagerly awaiting your company."

Before Alex could reply, Valerie spoke. "You should watch what you say, Countess dear. After all, you haven't had the best of luck lately. Plans going awry here and there. And of course, there was that little matter of your . . . pets."

The Countess turned white. "You dare," she managed to choke out, holding her napkin to her mouth, "You dare . . ."

"Oh, does the thought bother you?" asked Valerie, her voice dripping sugar. "I don't *see* why it should."

By now, all other conversations had stopped.

Everyone at the table was listening and watching the two women closely. Valerie seemed to relish the attention. "Perhaps I should say, *the eyes have it.*"

Alex had no idea what Valerie was talking about, but whatever it was, the words were getting the Countess very upset. Catching some drift of the conversation, he began to softly whistle *I Only Have Eyes for You.*

Turning a remarkable shade of green, the Countess rose from the table and quickly exited the room. Hannah followed at a rush, sparing the time for only a quick look of pure hate directed at the two of them.

"Ha. Ha. Ha." That was the fat black man directly across from Valerie. Each laugh was a distinct word, almost a bellow. The man's whole body shook like Jello as he spoke. "Very telling remarks, young lady. Marie never could take a joke. Especially if it was on her."

"She did seem a bit upset," said Valerie with a laugh.

"If looks could kill . . ." Alex began.

". . . the two of you would be very dead." This came from the thin, sallow faced man sitting right next to Valerie. "Fortunately for you, it is a spell far beyond the Countess's meager talents."

"Keep an eye on that ugly bitch," said the elderly gray-haired woman with bright blue eyes further down their side, who sat directly next to Ashmedai. "She'll kick the shit out of you if you don't guard your ass."

"I've had dealings with her twice," said Alex. He never knew little old ladies talked that way. "I've managed to hold my own both times."

"Better watch it, then," said the fat black man. "Third time is the charm. Hannah is not one to be taken lightly."

"She wouldn't have lasted five minutes in Nam," replied Alex. Out of the corner of one eye he caught one of the fat man's bodyguards nodding slightly in agreement. One professional paying his respects to another.

"Caesar salad," declared Claude, as two other servants wheeled in a large salad cart. The butler took in the two empty seats without a pause. "Will the absent ladies be returning shortly?"

"Undoubtedly," answered the fat man before anyone else could say anything. "Ha. Ha. Ha." His laughter sounded like bombs exploding. "The Countess would not miss this evening's entertainment for anything. Her wrinkles would not stand for it. She will be back."

"Then we will commence serving the salad." Claude looked at Ashmedai. Their host dropped his head in a barely noticeable nod. Without further remarks, the butler and his two helpers began tossing and then serving the salad.

The departure of the Countess had broken

the ice. Loud conversation flourished across
the table as they ate. Most of the guests knew
each other, if not by sight, by reputation. Alex
remained quiet, letting Valerie do most of the
talking. With her flashy good looks and her ever
present *glamour* she was the center of attention. Only Ashmedai remained silent. He
seemed quite relaxed and attentively listened to
all of the conversation swirling about him.

The Countess and Hannah arrived at the
same time as the entree. They took their seats
quietly, making no fuss. The other guests ignored them. Evidently, the Countess had few
friends in the black-magic field.

The main course was *Cassoulet de Camargue*.
It consisted of lamb, duck, smoked bacon and
haricot beans baked with herbs in a casserole.
Alex had never heard of the dish before and
was slightly apprehensive about trying it. One
bite convinced him of the error of his ways. All
about him, the other guests expressed the same
opinion about the delicacy. Ashmedai acknowledged the praise with a smile. He waved
one hand and Claude came forward with the
wine.

After the bottle had been decanted and
served, Ashmedai rose to his feet. Immediately,
all talking and eating stopped. Alex grinned.
There was no mistaking the true center of
attention at this gathering. When Ashmedai
moved, all other motion ceased.

"A toast," said their host in solemn tone. "To all of you here tonight. The greatest of the great. May that which you seek be all that you expect . . . and more."

"Bravo, bravo." This came from the fat black man whose name Alex had learned was Benedict Crosby. "Well put, sir." Then, without a second's pause, Crosby's voice grew cold. "But when shall we discover what it is we seek?"

"Aye," added Mary Zongran, the gray-haired woman right beside Ashmedai. "Toasts are fine, Ashmedai, but it's time for some straight talking. Betty, here," and the elderly woman waved a hand at her much younger female companion, "had to kill four people to get this damned Invitation. You gonna tell us what we're here for or not?" She chuckled. It was not a pleasant sound. "I bet Betty could make ya talk quick enough."

Alex was beyond surprise. No one at the table seemed particularly disturbed by Mary Zongran's revelations of murder. He could see why no one had been upset about the missing guest. Life was cheap here. The sharks were showing their teeth.

Valerie glanced at Alex and shrugged. He gently let his left upper arm nudge against his bowie knife. The feel of the steel blade was moderately reassuring.

With a quiet laugh, Ashmedai dropped back into his seat. He rested both hands on the edge of the table and rotated his head from side to side. Alex could sense the eyes behind the dark lenses staring at each of them in turn. "Come, come, my friends, we have not yet had dessert. My chef has prepared something very special. I refuse to conduct any business without my sweets."

"Ya refuse?" said Mary Zongran nastily, half-rising from her chair. "Betty . . ."

"*Sit down, Mary,*" commanded Ashmedai. The sound of his voice sent chills rippling down Alex's spine. Death might have such a voice. There was no arguing with an order delivered with such force.

It was obeyed. Mary sank back into her seat.

"Your grandmother, Hester Ann Curtis, was an impatient one, too," said Ashmedai, his tone perfectly relaxed and normal. "She fidgeted the whole evening till the Auction finally started." Ashmedai smiled. "Didn't make a bit of difference. She dropped out of the bidding quite early."

"You—you knew my grandmother?" Mary's voice was high pitched and hesitant. "She died when I was just a youngster. Must be seventy years gone."

"Did I say I knew her? Not at all. Don't jump to conclusions. There are records here of each and every auction. Very complete records, I might add, containing some very interesting facts."

"Notice how he didn't answer her question," whispered Valerie in Alex's ear.

"Records?" This was from Randolph Craig, the man who was sitting next to Valerie. He and his twin brother, Justice, had remained quiet through most of dinner. They were both clean-shaven thin men, wearing thick glasses, with perfect white teeth. They wore plain black suits and reminded Alex of undertakers. They had that lean and hungry look that Julius Caesar had feared with good cause. Randolph's voice was surprisingly full and deep. "How far back do these records go?"

"Yes, how far back?" That came from Justice Craig. His voice was nearly as deep as his brother's and equally powerful. "I've heard it said that these auctions have taken place for a thousand years."

"Longer than that," said Benedict Crosby, resting his huge arms on the table and leaning forward. His sharp eyes narrowed. "Much further in the past. In *The Devil's Apocrypha*, there is a passage that describes an Auction for the 'gift of eternity' taking place in A.D. 476. There are even hints that Constantine's conversion to Christianity might have been a direct result of that midnight gathering. An Auction, by the way, conducted by the Wandering Jew."

"Bah," said Ashmedai with a snort of disgust. "I thought you above such stories, Crosby. *The Devil's Apocrypha* is a foolish collection of old wives' tales and hoary legends. Needless to say, its unknown author proclaims it to be a true occult history of the first thousand years after the Crucifixion. As if that greater lie will substantiate all of the lesser ones. History is little more than a collection of convincing falsehoods. To the victor belongs the honor of rewriting the past. Legends become truth after a time. And just as often, truth becomes fable." Ashmedai's tone was mocking now. "A perfect example of the Church inventing history is the so-called Wandering Jew. The whole story is little more than a bizarre hoax conceived by the early Popes. Think of it. A man is cursed by Christ to live forever merely for verbally tormenting him. Nonsense. How can any Christian believe in the divinity of a God who would stoop to such pettiness? Come, come. An eternal soldier, fighting his way down through the Ages? Or a mysterious figure leaving his shoes with the Pope after performing fabulous acts of magic? You can't be serious."

"Yet Agrippa met him," said Alex. Ashmedai was playing word games. He couldn't let the opportunity slip by without baiting their host a little. "He was no friend of Rome. Are you saying that there was a world-wide conspiracy to create this mythical character?"

"Agrippa." Ashmedai's tone was reflective, as if remembering things long past. Alex suspected Ashmedai had a love of the dramatic.

He was toying with them, hinting at things but then denying them. "Cornelius Agrippa was a remarkable man." Ashmedai grinned. "Or so I have read. He definitely encountered a mysterious stranger in his lab many hundreds of years ago. But that person was not the Wandering Jew. At least, he was not the character enshrined in fable."

Before Alex could pursue that final, tantalizing remark, Claude stepped forward. "Dessert is served," the butler announced. Claude had been standing quietly by Ashmedai's chair for the past few moments, waiting for a break in the conversation. "This is a very special delight. *Millefeuille à la Creme Legere et aux Framboises*, prepared fresh. These are individual thousand-layer pastries filled with light cream, served on a raspberry sauce and showered with confectioner's sugar. Seconds," and for the first time all evening, the butler's solid expression cracked a little bit and he smiled for an instant, "are available upon request."

The table was clear; even the tablecloth had been removed. The lights had been turned down low. Outside, the storm had grown in intensity. A steady clatter of rain knocked against the high windows. From time to time, a stray flash of lightning illuminated the room. All were silent, their eyes focused on the one standing figure, Ashmedai.

He stood half-enveloped in darkness. He held an ebony cube some six inches on a side with both hands. Waist high he kept it, his large fingers spread out across its sides. Alex could barely make out recessed hinges near the top of the container. The lid on the box was held closed by a small but elaborately carved lock. Except for the latch, there was no break in the blackness. Ashmedai had brought it from another room only minutes before. No one seemed to breathe as Ashmedai began to speak. His voice was not loud, but the sound of it filled the room.

"Once each generation this Auction is held. For how long concerns us not. Suffice it to say that it has taken place before and shall take place again."

Ashmedai slowly raised the box in his hands until it was almost level with his face. "Inside this receptacle is the most powerful talisman that exists in the world today. Once, there were others of equal power: a spear, a crown, and a robe. They have disappeared over the ages, though, and now only this is left. How it came into my possession again does not concern us here tonight. My claim to it is the most telling one. *I have it*. In magic, might makes right. That is the only law."

Ashmedai turned to face each of them. Alex tried to pierce the darkness of the man's glasses, but met with little success. No one stirred. The silence was like a thick blanket spread across the room. Even the thunder outside seemed to have stopped.

Ashmedai continued. "I make no promises. The winner of the Auction will have the talisman. Others in the past have been overwhelmed by the power contained within this box. A few have been granted the one gift they desired above all else. I offer no information or aid. Let the buyer beware."

"Enough of this damned chatter," said Mary Zongran. "Open the damned box and let us see what's inside."

Surprisingly, Ashmedai smiled. It was a cruel, harsh smile. "Time bears down on you swiftly, Mary. You fear death, and with good reason. Your punishment will be great." He turned slightly. "And yours as well, Countess. The prize will not clean the blood from your fingers."

"Finish," said the little wizened man on Ashmedai's right. It was the first time he had spoken all evening. His voice sounded like the croaking of some huge bullfrog. "Finish already with your tale."

"You have no sense of the dramatic, Abraham," said Ashmedai, setting the box carefully down on the wood table. "I have so few guests. Let me enjoy my moment of glory."

With a flourish, Ashmedai waved his right hand above the box. With an audible click, the lock opened. Slowly, as if ghostly hands were raising it, the top of the box swung back.

Everyone inched forward in their chair. Only the old man Ashmedai had called Abraham didn't try to see what was inside the container. He folded his short little arms across his chest and closed his eyes. Only the look of intense concentration on his face proclaimed that he was still awake.

"The rules of the Auction are simple. In a few minutes, we shall break to give you time to think. In a half-hour, we will all meet again in this room. The bidding will commence at that time. There will be one round of bids. Then, after hearing what all others have bid, each of you will have a second chance to raise your offer. The best proposal after that second round will be the winner. The actual exchange will take place when the high bidder leaves in the morning."

"The *winner* leaves," said Crosby, his voice subdued, almost a whisper. "What about the others?"

Ashmedai sighed. "You all are free to leave any time you wish. Departing is never a problem. The spell is constructed so that the road out is always open. My aim was not to keep people here, only to keep them away. I value my solitude."

"There are stories," said Alex, "that no one ever returns from the Devil's Auction."

"I have to admit," replied the host, "that I am guilty of spreading such rumors. It comes from my desire to be alone. I am a very private person, and I have no desire to have hordes of curious treasure-hunters looking for my home. This box contains my greatest prize, but there are many temptations within these walls. A determined searcher could find this place if he worked hard enough. It has taken me years to discover such a quiet location. I do not want to move." The bantering tone of Ashmedai's voice was gone now. A veiled threat hung on every word. "While I expect no promises, your cooperation in not revealing any details of this Auction would be appreciated."

"Finish." It was Abraham again. "It grows late."

Ashmedai reached into the box with his right hand. Seconds later, he stretched out his arm, his hand clenched in a fist. Slowly, dramatically, Ashmedai's fingers uncurled. In the palm of his hand rested a solitary silver coin. Approximately an inch in diameter, it blazed with some inner light.

Benedict Crosby sighed heavily. Mary Zongran muttered softly to herself. The Countess licked her lips, her eyes never moving from the coin. Valerie sat frozen in her chair. She, too, seemed hypnotized by it.

"A silver Tyrian shekel," said Ashmedai. Thunder rolled as he spoke, echoing each word. "It is one of thirty identical silver coins. There are few in the box now, the others having been sold at earlier auctions. These pieces of silver date back twenty centuries. They amounted to four months' wages during the time of Pontius Pilate—a decent sum, but not a fortune. Not nearly enough to pay for the betrayal of a dream."

Ashmedai moved his hand back and forth, the coin shimmering in the dim light. "Blood money. Cursed for all time." Ashmedai closed his fingers around the coin again, clenching it tightly in his fist. His voice challenged all of them. "The power of Hell is locked in that coin. It is a tangible link with the most infamous crime in all history. Can there be a more fitting prize for the Devil's Auction?"

"Well," said Alex as he closed and locked the door of his room, "did you believe him?"

"Its the truth, Alex." Valerie's cheeks were flushed and her eyes burned with an inner fire. She rubbed her thumbs against her fingers as she talked. Back and forth in the room she paced, her whole body twitching with excitement. "You couldn't sense the power in that coin. I can still feel it. I felt like a flower suddenly exposed to intense sunshine. My whole body virtually exploded with energy."

"It has you a little jumpy."

Valerie laughed. "I feel supercharged.

Damn, the magical energy stored in that coin is frightening. Who knows what powers it might give the owner!"

"Eternal life, perhaps?"

"Hell yes." Valerie could not keep still. She bounced around the room as she spoke. "That thing *pulsated* with dark forces. No wonder Ashmedai is the most powerful wizard in the world. All thirty of those coins would give you the power of a god."

"Or a devil." Alex was edgy. "I still don't like this. There are too many unanswered questions. I'm the only one who seems to care. All the rest of you are running around like kids with a new toy."

"That's because you can't feel the Power," said Valerie, slowing down for a second. "It's addictive. As soon as I saw the coin I knew I had to have it. I *had* to."

"Sure. I'm not blaming you. Everyone else at the table felt the same way—I could see it in their faces. There were only two of us unaffected by the coin's magic."

"Two. You and . . . ?"

"Ashmedai. He didn't react a bit. Our host kept a close watch on the rest of you instead. For all it mattered, he could have been holding a lump of coal in his hand."

Valerie sat down. "I don't get it. He's a magician. I could feel his aura when we first entered. Why wouldn't the coins affect him. Unless . . ."

"He's grown used to their power over a very long time," finished Alex.

"But that's crazy," said Valerie. "Do you realize how long it would take for that to happen?"

"Two thousand years, maybe." Alex changed subjects. "What did you think of those dark glasses?"

"Spooky. He didn't seem to have any problem seeing through them. I don't believe he has vision problems."

Alex slipped his coat off and began sharpening his knife. The blade didn't need it, but the slow but steady motion relaxed him. "They say that a man's eyes are a reflection of his soul. I'm not sure if I want to know what lies hidden behind those lenses."

Valerie shuddered. "I once read a story about Lazarus. Christ brought him back from the dead, but four days had already passed. He remembered *the other side*. His body lived, but his eyes reflected death. Anyone who looked into them went mad." She shuddered again. "Finally the Emperor had him blinded and sent into the desert. He was never seen again."

"Lazarus," said Alex, thoughtfully. "Dead, then brought back to life. Would a man like that age and die again? Or would he live forever, unable to find peace?"

"No more questions we can't answer," replied Valerie. "Time to go downstairs. The

Auction should be starting any time now. I don't want to be the last one there."

Alex sheathed his knife. He had a feeling that he would need it before the night was over. All of the bidders in the Auction were intent on winning. None of them looked like they would be gracious losers.

CHAPTER THIRTEEN

The table was gone from the dining room. A half-circle of twelve chairs had been arranged around a small podium. The lights were still muted, but the drapes had been pulled back from the huge windows to reveal the storm still raging outside. Every few minutes violent splashes of lightning dazed the senses. Crashes of thunder rattled and shook the glass. The rain was a constant drumbeat assaulting the ears. It was as if the very heavens objected to the Auction.

When Alex and Valerie entered, the only other person in the room was Ashmedai. He stood behind the podium, resting both arms on it. The ebony box was slightly to the left of his hands. "Always," he remarked as if reading Alex's thoughts, "it always rains when these Auctions are held. This storm is typical. Please, sit wherever you like. We will begin as soon as the others arrive."

Alex steered Valerie over to the last two seats in the chain, farthest away from the windows. Every time he walked by the glass, he felt nervous. His luck had never been wrong before. Now, with Valerie's confession, he depended upon it. Thunder rolled once more and, for an instant, the solitary light in the room flickered. Alex began exercising his fingers.

The first to enter after them was Mary Zongran and her companion, Betty. Mary hobbled in using two canes. She shuffled slowly across the floor with Betty following close behind. Mary wore a plain brown dress with ruffled collar closed right to the top of her neck. She even wore brown high buttoned shoes. She looked like a typical midwestern grandmother. If Jack the Ripper had had a grandmother.

Betty wore black leather, and it suited her. She was a lot younger than the Countess and in much better shape. Her blouse, for want of a better name, was form-fitting and cut down the center from neck to waist, revealing plenty of cleavage. Her black leather pants were skin-tight and molded to her body from her waist to her narrow buttocks to her slender ankles. She had short, curly black hair; pleasant features; and a cute, inviting smile.

"Leather and all that," whispered Valerie to him, "it's still hard to believe she killed four people for the Invitation."

"Look at her hands," said Alex. "A pretty face doesn't tell you anything. Billy the Kid had a real baby face. See how rough her hands are? Notice the thickness of her fingers. The bones have broken and healed innumerable times, hardening in the process. It's common with advanced students of karate. Sweet little Betty can probably smash a brick into powder. Or, for that matter, a man's face."

The Countess and Hannah, the wizened little man Ashmedai had called Abraham, and the Craig brothers all came in at the same time. Abraham sat next to Betty. He sank back into the chair and closed his eyes without saying a word to anyone. Hannah snarled at Valerie and Alex then took the seat next to Abraham. The Countess remained standing, looking out at the storm. Her body was taut, her fingers clenched in fists. Each bolt of lightning made her flinch. Alex wondered what she had planned for tonight. He was sure the Countess was not going to give up the coin without a fight. After a few seconds more, she took her seat next to Hannah.

The Craig brothers sat next to Alex. They had been whispering in low tones when they entered the room, and they continued their conversation when seated.

"Who's the little guy with the eyes like a snake?" asked Alex, leaning over close to Valerie so no one else could hear him. "You know. The one called Abraham."

"That's Abraham the Provider," said Valerie in the same low voice. "I never met him, but he's pretty famous in magical circles. Nasty little man if even half the stories circulating about him are true." She smiled. "He's the world's greatest living authority on your favorite text, *The Kaballah*."

The arrival of Benedict Crosby and his two bodyguards completed their group. The big fat man nodded pleasantly to everyone and then took his seat. His companions ignored the chairs left for them and instead took up positions to either side of Crosby and slightly behind him. Ashmedai looked at them for a second and then shrugged. "No need for such actions, Crosby."

The black man laughed humorlessly. "I pay these fine young men to protect me. They insist on doing it their own way. No reflection on you or your hospitality, Ashmedai. They are just doing their job."

"Please instruct them to sit down. They are a distraction."

Crosby pursed his lips together. "I think not. They shall remain standing."

"Are we gonna get the show on the road or yap all night?" This was from Mary Zongran. Then she grinned, displaying a mouthful of yellowing teeth. "Crosby, don't be an asshole. Those jokers ain't any better standing or sitting. Maybe, after the auction, your two *bodyguards* could go a round or two with my girl, Betty? See how good they really are. How's that sound, fatty? Make a little wager, perhaps? Two against one, pretty good odds for you."

Betty was carefully working on her fingers with a thin metal nailfile. She looked up at the mention of her name and smiled pleasantly at Crosby. The fat black man looked suddenly uneasy. Both of the bodyguards faced Mary Zongran, their expressions calm. Beneath their jackets, the muscles in their back and arms were tensed.

"Sit," commanded Crosby, sweat beading on his forehead. "No reason to cause a scene. We will have out our differences after the Auction."

The bodyguards took their seats. Angry whispers rumbled between them and Crosby for nearly a minute. Unconcerned, Betty went back to her nails. Mary Zongran, still grinning, waved a hand at Ashmedai. "Well, whatcha waiting for? Those two bozos got the message. Let's start."

A look of disgust crossed Ashmedai's face. He drew in a deep breath and exhaled slowly. Locking his fingers together, he rested his elbows on the podium and leaned forward. "As Ms. Zongran wishes, we will begin the Auction. I will repeat the rules. There will be two rounds of bidding. We will proceed in a clockwise rotation. Each bidder will make his best offer when it is his turn. As all of the items are in my vault, a brief verbal description will suffice. I trust there will be no exaggeration or deception. The winner will be chosen by me, based on the relative value of the material. My decision is final. Any questions? I thought not. Let us begin. Mary, you are the first bidder."

"About time." The old woman peered about, her face tight with mistrust. Betty kept on filing her nails. "Got a really special item here. Had it most of my days." Mary grinned, again displaying her yellowing teeth. "Always had strong chompers. Came in handy that day. The damned fool thought he had me when I lost my knife. Still remember the sound he made dying with his throat ripped out."

"Delightful," said Benedict Crosby, wrinkling his nose in disgust. "Get to the point, you old witch."

"Yes, finish," said Abraham the Provider, his beady little eyes open and centered on Mary. "I am getting impatient."

Mary's face hardened. "I'm offering a deck of tarot cards. Not any pack, but the ones owned by the mad king, Charles VI. I know that some of the cards from that deck are supposed to be in a Paris museum, but those are counterfeits. *These* are the real ones, dating back to the late fourteenth century, which makes them the oldest known deck of tarot cards in the world. They have been used many thousands of times, but still look like new. They have served me well all my life. They're pretty damned accurate."

"A good offer," said Ashmedai. "Abraham, it is your turn."

The little man shook his head. "I brought only one thing with me. It can wait till the next round. It will be enough."

"As you wish. Countess, the floor is yours."

"Books. My bid is in books. They have been taken from my father's library, acknowledged by most to be the finest collection of occult lore ever assembled. With me tonight is John Dee's *Monas Hieroglyphica*; the *Grimorium Verum*, in the original French edition; and Peter of Abano's *The Magical Elements*. Three of the rarest grimoires in the world. Obviously," and the Countess turned slightly and sneered at Mary Zongran, "much more valuable than a deck of cards."

Ashmedai made no comment. He looked bored. "Crosby. What do you have to offer?"

"A secret." The fat man straightened in his chair. His powerful voice boomed out, dwarfing even the thunder outside. "It is the grand result of nearly twenty years of struggle. I have learned the true meaning of the Sator formula."

"Really?" Ashmedai sounded interested. "You are positive of your results?"

"Quite positive. Once the trick is revealed, the meaning becomes obvious. It is a powerful magical formula. I have tried it." Crosby's laughter boomed. "It works. It works perfectly."

The Sator formula was the most famous of all magic squares. It consisted of twenty-five letters forming a box of five letters across and five down. Like all magic squares, it read the same forwards or backwards, up or down. It had first been discovered inscribed on the wall of an ancient Roman villa in Cirencester. Later, others found the formula written on the boards of very early Bibles. Archaeologists all agreed that it was written in code. Many attempts had been made to translate the Sator square, but none had ever made any sense.

"Very interesting," said Ashmedai. The boredom was gone from his voice now. "Justice Craig. What do you offer?"

"Like Abraham the Provider, my brother and I have brought only one item. We will pass till the second round."

"As you wish. Miss Lancaster? Professor Warner?"

They had agreed that Alex would do all the bidding. "All of the items offered so far have been interesting," said Alex. "However, while they all promise power, they are not actual implements of magic. I offer that. For our bid, we offer a true Glory Hand, made according to the instructions of Little Albert. In this modern age, perhaps one of the few such charms still in existence."

Ashmedai rubbed his beard with one hand, his expression thoughtful. "Another very nice item. And a point well made." He stretched, rotating his neck to and fro. "The first round is over. Would anyone care for a drink? I didn't think so. Shall we begin the final round of bidding. Mary, you are again first."

Alex could feel the tension in the air. Mary Zongran no longer was so feisty. The old woman evidently realized her offer had little chance of winning. Her voice cracked as she spoke.

"I, too, have a book. It is the *Emerald Tablets* of Hermes Trismegistus. My copy is one of the earliest known copies, transcribed in Latin by—"

"I think we all know the book and its history," said Ashmedai. There was no attempt to disguise the revulsion in his voice. "How, when you were still a child, you killed your mother to obtain it. Your offer is noted."

Betty looked up again from her nails. She turned for an instant and looked at Mary Zongran. The old woman made a face and shook her head. Betty went back to her nails.

"Abraham. Your one and only chance."

"The secret of Rabbi Yehuda Loew is mine. I have discovered the mystical incantation of the Maharal."

The Maharal was the title given to the famous mystic and scholar of sixteenth century Prague, Yehuda Loew. Legends had it that to protect his people—the Jews of the Prague ghetto—the Maharal created a huge man of clay, the Golem. Using words of power he had discovered, the Maharal had brought the giant to life. For many years, the animate statue had protected Rabbi Loew's congregation. However, the Maharal never entrusted the words of power to any other, and when he died at age ninety-seven, the secret of the Golem had died with him. Until now.

"A major discovery," said Ashmedai, skeptically. "What proof do you offer?"

"Proof? You question my word?"

"Of course not. But many magicians have searched without success for the Maharal's secret. All know that he inscribed *emeth*, "truth" on the Golem's forehead to control it. None have ever found the words that gave the figure life. I need a little more evidence than just your word."

"You shall have it," said Abraham, with a grunt. He settled back in his chair and closed his eyes. "You shall have it."

"You have until the final bid is made, Abraham. Countess, you have another offer?"

"More books. A library full of books. I have no use for them." The Countess sounded desperate. "They won't do me any good when I'm dead. Take them all. My father's whole library. It took him most of his life to assemble the collection. You can have it all. Just let me have the coin."

"Crosby? You have something to add to your offer?"

"NO!" screamed the Countess. She leapt out of her chair. Hannah was up as well. The big woman moved incredibly fast. Before anyone could react, she jumped forward and grabbed Ashmedai around the waist. Hannah pulled the man tight to her. With a snarl of hate, she held their host as a living shield in front of her. The Countess rushed to Ashmedai's side. From some hidden pocket in her outfit, she had pulled a small .22 automatic. She waved it about meaningfully.

"I am an expert shot. This may not be a very powerful gun, but a bullet in the head would be fatal to anyone. Don't tempt me." The Countess rested her free hand on the ebony box. "This Auction is at an end. I am the winner."

Hannah pulled Ashmedai back away from

the podium. With a shove, she knocked him to the floor in the center of the circle of chairs. Ashmedai was breathing hard, but otherwise did not seem harmed . . . nor did he seem particularly disturbed by the turn of events.

The Countess waved her gun again. "Get up. All of you."

They all started to rise from their chairs. Alex kept his eyes fixed on the Countess. She was a cold-blooded killer. There was no trusting her. Whatever lies she told them, he knew she had no intention of letting them leave the room alive.

Evidently, he was not the only one who had come to that conclusion. Without warning, one of Benedict Crosby's bodyguards dropped from his chair and onto the floor. He rolled to the side, tugging out a pistol as he moved. The Countess' gun blasted, but she had been caught unprepared. The man came up in a crouch, his weapon roaring as he sprayed the podium. The Countess dropped safely to the floor instants before the bullets crashed above her. Then, Hannah was on the man.

The giant woman grabbed the bodyguard's outstretched arm with both her hands. With a savage roar, she whipped the man around. It was a terrible demonstration of pure brute strength. The bodyguard's arm broke with an audible crack and the man shrieked in pain. His scream came to a sudden, abrupt end as

Hannah released him and he went flying into the nearby wall. The black man's body remained standing for a second, flat up against the wallpaper, and then, without a sound, dropped to the floor. The impact left a mansized red blot where he had hit. The whole incident was over almost before it had begun. The rest of the bidders had remained frozen during the entire scenario.

The Countess fired again. Crosby's other bodyguard crumpled to the floor, a dark hole between his eyes oozing blood. Gun still smoking, the Countess rose to her feet. "He would have tried something sooner or later," she declared with finality. "Now, all the rest of you, get moving. Back to the far wall."

They were all on their feet now. Crosby had a stunned, confused look on his face. His two bodyguards lay dead at his feet. Abraham the Provider didn't seem very worried. His eyes were half open and he was muttering something under his breath, lips barely moving. Valerie looked at Alex, her face white and her expression grim. He let his head dip a bare fraction of an inch and winked. Valerie drew in a deep breath and slid closer to him.

Ashmedai was on his feet now, standing next to the Craig brothers. "You are wasting your time, Marie. Why not open the box before you continue with this charade?"

"What?" The Countess did not sound amused. "Hannah, assume your beast form. *Now*."

The giantess said something softly. Alex watched in astonishment. It was an unbelievable sight. The woman actually expanded before their eyes. The clothes ripped off her body. Her features seemed to flow like butter, rippling, changing into those of a beast. The whole process took only a few seconds. Then Hannah Stine was gone and in her place stood a creature of the night.

Almost immediately, the thing looked around and fastened its eyes on Alex. It opened its jaws, revealing huge fangs. The meaning was quite clear. Alex let his inner arm rest on the concealed bowie knife. One of them was not going to leave this room alive.

"Quiet," commanded the Countess. "You will have time enough for that one later. I promised him to you. Watch all of them for now." The Countess laughed harshly. "Hannah has been on edge of late. She is looking for an excuse to kill. Don't tempt her."

The Countess rested her gun on the podium and took the ebony box in both hands. She worked the lock for a minute and then looked up at Ashmedai in bewilderment. "It isn't even sealed."

"Of course not, you fool." Ashmedai's voice was harsh. "Do you think I would be stupid enough to bring the coin with me once all of you had seen it? The exchange was set for tomorrow morning. At the moment, the coin is safe where you can never find it. You stupid, arrogant bitch."

The Countess turned the box over, knocking the lid open. Her face contorted with rage. With a curse, she threw the ebony box to the floor and scooped up her gun from where she had put it down. "Tell me where it is. Tell me now. Or, I swear, no one will have it. If you value your life, talk."

Ashmedai threw back his head and roared with laughter. It was a bitter, almost tearful sound. "If I value my life," he managed to gasp out, holding his sides with his arms. Tears trickled down his cheeks. "Don't you understand. My life is a curse. You can't threaten me with death. I want to die."

He raised his hands to his head, pressing them against his skull. The laughter was gone now and only despair remained. "You still haven't guessed the truth. Even with all the hints and clues I provided. Don't you think I haven't tried to die? A hundred times, a thousand times I courted death, always without success. No matter what I do, I survive. I am cursed with life. There is no escape. Even suicide is denied me."

Ashmedai reached for his dark glasses. "Look," he said, pulling them off his face and facing the Countess. "If you want to know the truth about eternal life, look into my eyes."

Only the Countess, standing at the podium, could see Ashmedai's face. She stared directly at him. All motion stopped. Her eyes widened and then got wider still. A wild expression crossed her face. Fingers wrapped around her gun, loosened and then opened. The weapon tumbled to the floor. The Countess remained frozen. Her jaw fell. *"No-o-o."* The sound started softly and built in volume. *"No-O-O-O!"* She was howling now. *"NO-O-O-O!"*

Hannah spun around, her prisoners forgotten. Alex immediately grabbed Valerie and dragged her to the floor. He had a hunch things were going to get much worse before getting better. He ripped off his coat and pulled the bowie knife from its sheath.

Betty leapt into action. Without a wasted motion, she darted forward, the thin metal nail file held out in front of her. The Countess never saw her coming. With a savage thrust, Betty slammed the file deep into the older woman's stomach. The Countess grunted and took a step forward, an astonished expression on her face. Still gripping the nail file tightly, Betty slashed hard across and up. It was a killing blow. The Countesss' nose and mouth spurted blood as she crumpled to the floor. Thus ended her dreams of immortality.

With a shriek of pure animal rage, Hannah pounced on Betty from behind, her claws sinking deep into leather. The young woman tried to spin down and away, but the werewolf's long claws were sunk too deep into her flesh. Hannah roared and snapped at Betty's neck. She missed by inches as Betty dropped to the floor, dragging Hannah up and over her body. With a perfectly timed lunge, Betty snapped up, ramming her head into the werewolf's midsection.

The blow would have killed any normal foe. But Hannah was not normal. With a grunt of pain, she bore down on Betty, forcing the girl back to the floor. Blood was gushing from the werewolf's nose but it didn't slow her for an instant. One giant arm swept up and then down, slashing with yellow claws across Betty's face. The girl shrieked in agony. Again and again the clawed hand rose and fell. Each time, the werewolf's fingers were redder and redder. Finally, the form beneath the beast was still. Shakily, Hannah rose to her feet.

She turned and faced them. Ashmedai, glasses back in place, was at the far end of the room, backed up to the door. Next to him, quivering in fear, huddled Benedict Crosby. By the windows crouched Abraham the Provider. Next to him stood a defiant Mary Zongran. Lying flat on the floor, Alex and Valerie remained screened from the beast by the last few chairs. The Craig brothers had vanished.

The werewolf howled. A steady stream of

blood dripped from its nose, and its breath came in loud, ragged gasps. Madness burned bright in its eyes. As the creature moved its head from side to side, searching, Alex rose to his feet.

"Head for the door," he said to Valerie, keeping his eyes fixed on the werewolf. "Right now, before the thing charges. I can't fight it if I'm worrying about you."

Valerie scuttled away. The thing that was Hannah Stine didn't even notice. It was only interested in Alex. Hands raised, it stepped forward cautiously. It had not forgotten their earlier fight.

Alex retreated. The beast was quicker than he, with reflexes many times faster. Even badly wounded, its strength was enormous. The odds were all on its side. His only chance was to catch it by surprise. Drawing in a deep breath, he charged.

His attack was totally unexpected. Only a dozen feet separated him from the werewolf and Alex covered those in a second. The beast had no time to react. One huge hand swatted at him—too late. He was inside its guard. The bowie knife flashed as he plunged it deep into the monster's stomach. Teeth snapped only inches from his face. He wrenched the knife hard, pulling it free. Hot blood gushed out of the gaping wound. The werewolf staggered back.

Trying to keep the monster off balance, Alex pressed forward. He stabbed again with the bowie knife, slicing through muscle and flesh. He twisted and tried to pull the blade free. It didn't move. It had wedged hard against a bone. He hesitated for a second.

It was all the time the werewolf needed. A huge hand slammed into the side of Alex's head. Blood filled his mouth and his vision blurred. Desperately, he fell back and to the side. Another clawed hand swept by him, only inches from his eyes. He stumbled over the few remaining chairs, his senses reeling. Far in the distance, he could hear Valerie screaming.

The werewolf howled in triumph. Remembering their first encounter, Alex dropped and rolled. The beast went charging past him. It was still a creature of habit. Alex shook his head hard, clearing his vision. The monster was a dozen feet away, doubled over in pain, the bowie knife still embedded in its side. Blood bubbled out of its earlier wounds, forming a red pool on the carpet. Any other living thing would be long dead with wounds like that, but not this supernatural horror. As Alex watched, the werewolf straightened. It was huffing and puffing like a steam shovel. It couldn't last more than a few minutes, losing blood so quickly. Unfortunately, Alex knew he would not be alive to enjoy his triumph.

"Alex, catch!" screamed Valerie. He had no time to think. He reacted, grabbing at what she threw. His both hands wrapped onto cold metal as the werewolf attacked. Jaws gaping wide, the beast leaped straight for him.

Alex's feet spun out from under him as he tried to escape. He had forgotten the polished wood floor. Blood from his own wounds had dripped onto the surface, making it incredibly slick. He crashed to the floor as the werewolf went flying over his head.

He rolled. The werewolf scrambled around on all fours. For a mad instant, they were face to face, both of them flat. The monster's open jaws were inches away from Alex. He could feel its breath like a hot wind out of Hell burning across his skin. The beast snapped. Alex lunged back. The werewolf raised itself up on both arms, in a half crouch, and Alex saw death staring at him from red eyes.

There was cold metal in his hand. He had never let go of the object Valerie had thrown to him. It was his only chance. As the werewolf hurtled forward, Alex wrenched up the metal and shoved it into the creature's face with all of his strength. By reflex action alone, the werewolf clamped its jaws shut. Teeth smashed and broke as they crunched down hard on steel. Alex's grip tightened involuntarily. The gun he was holding exploded in the werewolf's mouth.

Wildly, Alex pulled the trigger again and again. Long after all of the bullets were gone, he kept on squeezing.

Finally he stopped. Trembling, he rose to his feet. Valerie cried out in relief when she saw him stand, and she came running forward. The others moved much more cautiously. There was little reason for concern, though. The gun Valerie had retrieved from the dead bodyguard had been very effective. Using it, Alex had blown away most of the werewolf's skull. Hannah Stine had joined her mistress.

Now, Alex sucked in air, trying to regain some of his strength. He was bleeding from a score of cuts, but he had suffered no serious injury. Valerie fussed over him, trying to get him to sit down. Alex refused. Somehow, he knew that it wasn't over yet.

"Well, now what?" Benedict Crosby's voice boomed like a foghorn, breaking the silence. He nudged the dead werewolf with one large foot, as if to convince himself it was really dead.

"The Auction is not yet complete," said Ashmedai. "We have yet to finish the second round."

"It *is* over," said Abraham the Provider, with a crackling laugh. The little man stood alone, by the main entrance to the room, beside the row of long glass windows. "Over for all of you. I have the winning bid."

Abraham waved one small arm in a signal. Outside, in the rain, something big and bulky cast a giant shadow on the windows. Glass and wood crashed as the thing smashed through wall and window and lumbered into the room.

Alex recognized the metal giant at once. Eight feet tall, deep green in color, armed with a long cavalry sword, it was the missing statue of Casimir Pulaski. Pasted high on its forehead was a white slip of paper inscribed with the word *emeth*.

This was the thing that had roamed the woods dealing death to all it encountered. It was a juggernaut of living bronze. Abraham the Provider pointed an accusing finger at their host. "Let us put your immortality to the test, Ashmedai. How much pain before you go mad? Can your immortal body survive being crushed to a pulp?" There was madness in Abraham's voice. The old man's tone grew harsh and cold. "Kill them. Kill them all."

CHAPTER FOURTEEN

The statue marched forward. Each step it took shook the room. **Thump. Thump. Thump**. It moved slowly but steadily. Its footsteps were like the beating of some giant heart. In one huge hand it held a long sword of bronze. Its other hand was empty. Huge unfinished metal fingers opened and closed with each step it took.

The Golem had no eyes, yet it seemed to know where they all were. For an instant, they stood frozen in place. Five steps and it was nearly upon them. With a high-pitched scream, Benedict Crosby dashed around the animate statue, making for the door. Alex grabbed Valerie by the waist before she could follow, dragging her back behind the podium. Ashmedai followed them hastily, pushing chairs out of his way.

Crosby had the right idea. The statue could not think; it was little more than an extension of Abraham's will. It did not react quickly. The fat man was by the statue before the man of metal reacted to what was happening. Then the Golem hesitated in mid-stride. Its head followed the fat man's path, rotating 180 degrees on a motionless body. It was an eerie sight.

Huffing and puffing, Crosby had eyes only for the double doors a dozen feet away. His arms flailed wildly as he ran. In doing so, Crosby totally forgot the carnage that littered the floor. It was the body of the bodyguard Marie Lamont had shot without provocation that proved to be his undoing. One misplaced step caught his foot beneath the dead man's torso. With a sharp cry of pain, Crosby stumbled and fell to his knees.

The sound was what decided the Golem. It swung around. Metal grated on metal as it marched after the fat man.

Crosby saw it coming. Desperately, he pushed hard with both hands against the floor, trying to regain his footing, but his huge bulk was not made for speed. He barely made it upright when the golem grabbed at him. Metal fingers sank deep into the back of his white jacket.

The fat man shrieked. The coat ripped like cheesecloth beneath powerful bronze fingers. Blood gushed where the metal fingers ripped away flesh. Crosby crashed forward, his momentum carrying him free. He raced desperately for the door, huge legs pumping like pistons. The Golem marched after him.

Alex grabbed one of the loose chairs and raised it over his head. It was too late to help Crosby. Their own survival was his main concern. When it finished with the fat man, the statue would come after them—and Alex had no intention of waiting for it to attack. With a powerful lunge, he threw the chair into the long windows at his left. Glass shattered, leaving a large hole to the outside. Valerie ran forward. She had her heels off and held them like hammers in her hands. A few well-placed sweeps and the jagged fragments of glass on the lower sill were gone.

The storm howled its welcome. Alex swung Valerie up and out. Mary Zongran, using her canes, hobbled forward from the rear of the room and went next. Ashmedai followed. Only Alex remained. He had one leg over the sill when Crosby shrieked in pain.

Alex risked a quick look over his shoulder. The Golem's arms were wrapped around Crosby's waist now, and the black man dangled several feet off the floor. The thing had him tight against its body and was squeezing hard.

Metal grated again as the Golem pulled one arm around the other. Crosby's face turned beet red as he screamed in pain. His legs kicked helplessly in the air.

The Golem continued to squeeze. Crosby's screams rose in volume. His arms clawed at the metal arms that encircled his waist. Desperately he tried to wrench loose from that unbreakable grip. There was nothing the black man could do. Blood spurted from his nose. His arms dropped limply to his sides.

Inside his body, bones cracked under the pressure. His rib cage collapsed in ruin. Blood burst from his chest as broken bone was shoved up through muscle and flesh. Crosby screamed one last time.

Hands grabbed Alex's shoulders and pulled him outside. It was Valerie. Ashmedai stood close by. Mary Zongran was already twenty feet away, heading for the cars parked at the end of the long circular driveway. Hard, driving rain pelted them like a thousand tiny bullets. "We have to get back in the house," said Ashmedai. "We stand no chance against the Golem in the open."

Glass and wood shattered behind them. There was no time to talk. The statue was coming for them. It smashed through the broken window and wood frame, arms outstretched. The monster's chest and arms were no longer green, but a bright shade of red. Alex grabbed Valerie's hand and together they ran.

Ashmedai was right. They could not fight the metal man in the storm. Thunder rolled and lightning flashed. Icy rain slashed at their bodies as wind ripped through their clothing.

They were mere flesh and blood. The Golem was hard, unyielding metal, unfazed by the storm. **Thump. Thump. Thump**. It marched after them; relentless, never yielding. Behind them, floating on the wind, Alex could hear Abraham the Provider yelling instructions to his creation. "The old woman. She's slow and feeble. Get her! *Crush her*!"

"The other way!" said Ashmedai. "There is nothing we can do for her. Make for the far end of the building. There is another entrance there."

Alex and Valerie chased after Ashmedai. He was right about Mary. Every one of the Golem's strides brought it closer to the old woman. She had no chance. Alex didn't miss a step when a thin, wailing cry filled the night. Soon the Golem would be coming after them.

The door was locked. Ashmedai pounded desperately with his fists against the upper panelling. "The servants are quartered at the end of the other wing. They know better than to meddle in my affairs. We can expect no aid from them. I must have lost my keys in the scramble. We're locked out."

Alex fought off exhaustion. His body felt on

the verge of collapse; the fight with Hannah had pushed him to the limit. He ached all over and his muscles screamed for rest. He sucked air into his chest, filling his lungs with oxygen. There was no time for finesse. Already, he could hear the monstrous steps of the Golem somewhere behind them.

He spread his legs for maximum balance, bending them slightly at the knees. One hand outstretched, the other pulled back even with his chest, Alex focused all of his mental energy on his fingers. Another deep breath, and then he was ready. *"Hai!"* he shouted, pulling back his one arm and lashing out with the other. His fist slammed into the wood panelling with the force of a pile-driver. Into and through. With a quick wrench, Alex had the lock undone. The three of them dashed into the hallway.

Thump. Thump. The Golem was very close.

"Up the stairs," said Ashmedai. He led the way, mounting the steps two at a time. Valerie helped pull Alex along. Every step was an effort for him. His arms and legs felt like lead weights now. His lungs burned and a red haze clouded his vision. Up to the second floor they raced. Valerie had one of his arms over her shoulders. Ashmedai supported him on the other side. They half-dragged, half-carried him down the long hallway. Behind them, the stairs were quiet.

"This room has two exits," said Ashmedai,

pulling open one door. "We can rest inside."

They staggered in. Alex collapsed onto the bed, gasping for breath. Valerie sank into one of the plush chairs off to the side. Only Ashmedai remained standing.

"We are probably safe for now. The statue is too heavy to climb that staircase. It will have to circle back to the main entrance and come up the main hallway. That gives us a little time."

Alex forced himself to a sitting position. Gingerly, he rubbed his knuckles. "Time for what? I doubt if my karate would even dent that thing. You have any tricks up your sleeve?"

"I remember reading the legend of the Golem," said Valerie. "The word inscribed on its forehead gives it life. According to the story, to stop the Golem, you have to erase the first letter of *emeth*. That changes the word to *meth*, meaning 'death'. Nothing else works."

"Perhaps," said Ashmedai, stroking his beard, his dark brows furled in thought. "There was a tendency in such stories to exaggerate the magic involved. Remember, Rabbi Loew lived long before modern weaponry. For all of its unnatural strength, the Golem is a thing of metal. I suspect a well-placed bazooka shell would stop it, and dynamite would probably blast it to pieces."

Alex pounded the bed with his sore hand. "That's the answer! Not dynamite, but something just as good. Only it's back on the roadway at the edge of the forest. I'll have to go get it."

"Get what, Alex?" asked Valerie, her voice tight with worry.

"Plastique. There was a brick of plastic explosive and a small detonator in my duffel bag. I told you I was ready to fight a small war. The explosive can be molded into a small but very powerful bomb. I was pretty handy with the stuff once upon a time. Those are lessons you don't forget."

"It will be powerful enough to stop the Golem?" asked Ashmedai.

"You'll be scraping bronze off your roof for a week. The biggest difficulty is getting into the forest and back. Do you have any of those Invitations lying around somewhere?"

Ashmedai shook his head. "No need. The paper was a mere extension of my will. You will have no trouble leaving. But the spell would keep you from returning." He reached out with his left hand. "Do not move for a second."

The sorcerer touched Alex on the forehead with one finger, tracing a strange pattern. The design burned for an instant. "You will not have any problems. Come, we must leave this room. I can sense the Golem climbing the other stairs."

They hurried back the way they had come.

"We'll split up," said Alex. "Valerie, you go with Ashmedai. I'll get the plastique on my own."

Valerie started to protest, but he cut her off with a wave of his hand. "No time to argue. I know what I said about sticking together, but this is different. I can make a lot better time on my own. Ashmedai knows the mansion. The two of you can keep the Golem distracted until I get back."

They emerged from the hallway onto the second-floor landing. Alex was in the lead now. "Seems like we're forgetting one thing," said Valerie, right behind Alex. "What about Abraham the Provider?"

"Yes. What *about* me?"

Abraham the Provider stood in the broken doorway. The skin of his face was pulled back in an evil grin. Mad eyes glared at them. Both his hands were raised. His middle three fingers were pressed together and pointed right at them, his pinky and thumb at right angles to the other digits. Electrical sparks leapt across his fingers. The little man stepped forward, mounting the first step. "Did you think you could escape me? The Golem is behind you. I guard this door. You are trapped."

Ashmedai pushed forward past Alex on the steps. "Arrogant little snake. You dare challenge me?"

Behind them, the floor shook as the Golem

approached. Abraham laughed wildly. He dug one hand into his pocket and brought it out clutching a handful of silver coins. *"I* have the power now, Ashmedai. I found your precious talismans. This is the final Auction."

Ashmedai took another step forward. Then another. He did not seem particularly worried. "You bore me, little man. And, you have made a mess of my home." Alex noted that Ashmedai did not seem overly concerned about the murder of his guests. "It is time to pay the price for your greed."

Swiftly Ashmedai descended the steps. Alex and Valerie followed, keeping well back from the man. Abraham's body began to shake. He threw both hands over his head and quickly started to chant a spell. Ashmedai kept coming.

"I conjure thee, Fire, by Him who made thee and all other creatures of this world, to burn, torture and consume this one before me. Let him suffer the agonies of Hell in thy fire."

With a roar, a curtain of white fire surrounded Ashmedai. Flame engulfed him. In seconds, he stood in the midst of a raging inferno. Abraham the Provider fell back away from the blaze, his hands still held up over his head. "I have won!" he shouted. *"I have won!"*

The door at the top of the stairs burst open. The Golem had arrived at the landing. At the same time, Abraham's cry of triumph turned into a scream of horror. The burning figure before him had not stopped moving. Fiery arms reached out and grabbed ahold of his shoulders. Abraham shrieked as Ashmedai wrenched him forward. The little man tried to pull away, but it was too late. Fire enveloped him. His body sizzled in Ashmedai's terrible embrace. The smell of burning flesh filled the air.

The Golem lurched forward as if to save its creator. One foot descended on the fragile wooden landing, then the other. For a bare instant, the frame held. Then, with a loud crack, the whole stairway collapsed.

Alex and Valerie were almost at ground level. A quick leap forward and they were safe. When they looked back, the Golem was nowhere to be seen. It lay buried under a mound of wood beams. Then Alex turned back to the burning figures. He took a step forward, then had to retreat. The fire was just too hot. The flames roared furiously. Then, as suddenly as they had appeared, the flames began to fade.

"Alex," said Valerie. "It can't be. No one could live through that."

The fire vanished, revealing two standing figures. Ashmedai looked completely untouched by the flames. He released the blackened body of Abraham the Disciple, and the charred corpse collapsed to the floor. Then Ashmedai turned to them, a wry smile on his face. "You are quite mistaken, Miss Lancaster. Look at the floor. Not a mark on it. Those magical flames only consume *mortal* flesh. Abraham was destroyed by his own sending."

Behind them, the wooden beams groaned in protest. One huge green hand thrust up out of the collapsed landing. Then another. The whole pile trembled. Even though its master was dead, the Golem still lived. Wooden beams went flying as the bronze statue struggled to its feet.

Alex shoved Valerie into Ashmedai's arms. "Get going. Make for the cars. I'll meet you there. *Run.*"

Back out into the storm they ran. A flash of lightning greeted them as they emerged from the house. Thunder rolled. Valerie and Ashmedai struggled up the driveway towards the cars.

Alex stood waiting. He didn't want the Golem following the others. He was human bait for the metal man.

The Golem burst out through the door. It held its sword high over its head. It spotted Alex immediately. Without hesitation, it came pounding forward. Alex turned and ran.

He deliberately cut across the huge open lawn. The ground was soaking wet and heavy rain had turned it into a swamp. It was like running through Jello. It was difficult for Alex to make much progress, but for the Golem it was nearly impossible. It sank six inches down in mud with each step.

Alex risked a quick look over his shoulder. He was pulling away from the monster. With luck, he would make it to the forest before the Golem got to the end of the huge lawn.

Lightning flashed, momentarily blinding him. Thunder roared. Without warning, something incredibly heavy smashed into his right leg. With a cry of pain, he collapsed to the ground. Mud splattered in his face as he hit the earth. His leg felt like it was on fire. Using all of his strength, he rolled onto his back. Pain lanced through him each time he tried to move his leg. A hurried examination confirmed his worst fears. The bone was broken.

A few feet away, Alex spotted a long green metal shaft on the ground. It was the Golem's sword. The metal man must have thrown it at him like a spear. It had missed his back but had gotten his leg. Alex looked up. The Golem was a score of feet away and advancing steadily. If he didn't get moving, he was a dead man.

Frantically, Alex tried to grab hold of the bronze sword. If he could get it, he might be able to use it as a crutch. He stretched out as far as he could without shifting his leg. It was no use. The metal rod was just beyond his grip. Gritting his teeth, he tried raising himself up on his hands. Red mists swept across his vision as he thrust himself forward. With a whimper, he collapsed only a foot away from the sword. He struggled to remain conscious. There was no strength left in his arms. The sword was only inches from his face, but he couldn't raise a hand to grab it. Then, the Golem was there.

It towered over him, a green bronze giant. Slowly, the Golem bent down and grasped its weapon For a second, the metal head was so close that Alex could see the strip of white paper glued to its brow. There was nothing he could do. Pain held him in an unbreakable grip. His eyes opened wide as the Golem raised the sword over its head. It paused for a second, as if saluting a fallen foe.

In that instant, the sky exploded.

Chapter Fifteen

Touch returned to him first. Alex could feel the crisp, clean sheets beneath his fingers. The digits of his hands curled, sending shivers through his arms and up across his shoulders. Without thinking, he drew in a deep breath. The scent of Valerie's perfume filled the air. He opened his mouth to speak, but no sound came forth.

"Alex. Don't panic. It's me, Valerie." At first, she sounded far distant, but as she continued to speak, his hearing seemed to improve. "You're okay. There is nothing to worry about. Your body has been through quite a lot. It's mending, but it takes time. Just rest. All you have to do is rest."

He tried to open his eyes. It felt like there was a heavy weight resting on each eyelid, holding them shut. Again, he drew in a deep breath and tried to speak. A soft croaking noise was all he could manage. Resigned to his fate, he stopped struggling. In seconds, he was asleep.

The next time he awoke, he was immediately conscious of bright sunshine. Without effort, he opened his eyes. He blinked a few times, unaccustomed to the glare. Squinting, he spotted Valerie on a chair only a few feet from the bed. She was watching him anxiously. When he moved his head, she smiled.

"What the Hell is going on?" he asked. His voice was a little hoarse, but otherwise back to normal.

Ashmedai moved into his line of sight. The bearded man shook his head in disbelief and smiled. "You are the luckiest man I have ever met, Professor Warner. In all my days, I have never seen anything like it."

With a groan, Alex rolled over and pushed himself up. It took some effort, but he raised himself on a bent arm so that his head was off the bed. He was naked beneath the sheets, but he didn't care. Looking around, he recognized the room where he had changed for dinner. The curtains had been drawn back and sunshine streamed in.

"You've been out for nearly two days," said Valerie with a grin. "It took time for

Ashmedai's magic to work. How do you feel?"

"Pretty weak, but otherwise, not too bad." Alex paused for a second. "My leg. It was broken." He bent his injured leg without any pain. "The bone snapped. I felt it break."

"It healed while you slept, Professor. As did your eyes and ears and the burns over much of your body."

"Burns." Alex remembered the sky exploding. "Lightning. The statue was hit by lightning."

Ashmedai nodded. "It was incredible. We saw the whole thing from the driveway. The upraised metal sword acted like a lightning rod. The sky erupted with electricity. One bolt after another came hurtling out of the storm, and the sword drew them down to the Golem. Nothing of this Earth could exist in that blaze of energy. The Golem shattered, blown to bits. Much of it was reduced to smoldering slag. It was the most incredible display of nature's fury I have ever witnessed. I was positive you had been killed, either by the Golem or by the force of the lightning. Miss Lancaster refused to accept my judgment. She was sure the Golem's destruction was a direct result of your astonishing luck. Reluctantly, I accompanied her to inspect your body. You were not a pretty sight, but you were still alive."

Valerie came and sat down on the bed next

to him. She covered one of his hands with her own. "So we carried you back here. Ashmedai's magic did the rest. It took time, but you're just about healed now. He assures me you'll be as good as new."

"Better," said Ashmedai, with a laugh. "You will find that all of your scars have disappeared as well. And any other minor medical nuisances like allergies will no longer bother you, either. The Coins are quite thorough."

"The Coins," said Alex. "They actually work?"

"Yes. They do work." Ashmedai walked over and pulled the curtains closed. "But even they need some help. You have remained awake long enough, Professor. Your body has still not fully recovered. Time for you to sleep again."

Alex did feel tired. But there were so many questions left unanswered. "The Craig brothers?"

"No sign of them. Their car was gone as well. They must have fled as soon as the opportunity presented itself. Now go to sleep, Professor."

"Then we are the only ones left," Alex murmured as Valerie joined Ashmedai by the door. "We won the Auction."

"You are the winners," said Ashmedai in soft tones. "The only ones left are always the winners."

* * *

They were in a library lined with thousands of books of magical lore. Ashmedai sat in a huge, carved chair, made of the same dark wood as the mysterious ebon-colored box. Grinning gargoyles leered at Alex and Valerie from the high posts of the chair. Valerie sat directly across from Ashmedai. Alex remained standing. It was hard to concentrate surrounded by this treasure-trove of occult references.

Ashmedai finished his examination of *The Secrets of the Hanged Man* and closed the cover. "A very fine copy," he said. "Much better than the one I already own. It will make a nice addition to the Library."

"What about the other items in your safe? The ones brought by the Countess and your other guests. What happens to them?"

Ashmedai shrugged. "I plan to keep them. What else would you have me do? Who has a better claim to them than I. Call it a small measure of repayment for the destruction done to my home and grounds."

Valerie snapped her fingers. Her face was flushed with excitement. "Of course. I should have guessed. The answer was obvious all the time. You expected something like this to happen. *You planned the whole thing.*

"It was easy. You invited the most powerful black magicians in the world to this mysterious Auction, every one of them an arrogant, self-centered individual, accustomed to getting his own way. Even my father fit that description. Then you show them something which they all *must* have, but only one can win. What a set-up. The suckers don't even realize they are being manipulated. All you have to do is sit back and watch them kill each other off—leaving you in possession of all the rarities they brought as part of the bargain."

Ashmedai gently drummed his fingers on the desktop. "So? I told no lies. I deceived no one. But you are only seeing a small part of the whole picture. Weren't you ever curious about all the rumors and stories concerning the Auction? If it is so secret, how did so many people know something about it? Especially if no one ever returns to tell the tale? I came close to revealing the truth that evening at dinner. *I* am responsible for spreading all of the half-truths and hints about the Auction. You can't catch any fish without spreading your net."

"But why do you bother?" asked Valerie. She waved an arm about, taking in the whole library. "You are the most powerful magician in the world. No one can equal you in power. Your library and collection of occult talismans is the greatest in existence." Her voice got louder and louder as she continued, until she was nearly shouting. "Was Alex right? Are we puppets dancing to the strings of an immortal toyman? Is this all just some sort of sadistic game?"

"No." Ashmedai pushed back his chair and rose to his feet. He walked to the rear of the room. On a small teak table rested the ebony box. Ashmedai took it with both hands and brought it back to the desk.

"I am immortal. That one fact rules my actions. You are bound by a span of decades. I have lived for centuries. My plans are not yours to understand. I take the long view. I am preparing for . . . Armageddon."

"Armageddon?" asked Alex. "The Day of Judgment?"

"The final confrontation," corrected Ashmedai. His expression was grim, "when Good and Evil battle for the fate of mankind. It will be a war fought between unimaginable foes. They will be armed with the darkest secrets of magic. Suffice it to say that I am collecting weapons for that conflict."

"Which side?" asked Alex in a whisper. "Is this truly the Devil's Auction?"

Ashmedai laughed. He reached for the lock holding the ebony box closed. "I will leave that for you to decide, my friends."

With a touch, the lock opened. Bright light filled the study. "The time has come," said Ashmedai, pushing the box across the top of his desk. He let it rest in front of Valerie. Leaning forward, Ashmedai pulled the lid completely open. Resting inside the container were three stacks of silver shekels.

"The Auction was not a sham. For all of the manipulation and deceit, no lies were told. The violence was a result of greed, not any of my actions. The Auction was designed for the greatest return possible, but I never cheated anyone. The bargain is always kept."

He took a deep breath and continued. "As the only bidder left, your bid is the winning one." His voice sounded odd. It was as if he was trying to warn them of something but could not. His face had a grim, desperate look to it. "Here are the thirty pieces of silver."

Valerie reached for the box. Without knowing exactly why, Alex grabbed her wrist. "Not yet." A vague feeling of wrongness had swept through him when Ashmedai spoke. There was a message in those words.

"Alex." Valerie sounded annoyed. "What is this all about? You're hurting me."

"Sorry." He released her arm. "Leave the Coins alone for now . . . please. At least until I get a few things straight in my mind. Okay?"

Valerie rubbed her wrist and grimaced. Her eyes were fixed on the pieces of silver. Reluctantly, she nodded. "Okay. But I think you're crazy."

"Humor me."

Alex stood silent for a moment. All of the explanations made sense. The secrets of the

Robert Weinberg

Auction were revealed. Yet, he felt uneasy. It was as if one piece of a giant puzzle was still missing. His eyes were drawn to the ebony box. It was hard to believe that it held thirty pieces of silver over two thousand years old. "Thirty pieces," whispered Alex. And then he knew.

"You've been holding these Auctions for a long time. For a thousand years or more. Each time, the prize is one of these silver shekels?"

"That is correct," said Ashmedai. A smile crossed his lips and he nodded, as if urging Alex to continue his line of reasoning. "One coin for the winner."

"Yet," said Alex, pointing an accusing finger at the three stacks of coins shining brightly amidst the ebony, "there are thirty pieces of silver in the box."

Ashmedai laughed. The dark shadow was gone from his face. "You are one of the very few to notice, Professor. Most act without thinking. Their greed blinds them to the truth. I want to warn the winners, but cannot. Long ago, I vowed never again to interfere with another's destiny.

"The Coins have a history of returning to my possession after a short time—often, within a few days. Like me, they are cursed.

"A long, long time ago, I tried to give them away. I tried many times. Agrippa, whom you mentioned, was just one of many who had them in his possession for a short time. Like all of the others, they brought him only disaster. No matter how I tried to dispose of the Coins, sooner or later they returned to me. Finally I decided to take advantage of my burden. Thus, I began holding the Auctions."

Valerie looked down at the silver and shuddered. "With all of the power in the Coins, I can guess the only way the winner relinquishes his prize."

"They are worthless to the Dead," said Ashmedai, as if reading her thoughts. "That is the final irony. Magicians come here seeking eternal life. They never realize that the prize they desire brings only death."

Alex pushed the lid closed on the ebony box. "Keep the Geoffrey book and the Glory Hand. And the Coins as well." Valerie had gotten to her feet and Alex pulled her close. "We have the greatest prize of all. Our lives and each other."

"Nicely put," said Ashmedai, "though I still feel in your debt. Defeating the Golem would have been a problem even for my powers. Let me think. Ah, I know one thing I can do!"

He pointed a finger at Valerie and muttered something under his breath. "You will no longer suffer for your adolescent mistake. The *glamour* is gone. I removed the spell. I would advise," he said with a chuckle, "you to be a bit more careful practicing sorcery in the future."

Impulsively, Valerie grabbed Ashmedai and hugged him for an instant. The sorcerer quickly disentangled himself from her grip. "Enough. I am not fond of emotional scenes."

He turned to Alex. "For you, Professor, I have something much more precious. You asked me a question at dinner. It was not the right time or place for a reply. If you like, I will answer you now. Are you sure you want to know the truth?"

Alex drew in a deep breath. "Tell me."

Ashmedai picked up the Justin Geoffrey volume. "Who is the Hanged Man? Geoffrey knew his identity. But Geoffrey was a madman. He feared some sort of divine retribution if he revealed too much, so he disguised the answer. The truth was hidden in the Latin verse that began his book. The rest of the work is gibberish, meant only to deceive the unwary."

Ashmedai opened the book to the title page. "Read between the lines. 'We have signed a treaty with death'. Why a *treaty* with death? What bargain could there be with the Dark Angel? Only one covenant would matter. Geoffrey knew that the Hanged Man was undying, immortal. 'With Hell we have made a pact' signifies a man damned for all eternity."

"The picture of the Hanged Man in the tarot deck," said Alex, trying to follow what Ashmedai was saying, "a man hanging from a gibbet by one foot, touching neither earth or sky."

"Cursed on the Earth, he is denied entrance forever to Heaven," replied Ashmedai. "The most telling point is that he is hanging but not dead. His face shows no sign of either suffering or remorse. He is the suicide who hung himself but did not die."

A cold chill passed through Alex. "In fortune-telling, the Hanged Man is the sign of treachery."

"Betrayal." Ashmedai spat the word out like a curse. "The Hanged Man is twelfth of the major trumps. He stands between death and justice. It was the twelfth disciple who betrayed his master that night in the olive grove, Gethsemane."

Alex could feel the tension within him. Everything Ashmedai said pointed to only one conclusion. "*Woe to that man by whom the Son of man is betrayed. It would have been better for that man if he had not been born.*"

Silently, Ashmedai returned to his ebony chair. "John knew the truth before he died. In the *New Testament*, chapter 21, verse 22, he described the true fate of the Betrayer. He was to tarry until their Master returned." Ashmedai laughed harshly. His voice was filled with bitterness and despair. "Tarry."

Valerie shook her head, bewildered by the

conversation. "What does all this have to do with the Wandering Jew?"

"The Wandering Jew is the Hanged Man," said Ashmedai quietly. "And the Hanged Man is the betrayer of Jesus Christ." The weight of two thousand years was in Ashmedai's voice. "I am the Hanged Man. I am Judas Iscariot."

Buy two books by
SHAUN HUTSON
and get a third
FREE!

_____2511-6 **SLUGS** $3.95US/$4.95CAN

_____2544-2 **BREEDING GROUND** $3.95US/$4.95CAN

_____2622-8 **SPAWN** $3.95US/$4.95CAN

Please send me the following titles:

Quantity	Book Number	Price
_____	_____	_____
_____	_____	_____
	Postage & Handling*	_____
	Total Amount Enclosed	_____

Your third FREE book by Shaun Hutson will be selected by us and included in your shipment!

*Please include $1.25 shipping and handling for the first book ordered and $.30 for each book thereafter in the same order. All orders are shipped within approximately 4 weeks via postal service book rate. PAYMENT MUST ACCOMPANY ALL ORDERS.**

**Canadian orders must be paid in U.S. dollars payable through a New York banking facility.

Mail coupon to: **Dorchester Publishing Co., Inc.**
                        276 Fifth Avenue
                        New York, N.Y. 10001

                        ATTN: Customer Service